THE
WARLOCK'S
SHADOW

THE
WARLOCK'S
SHADOW

STEPHEN DEAS

GOLLANCZ
LONDON

The right of Stephen Deas to be identified as the author
of this work has been asserted by him in accordance with
the Copyright, Designs and Patents Act 1988.

First published in Great Britain in 2011 by Gollancz
An imprint of the Orion Publishing Group
Orion House, 5 Upper St Martin's Lane,
London WC2H 9EA
An Hachette UK Company

A CIP catalogue record for this book
is available from the British Library

ISBN 978 0 575 09451 2 (Cased)
ISBN 978 0 575 09452 9 (Trade Paperback)

1 3 5 7 9 10 8 6 4 2

Typeset by Deltatype Ltd, Birkenhead, Merseyside

Printed in Great Britain by Clays Ltd, St Ives plc

The Orion Publishing Group's policy is to use papers
that are natural, renewable and recyclable products and
made from wood grown in sustainable forests. The logging
and manufacturing processes are expected to conform to
the environmental regulations of the country of origin.

www.stephendeas.com
www.orionbooks.co.uk

For Lucca, who had to be free no matter how high the fences around him.

The evil that men do lives after them.
The good is oft interred with their bones.

Julius Caesar, Act III

PROLOGUE
THE WARLOCK'S SHADOW

Kasmin didn't see the three men come into the tavern but he knew they were there almost at once. There was a subtle stutter in the mood of the place, a difference in tone, conversations falling quiet, tankards pausing for a moment as heads turned. Strangers. He didn't get strangers very often. The press of dark narrow streets and alleys that was The Maze had made an unfriendly name for itself, one it mostly deserved. The inside of the Barrow of Beer was a safe enough place to be – it was Kasmin's place and he had a reputation to keep – but the outside was a wholly different matter.

He tried not to look but he couldn't resist. Three men had come in together. He couldn't make out much through the press of his regulars but they had an air to them, the sort that said they were used to trouble. They didn't look like they were local, either. Not city folk. Most likely they were sailors up from the docks, although the Barrow of Beer was closer to the market side of the Maze and not many sailors made it this far. The taverns and the Moongrass dens and the brothels and the muggers and the press gangs saw to that.

The three of them settled into a corner near the door, crowding tightly onto wooden stools around a tiny table. An unspoken accommodation was reached and the mood in the Barrow sighed and relaxed back to its usual loudness. Three men who were used to trouble, but they weren't

1

looking for it here and that was all that mattered. Kasmin finished what he was doing, wiping empty tankards and poured a couple more. Most of the men in here passed as friends, people who'd been coming to the Barrow for years. They were his family, his safe place. He took comfort from that. Strangers made him uneasy. He hadn't always kept a tavern.

That done, he did what was expected of him and wandered across the floor, easing himself between the knots of drinkers until he reached the three strangers by the door.

'Evening, gentlemen ...'

His words froze in his mouth. He'd never seen two of them before, but the third ... the third he knew all right. It was a face ten years older than when he'd seen it last, but there was no mistake. If Kasmin had had a sword with him, there would have been a fight, right there and then, and one of them would have been dead.

But he didn't have a sword and the three men had knives. Long curved knives, a sort he knew all too well. They were looking at him blankly, wondering what was wrong with him. The man he wanted to kill didn't remember him!

'Ale or wine?' he asked brusquely.

The man he wanted to kill spat on the floor. 'Wine.'

The voice. He remembered that voice, too. Shouting out orders across the deck of a ship and swearing murder over a narrow gap of sea. Kasmin had sworn something back, something about revenge.

'Wine.' He gave them a curt nod and pushed his way back to the other end of the tavern, almost stumbling in his own house. There was a fury inside him now, a rage he hadn't felt for – how long had the Emperor sat on the throne of Varr? Eleven years now? That long and a couple of years more. A killing rage. His hands were shaking. Men who'd known him for years were looking at him, brows furrowed.

'You all right, Kas?'

He shook them away and steadied himself, then took a bottle of wine and three cups from a shelf. He looked at the secret place where he kept his own long curved knife, exactly like the ones the three men had on their hips. He hadn't used it, not in anger, not for the same number of years since he'd felt this fury, but he still knew how. Straight into the neck of one of them, into the face of the second …

And then the third man, the one with his back to the wall, the one sat in the corner with the table in front of him, the one Kasmin *really* wanted to kill, he'd be on his feet by then, blade drawn and ready for a fight. It wouldn't take much to go wrong for Kasmin to be the one who came off worse from that.

His eyes left the knife. He took a deep breath. There were other ways. Syannis – he'd have to tell Syannis. *Then* there would be blood, no two ways about it. Syannis would come like a hurricane and carve them into pieces.

He wormed his way back to their table and put the cups and the bottle down in front of them. 'Half a crown.'

The man he wanted to kill tipped a handful of pennies out of his purse. Kasmin counted them. Too many. He left a couple behind. The man was watching him, peering at him, looking too hard for comfort.

'Better be good, this,' he grunted. 'Came here special, we did. You must be right friendly with that weird old fellow down by the river. Said this was the best place in the Maze for a drink. Don't look it.'

Kasmin shrugged. He took his pennies and backed away. So the witch-doctor had sent them here. Saffran Kuy, another refugee from a kingdom that didn't exist any more. Syannis and Kuy, the thief-taker who hadn't always been a thief-taker, the witch-doctor who hadn't always been a witch-doctor. And him, the tavern-keeper who'd once been a soldier. They'd all come here because it was far, far away, because they had no home and nowhere was safe any more, and it was all thanks to one man. Radek of Kalda.

And here, sitting in the corner of Kasmin's tavern was the Headsman. One of Radek's lieutenants. The one Kasmin hated the most.

⚔ PART ONE ⚔

A PRINCE'S GIFT

1

KELM'S TEETH

Deephaven! Great northern port of the Empire, young and vibrant and alive with a wild frantic energy! While cities like Varr slipped into decadence with a fatal resignation, Deephaven ran out to embrace it and offer up its heart. Here anything was possible, here north met south, all that was Aria collided with all that was not; it was a place where swords and lives and even kingdoms were bought and sold, a place always humming with anticipation of what the next moment would bring even as it revelled in the last.

Berren sat slumped in the corner of a cold stone room, drumming his fingers on his knee. The world outside the sun-temple was rousing itself from the torpor of winter and sniffing the possibilities of spring. Barges from the City of Spires were riding the thaw down the river and the first boats from distant Varr wouldn't be far behind. The world outside was waking up.

The world *inside* the temple, however, had largely gone to sleep. At the front of the class, Teacher Sterm was droning on about something that didn't interest Berren in the least. Berren was daydreaming. If the little teaching cell had had a window, he'd have been staring out of it, counting the leaves on the trees. He could hear the hiss of rain, slithering in through the half-closed door. After a bit he started to count the drips falling off the lintel instead. Anything.

Whatever it took to make the seconds hurry on past. After all, it wasn't every day you got to meet a prince.

A stinging blow on his cheek summoned his thoughts back. Sterm had a cane and in the month since he'd first counted Berren among his students, he'd had a lot of practice using it. He was getting quite good with it, but Berren thought he'd best not tell him. Not yet. He was saving that.

'Your master pays me money to teach you, boy,' snapped the priest. 'It's no bother to me if you sleep through everything I have to say, but I imagine he will have a different view when I tell him. Get up.'

Berren wasn't so sure about that. Master Sy was a more religious man than some, but he generally had enough reasons to be annoyed at Berren without anything Teacher Sterm might have to say.

With a sigh, he got up. It was going to be one of those make-an-example-of-Berren afternoons. There were a lot of those with Sterm. He weathered them with an indifference that only made Sterm even angrier. In another month, he'd move on to a different teacher. They all knew him by now. None of them liked him. That was fine – he didn't like them either. He didn't like priests, he didn't like temples, he didn't like gods, didn't like any of it. They were all just something he had to put up with to get what he wanted. What he wanted was Master Sy, teaching him to use a sword.

'Come to the front, boy.'

Berren shuffled forward. He was here because nearly two years ago, Master Sy had promised to teach him swords on the day he mastered his letters; now, even despite his complete apathy, he could read and write. He was slow, he was clumsy, but he could do it.

'Right.' Sterm's voice was clipped and sharp. The cell smelled of damp but as Berren walked to the front, he picked out a whiff of sugarleaf on Sterm's breath. 'Berren will now tell us everything he knows about Saint Kelm.' Sterm smiled, stepped back and stared at Berren. Around him, a dozen novices looked up. They all hated Berren too. They were envious, he thought. Envious because they had to stay at the temple every evening and every night with nothing to look forward to except more of the same for the rest of their lives, while he, Berren, was apprenticed to the best thief-taker in the city. *He* spent his evenings in taverns and markets and walking the twilight streets.

He sighed. Envious or not, when it came to letters and words and the histories of pointless saints that no one else cared about, they all knew a lot more than he did. He had no idea at all what Sterm had been talking about. Something about some priest who'd done something incredibly dull, most likely. Probably in some part of the world that didn't exist any more, and all so long ago that no one apart from Sterm even remembered it.

'We're waiting, Berren.' Sterm the Worm, Berren called him behind his back. Master Sy had tried to tell him off the first few times. He'd also been trying not to laugh, so it hadn't really worked. Here, though, the other novices all gasped and tutted. Such insolence! Such disrespect! Such a bunch of boring ...

'Kelm, boy!'

One of the novices at the front grinned and bared his teeth.

'Teeth!' blurted Berren. 'He had teeth!' *Kelm's Teeth!* He heard someone utter that curse almost every day.

'Yes, boy. And horses have teeth and so do little rats and weasels and sleepy little sloths who doze in the corner of my class. Sit down!'

The priest slapped his cane across Berren's arm, more out of a bored sense of duty than anything else. Berren ignored the sting. He got much worse from Master Sy when

9

they sparred. The wasters, the wooden practice swords they used, were about the same length as Sterm's cane. They were heavier and harder and Master Sy didn't pull his blows.

'Kelm.' Teacher Sterm grimaced and started to pace. 'The greatest saint in the illustrious history of the sun. Berren tells us he had teeth. I imagine we can do a bit better.' Somewhere outside, one of the temple bells started to ring, warning them all that it was an hour until sunset. Time for novices to ready themselves for their prayers; time for Berren to run through the city streets to the Watchman's Arms and finally see a prince. He could barely stop his toes from wriggling. None of the other novices seemed to be in the least impressed but surely they were just pretending; underneath they had to be green with envy. A prince! How many people ever got to meet a prince? How many poor orphans from Shipwrights' ... ?

The cane caught him round the ear and this time Sterm didn't hold back. Berren gulped down a squeal of pain.

'For the love of all that's bright, will you keep *still*, boy!' Sterm's knuckles were white. 'Kelm! You will devote your evening to study and you will learn about Kelm.' He gave Berren a withering look. 'You may wish to use the temple library. You may wish to learn from the wisdom of your forebears. You may wish to read their words and their histories. Unless you are Berren, of course, who believes he will attract knowledge like a lodestone; that it will appear out of the very air and force itself in through his ears despite his every effort to the contrary. Or is there some other explanation for your lack of attention, boy?' For a moment the priest looked pleased with himself. His eyes scanned the class. 'We will have visitors in the temple soon. The Autarch himself is coming from Torpreah. He plans a great summer tour of the empire. He will bring many priests and many holy artefacts with him and he has chosen

Deephaven as the place where he will begin. In a few days his dragon-monks will be coming here.' He looked at Berren now and smiled. 'Whatever else *some* of you may have heard, the Autarch's dragon-monks are the best swordsmen in the world. They are his personal guard and a score of them will be coming to make sure our temple is safe. Each monk will be given a novice to assist them in their duties.' Sterm's eyes stayed on Berren. 'Those novices who are most gracious and penitent and have best applied themselves to their studies. For the rest of you ...' His smile turned sickly. 'The rest of you will still have me. And since our numbers will be so few, you will have the opportunity for some very personal teaching. You may go. Tomorrow you will tell me what you know of Kelm.'

On other days Berren might have patiently taken his place in the line of novices that filed slowly towards the door, heads bowed, mumbling prayers to themselves as they crossed the threshold into the open yard outside. Today he couldn't get out fast enough. He barged through the line, dashed outside into the rain and the smell of the sea blowing in from the harbour and ran for the temple gates. The soldiers who stood guard there in their bright yellow sunburst shirts threw him a half-hearted glare. Heavy grey clouds pressed down against grey streets. The cobbles were slick with water but Berren was far too busy to be worrying about that. He skittered and slid across Deephaven Square, splashing through puddles, paying no heed to the angry shouts that followed him. Down the sprawling Avenue of the Sun and into the city's second great square, the square of the Four Winds. Here men and women scurried back and forth, heads bowed against the weather. A steady line of carts trudged from one side to the other. They came up the Godsway from the river docks, then went down the Avenue of Emperors to the harbour and the sea. They were

11

the city's blood, the flow that never stopped, up and down from river to sea and back again, filling the coffers of rich men with gold.

Habit made him stop at the top of the Avenue of Emperors. Rain hissed into steam from the braziers pressed against the walls, smells of hot fat and butter and onions and spices mingling with the smell of the damp street and the ox-carts and the ever-present whiff of rotting fish. The noise was a cacophony of shouting, offers of everything from fried dough-balls to strips of pickled fish to spiced rat-sticks and baked weevils, all hurled and battered against one another by the whirl of the wind. Berren hardly noticed it. He came here every day, and every day here was the same, rain or shine.

You see those ships, boy? On the day the thief-taker had bought Berren from Master Hatchet and his gang of dung-collectors, they'd come here too. Before he'd even taken Berren home, he'd turned Berren around and pointed him down the Avenue of Emperors to the jumble of ships and masts anchored out in Deephaven Bay. *When I'm done with you, you'll come here every day and you'll look at the flags. You'll tell me if you see four white ships on a red field. If ever you do, there's an emperor in it for you.*

Back then an emperor had seemed like a fortune big enough to buy the world. He knew better now but it was still a lot, still worth a pause and a quick look every day. You couldn't make out the flags themselves from so far away, but the top of the Avenue of Emperors was as good a place as any to see if there were new ships in the harbour, to see whether it was worth a closer look.

Habit made him pause, but it was raining. The harbour vanished into a murky grey haze. If any ships had weighed anchor since yesterday, they'd still be there tomorrow. Berren's prince, on the other hand, might not.

Stopping to look at the ships wasn't the only old habit that refused to die. He snatched a hot dough-ball while no one was looking and ate it, laughing, as he ran on.

2

PENNIES AND PRINCES IN A POOL

By the time he reached the Watchman's Arms he was soaked. His shirt and breeches stuck to him like a second skin. He ran straight through the commoners room up the stairs to the rooms above, dived through a door, slammed it closed and had already pulled his shirt half off when he realised that he wasn't alone.

'Hello, Berren.'

'Master Mardan.' Berren paused. On the one hand, Mardan was a thief-taker like Syannis, his own master. Whenever he went with Master Sy to the Eight Pillars of Smoke, the tavern behind the city Courthouse where the thief-takers gathered, Mardan was always there. He and Master Sy were old friends.

On the other hand, as far as Berren knew, Mardan wasn't supposed to be here. He finished taking off his shirt and then stood, tense, holding it, idly twirling it. A wet shirt all twisted up tight made a fine enough weapon in a pinch. At least it did when you had nothing else.

'Syannis is down below.' Mardan was watching the shirt too closely not to have realised what Berren was doing. He chuckled and looked down at the floor. There were three mattresses where this morning there had been two. 'The justicar still isn't happy that His Highness has enough of us around him. Me, I try telling him – the more people you put here, the more chance one of them has itchy pockets.

I try telling him he should keep Syannis here and send everyone else away, but he just doesn't listen.' Mardan gave an exaggerated shrug. 'Or maybe Kol sent me here for my wit and charm. I hear His Highness finds Syannis a tad dismal and dull. Who'd have thought, eh?' He shrugged. 'Trouble is, doesn't matter how many thief-takers and so forth you pack together, it doesn't change how many rooms they have.'

Berren dropped his shirt. Still wary, he dried himself and dressed in his best clothes, the one set he had that didn't make him look like what he was – an orphan boy from Shipwrights' who happened to fall out the right side of the ship. A white shirt with frills around the bottom and dark blue breeches with a bright strip of yellow down either side. Master Sy had gone on and on about how hard it had been getting the colours right. Picking ones that wouldn't *mean* something. Apparently that was extraordinarily difficult around this particular prince.

'Have you ... Have you met him?'

'Syannis? Yes, he's down ...'

Berren shook his head. 'The Prince, Master Mardan.'

Mardan laughed. 'His Highness, I think you mean. No, not me. Syannis gets the special treatment because he knows his manners. The rest of us, we guard the doors and frisk the commoners.' He shook his head. 'Besides, from what I hear His Highness was up for most of the night. I imagine he's nursing a crippling hangover. I think he might have a couple of ladies from up on Reeper Hill helping him to get his strength back too.' Mardan smirked. 'Mind, from what I've *seen*, I reckon I'm going to enjoy frisking some of the commoners here.' He wiggled his fingers suggestively. 'Come on, lad. Let's see if we can't find your master down below. And if we can't, let's see if we can't find us a bed-warmer or two, eh?'

Berren shrugged. Truth was, he didn't much like Master

Mardan. He didn't much like the justicar or Teacher Sterm either, but Mardan was different. Mardan was creepy. The rest of them treated him like he was still a child. Mardan did that too, but he kept acting like he was trying to be friends as well.

'Are you ready?' When Berren nodded, Master Mardan bounded to the door and flung it open. 'Then I'll show you the way. Come on, lad! Let's find your master.'

Berren muttered something rude under his breath. He followed Mardan across the landing outside and up to a door guarded by a pair of stiff soldiers, ramrod straight. They wore heavy sleeved brigandine armour, with metal greaves and vambraces protecting their lower legs and arms. Over the armour they wore pale moonlight-silver cloth and on their chests was a black triangle. Within the triangle, the tips of its wings and its claws poking out, was the design of a flaming red eagle. Red, black and silver, the colours of the Imperial Throne, of House Falandawn, raised for the first time over the palace of Varr by Khrozus the Butcher not long before Berren had been born. Probably. Everyone – Berren included – simply assumed that Berren was one of Khrozus' Boys, the unwanted bastards that Khrozus' army had left behind after the siege of Deephaven. If that was true, then Berren was fifteen years old, give or take, and by any reckoning almost a man.

The two imperial soldiers held naked steel in their hands. It wasn't any ordinary steel either. The swords glowed faintly in the gloom and sometimes seemed to flash with colour, a slight shimmer of gold or a deep red, depending how they caught the torchlight. Sunsteel, forged by the priests of Torpreah, a holy metal if Teacher Sterm was to be believed. It might even have been enchanted. Master Sy had a light mail shirt made of the stuff and swore it would turn anything.

The soldiers hadn't moved. They were looking at Berren. Mardan frowned.

'It's not like you don't know who both of us are,' he grumbled.

One of the soldiers growled and tried to look fierce. He might have done a better job of it if he hadn't been sweating so much under all that armour that he was bright red in the face. Berren thought he looked a bit like a lobster. They were the prince's soldiers from Varr, where winter locked everything in snow for months on end. No one who'd lived here through a Deephaven summer would ever think of dressing like that.

The other one sniffed. 'Ser Syannis' squire – does he know how to behave, Ser Mardan? His Highness is present.'

'Er ... Yes.' Mardan beamed brightly. 'Yes he does. He knows exactly how to behave. Master Syannis is the best teacher in the city when it comes to behaving.'

Berren nodded. *That* was certainly true. Most days it seemed like Master Sy spent more time teaching him how to hold his cutlery than teaching him how to hold his sword.

The soldiers moved aside. 'Ser Syannis is in there,' grunted the sniffy one. 'He's in one of his moods.'

Berren nodded. He walked on behind Mardan, past the soldiers and down some stairs into a part of the Watchman's Arms he hadn't seen before. It was a lot nicer here; it reminded him a bit of the Captain's Rest down the end of the Avenue of Emperors near the sea-docks. *That* was supposed to be the richest tavern in town. Odd that a prince would stay here instead.

The stairs led them out into another hall. It was empty except for a pair of soldiers by an arch into an open courtyard. There were voices, several, wafting in from outside, and laughter, the too-loud braying of drunk people. The soldiers stood aside and then Berren was through, into the fresh damp air. He looked about. He couldn't see Master

Sy but then it was hard to tear his eyes away from the centre of the yard. A shallow circle of water sat there, enclosed by a wide stone wall about as high as Berren's knees and engraved with the phases of the moon. A moonpool. Throwing a penny into the reflection of the moon, even in a puddle on the street, was supposed to bring good luck, and there were hundreds of pools like this one dotted around the city. Penny collectors from those who could afford to throw pennies away. Most temples had them, priests claimed they were holy places, but as far as Berren was concerned they were free money.

Apparently what got thrown into this one was people rather than pennies. A man sat in the water, stripped to the waist with a bottle of wine in one hand and the other up the dress of some expensive ground-floor girl from the brothels of Reeper Hill. There were two other women in the pool with him, all of them laughing and splashing and wearing flimsy white cotton that was soaking wet and left next to nothing to the imagination. As Berren stared, the man in the water pulled the closest of the woman down beside him and tipped his wine over her neck, lapping it up as it ran down her skin.

Mardan leaned over and whispered. 'Your luck's in, Berren. There he is. The prince. His Imperial Highness Prince Sharda. Second in line to the throne. From what I've heard this looks like it's one of his better days.'

Berren stared. The women in the water were mesmerising. He hadn't seen anyone look this gorgeous since ... since Lilissa.

Best not to think about *her*. Her and her fishmonger's son. He shivered.

'Berren, lad.'

'Master Mardan?'

'You're gawping.'

'Huh?'

18

'Mouth, lad. Close it.'

Someone landed him a heavy cuff round the back of the head. Berren staggered and spun around and there was Master Sy. They were almost the same height now, neither of them particularly tall for men of Deephaven. Master Sy came from some land far across the sea where they were probably all short, but it sometimes made Berren wonder who his own father was. Most likely he'd been some soldier in the army of General Kyra, a soldier who'd sired him in exchange for a crust of mouldy bread during the siege. The sad truth was that he was never going to know.

'Eyes to the floor,' hissed Master Sy through clenched teeth. 'And bow your head. You are in the company of a prince.' Berren did as he was told. He saw Master Sy kick Master Mardan in the ankle. There were some angry whispers but Berren wasn't paying attention. He was still peering through his eyelashes at the women in the water. He understood now what Master Mardan had meant about the frisking.

The prince swivelled his head and gave Berren and the two thief-takers a languid look. He sat up straight. For a moment he might have been about to say something; then, with a great splash, he toppled over backwards. Everyone stood in shocked silence; Master Sy took a step forward, but then the prince reared out of the water, shaking his hair and laughing fit to burst. He pulled himself to his feet, staggered sideways and leaned heavily on two of his ladies. He cocked his head and screwed up his eyes and looked vaguely around the yard. 'What I would like to see is ... They say the ... whoever they are. The ones who come across the sea in the sharp ships. With the ...' He frowned and growled something to himself. 'Anyway, whoever they are, I hear they make black powder rockets that fill the sky with coloured stars. Someone told me that. I want to see *them*. If they could do that ... They had them for Ashahn and Arianne. I missed it.' He slipped then and nearly fell over. Beside Berren, Master Sy was almost rigid, fists clenched.

The prince and his women stumbled out of the pool and walked away, lurching from side to side. Berren stared after them, transfixed. Even after they vanished through a door on the other side of the yard, he still couldn't move. Master Sy stayed where he was, head bowed until the prince was out of sight. Then he took a deep breath and sighed and slowly began to relax.

'Oh. My. Gods,' moaned Master Mardan. 'Now was that a sight or was that a sight?' He grunted as Master Sy elbowed him in the ribs. Then the thief-taker had Berren's ear between his fingers, practically tearing it off as he dragged Berren away.

'Ow!'

'Sit down, boy.' Master Sy pushed him back onto an ornate carved stone bench. Around the yard were at least a dozen soldiers, most of them standing stiffly to attention and acting as though they hadn't seen anything, although Berren thought he heard a snicker or two. There was no way to know whether they were snickering at him or at the departed prince.

'Sorry, master.' Berren bowed his head. That was always the best way to start. Arguing with Master Sy only made him even more angry. Looking penitent always seemed to catch him off-guard.

'Boy, do you know who that was? That was His Imperial Highness Prince Sharda of Varr. So: What do you think?'

3

THE SCENT GARDEN

Berren kept quiet. Saying that yes, thanks, he'd already guessed it was the prince probably wasn't going to take the conversation anywhere useful. Instead he stared at the flagstones on the floor. The rain had stopped but it had left puddles. The stones were carved in some faded motif, worn down by countless booted feet. The thief-taker looked him up and down, frowning fiercely, straightening a fold in his clothes here, brushing away a fleck of dirt there. 'He's dangerous, that one. Unpredictable. A drunk. Prone to be morose and violent. You don't want to catch his eye, boy. He'll rip you to pieces.'

Unpredictable? Prone to be morose and violent? Sounds familiar, that does. Berren wasn't sure *what* he'd been expecting, but certainly it hadn't been a drunkard, stripped to the waist like some dock-worker, someone only a few years older than him, full of swagger and yet with enough chips on his shoulder to start a fire. Not someone who had staggered off almost too drunk to stand with three of the prettiest ladies of Reeper Hill. Impressed? Disappointment and envy in roughly equal measure, that was more like it. He shrugged. 'I didn't ...'

Master Sy's glare shut him up. 'Look and listen but say nothing. Everyone here has wealth and power far more than us. You see those soldiers?' He pointed to the men by

21

the door, sweating under their armour. 'You think they're nothing more than snuffers?'

Berren shook his head. Snuffers were mostly relics of the war, the remnants of Khrozus' army who'd never gone home after the siege. Men who'd stolen swords and maybe a bit of mail from the corpses of their comrades and now hired themselves out to whoever would pay. The ones that had lasted were the brutal ones, the savage, the murderous. No, Justicar Kol would never hire a snuffer for something that actually mattered. Snuffers served whoever held the biggest bag of gold and that was that, not like a thief-taker.

'These are the Imperial Guard, boy. To be in the Imperial Guard you have to be the son or daughter of land and a title. Every one of them has sat in the imperial court. These will be lords and ladies of the empire one day. Now imagine having all that power and having to stand here all day as though you're one of that prince's pet monkeys. So mind your tongue. Watch the way they act, the way they dress. Listen to the way they talk. Learn from that but do it silently and with your head bowed. You understand me?'

Berren nodded, secretly rolling his eyes. He'd come from the temple to the Watchman's Arms full of excitement; now it was starting to look as though he might as well never have left. *Silently with your head bowed?* If he closed his eyes, he could hear those exact words coming out of Teacher Sterm's mouth.

'And for the love of the sun, don't steal anything!'

'Master!' Berren made a good show of looking shocked and hurt. Old habits *did* die hard, but as far as Master Sy knew, he hadn't stolen anything for more than a year. Ever since ...

He glanced wistfully back at the archway where the prince and his three ground-floor girls had gone. Ever since Lilissa had gone and married her fishmonger's son. He'd hated her for that. Hated the fishmonger's son, too. Dorrm. Dorrm the dumb, Berren called him, quietly when no one was listening. Dorrm was four years older than Berren, probably about twice his bulk, dim as a plank and disgustingly amiable. If he'd been anyone else, Berren would probably have liked him. Things being as they were, he quietly hated Dorrm and wished he'd die. Or get grabbed by the voracious press-gangs that festered down by the sea-docks these days.

Yeah, and after Lilissa had chosen Dorrm instead of him, he'd started stealing again and buying her presents that Dorrm could never afford. When that didn't work, he got to showing off, trying to goad Dorrm into a fight. Stupid, now he looked back on it. Embarrassing. Humiliating. Worst of all, Dorrm had never made anything of it. *That* had made Berren hate him even more.

Master Sy had taken him away across the river, into the maze of mud-islands and channels and creeks and swamps where no one lived except the most desperately wanted men with nowhere else to hide and the thief-takers sent to catch them. They were away for a month. When they came back, Lilissa and Dorrm were married. She was living with him in his father's shop somewhere on the eastern edge of The Maze. As far as Berren knew, she still was. Master Sy wouldn't tell him where and he'd somehow never found the time to go and look. And that was the end of that.

Yes, as far as Master Sy knew, Berren had stopped stealing.

'Come on, lad. I'll show you around.' There were arches leading away from the yard in all four walls. One led back to the rooms where Berren and the other thief-takers were staying. One led to the prince's wing. Master Sy picked the nearest of the other two, where another pair of imperial soldiers stood on guard. Beyond the arch lay a second square yard. Here, instead of open space, everywhere was overgrown. Tiny paths wound through leaves and flowers, punctuated by little marble benches like the ones in the yard before.

'Look familiar?'

Berren blinked. 'Yes!' Yes, suddenly it did. 'It's like the Captain's Rest.'

Master Sy half-smiled and nodded. 'Yes. Built and owned by the same guild-master.' He started to wander the paths. 'I've heard there are gardens like this in Varr too but much bigger. Scent gardens, they call them. Use your nose. I imagine they'll be at their best about a month from now.' Berren looked around. Scented and flowering bushes and even two small trees grew up from the ground, masking the usual city-smell of bad fish. Variegated ivies competed for domination of the walls. There were no birds here, though. The Captain's Rest, he remembered, had had birds.

'You have to be a sea captain or one of their ilk to make your business in the Captain's Rest. Everyone else comes here. Or they did, until His Highness took over the place.' He pointed back the way they'd come, through the archway to the yard and on through to the other side. 'Those are the rooms and lodgings for the Imperial Guard. We don't go there.' He gestured up at the windows overlooking the scent gardens. 'Up there is where the prince sleeps. We don't go *there* either.' He walked closer until they were on a path right underneath the windows, one so crowded by greenery that it brushed Berren's legs as he walked. Berren stopped. One of the windows was open. He could hear a gentle moaning and soft throaty laughter wafting out of it. Master Sy pursed his lips. 'That's where he has his rooms. There are baths in there and, well, the usual other diversions.'

By which Master Sy meant women. Berren grinned to himself. Master Sy was deadly deft and agile about everything else, but when it came to women he was as clumsy as a coconut. Berren, on the other hand, had grown up two doors away from a cheap whorehouse. He'd already seen about as much as there was to be seen before he even knew what it was all for; and while he was waiting for Dorrm the Dumb to trip over and impale himself on a swordfish, he was quietly working his way through the various houses on Reeper Hill whenever he could slip away for an evening and had enough crowns in his purse to pay for it.

Yes. Another thing Master Sy wasn't supposed to know.

The thief-taker held up his hand. 'Stop for a moment.' They were right under the prince's window, about ten feet above them. The noises coming down from there didn't leave much to the imagination. Berren puffed his cheeks, trying to ignore them.

'Look around you.'

Plants and paths and walls covered in ivy. If he peered a bit, he could see the archway and the moonpool yard and the soldiers standing there.

'Do you think anyone can see us?'

Berren shrugged. 'I suppose. If they look hard enough.'

'Go over to the archway. Tell me if you can see me.'

Berren trotted off as he was told. When he looked back, he was surprised to see that Master Sy was almost invisible between the leaves of the bushes and the trees. Easy enough to see him if you knew he was there to be seen in the first place, but even then he had to peer a bit to be sure. He trotted back. Master Sy glanced up at the window and the ivy-covered wall below it.

'How long would it take you to climb up there?'

'There?' Berren laughed. 'Easy! I'd be up in a flash.'

'Yes. That's what I thought.' Master Sy nodded. 'Right. Well. Off to bed with you then.'

'What?!' Berren looked up at the sky. The sun might have set but the sky was still light and they hadn't even reached the spring festival. 'There's half the day left!'

The thief-taker gave him his best baleful look. It was the look he put on every time Berren forgot that he was a worthless apprentice who should be grateful to even exist. 'We are here to perform a duty, boy. I will take my turn on watch here until the small hours. Then *you* will take *your* watch. At dawn, you will leave here and go to the temple for your daily lessons. Master Mardan or Master Fennis will relieve you.'

'But ... !'

'Boy, you will do as you're told. We are taking the justicar's gold to protect the life of His Highness. Whatever you may think of him.'

Berren closed his eyes. He could see the future, clear as the sun. *This* was how it would be. *Forever*, probably. After all, if you were the prince, with women like that to take to your bed and soldiers and thief-takers to fawn at your feet, why would you ever leave? 'You were going to show me how to fight with short steel. Before spring! You promised!'

The thief-taker growled. 'In good time, boy. The festival of the equinox is weeks away. Now do as you're told!'

They glowered at each other but that was a fight that only one of them was ever going to win. Berren walked away, saving his storming and stomping until he was out of Master Sy's sight. The thief-taker had promised to teach him to fight with steel more than a year ago and still all they ever did was fight with sticks. He'd promised again for midsummer, spent a week showing Berren how to hold a real sword properly and then promptly gone back to sticks again. Then he'd promised for midwinter and just forgotten all about it.

Berren reached the room where he and Mardan and Master Sy would all sleep together. Thank the sun, Master Mardan wasn't there. Berren threw himself down on the mattress. He was *never* going to learn swords. Master Sy just didn't want to teach him, that was it.

Trouble was, neither would anyone else. Not for the meagre purse that Berren could muster. Sword-masters were paid in gold.

4

SECRETS BY MOONLIGHT

Most evenings, before this drunkard prince had come to Deephaven, Berren came back from the temple and had his supper with Master Sy. Then they'd go off about their errands, the sort that were best run after dark. They'd wander down into the night market to make a nuisance of themselves among the wagoners, or else they'd amble down to the taverns near the docks and listen in on who was selling what and who wanted to buy it. Sometimes they went as far as Reeper Hill or wandered the streets around The Peak. The thief-taker would talk to the snuffers, the ones who still had a vestige of decency to them. Once or twice every month they'd dodge the press gangs and head into The Maze, to the Barrow of Beer and Master Sy's friend Kasmin from the old days that he never liked to talk about. Sometimes they didn't go any further than the yard outside Master Sy's little house, the thief-taker clucking and shaking his head while Berren tried to cut and lunge with his waster until the light failed.

That was before.

It seemed he'd only just managed to fall asleep when Master Sy was shaking him awake again to sit for hours in the dark of the scent garden, bleary and cold, listening to people snore. And then, as everyone else was getting up and thinking about breakfast, there was Master Fennis, chasing him on his way with nothing but a crust of yesterday's bread in his pocket, back up the hill to Deephaven Square and the temple in time to catch a lash of Teacher Sterm's cane for being late. And *that* was when he realised that he hadn't asked Master Sy about Kelm, whoever he was, and sure enough, Sterm had him straight up to the front first to share his ignorance.

That was the way his days became – woken up in the middle of the night, cold and thankless hours sitting in the dark of the garden, more cold and thankless hours of sitting in the gloom at the temple, snatching leftovers to eat whenever he had a spare moment, always rushing from one misery to the next. His head was full of things he wanted, of princes and their women, swordplay and blade-dancing, and he was getting none of it, no swords, no thief-taking, nothing. He barely even saw the prince he was supposed to be guarding. In the temple, the other novices only jeered at him when he tried to tell them how important he was. The solar priests, it turned out, didn't much care for Prince Sharda of Varr. If they'd known half the truth, they'd probably have rolled on the floor and wept with laughter.

The novices to serve the monks from Torpreah were chosen – not Berren of course. They might have been the most gracious and the most penitent but that didn't stop them strutting like peacocks when none of the priests were looking, and for once Berren envied them. Monks of the fire-dragon *were* the best fighters in the world, even Master Sy said so, and now he'd probably never even see them. His misery was complete.

'Here.' Master Velgian beckoned Berren over one evening when the Watchman's Arms was busier than usual. Velgian had replaced Master Mardan, who had apparently said something he shouldn't and been thrown out. Velgian fancied himself a poet and always carried the same battered old book of verses from Caladir and Brons with him wherever he went. On quiet evenings in The

Eight, he sometimes read to the other thief-takers whether they wanted him to or not. There were more soldiers than Berren was used to tonight; there were other faces too, men and women he hadn't seen before, wandering in and out through the yard around the moonpool. They were dressed in the silks and satins of rich city lords from The Peak, laced with gold and silver and decked with jewels. They looked agitated.

Berren shrugged. It wasn't as if he had anything better to do. As best he could tell, the prince was somewhere off and about, most likely up on Reeper Hill again. He'd taken Master Sy with him too.

'Get a torch, lad.'

Velgian was sitting beside the archway to the scent garden with a square piece of metal on the ground in front of him. Berren got a torch and sat down beside him.

'Keep that away for a moment.' Velgian had a waxed paper pouch in his hand. He tipped it over the metal plate, shook out a little pile of black powder then shuffled back a little. 'Go on. Touch the torch to that then.'

Berren poked the torch at the metal plate. There was a whoosh, a flash of orange light, a puff of smoke and a wave of heat. Berren reeled away. The smoke stung his eyes and the air stank of bad eggs.

'What was *that*?' He stared in awe at the black stain on the metal plate.

Master Velgian shrugged. 'I don't know what they call it. Comes from Caladir. Black powder but with something else as well.'

'Does the witch-doctor make it?' The witch-doctor, Master Sy's old friend from across the sea who lived in an old warehouse by the river, was the only person Berren knew who dealt in potions and powders. Velgian, for some reason, looked petrified.

'That devil?' He shuddered. 'I know Syannis speaks

with him sometimes, but take it from me, Saffran Kuy is evil and nothing good comes from any who deal with him.' He glanced up into the sky and leaned closer. 'You know how everyone who goes to see him leaves a basket of fish outside when they leave? That's because he has a pact with the cats and the gulls who live there. They're his spies. He rides inside them, seeing the world through their eyes, listening to what people say with their ears!' He shuddered again and then sat back. 'No, this is what the Taiytakei use to make things that fly up into the air and make pretty lights. A ship came in with some kegs of it a few weeks back, a present ready for the Emperor's spring festival in Varr. Turns out one or two fell off the back of a wagon on the way and ended up in the night market. Fancy, eh?' He rolled his eyes and then shrugged again. 'Bought a pouch of it. Too much money from standing watch over this prick of a prince. Bloody waste. Here, come look at this though.' Master Velgian led Berren across the moonpool yard and back inside the Arms, into a wide hall that Berren hadn't seen before. A delicious smell of food laced the air. Paintings and hangings lined the walls here, faces of men from Aria's history that Berren had had beaten into him by Teacher Sterm, and other faces that he didn't know. Uniformed servants hurried around them, speaking in whispers. Berren watched them.

'What's happening?'

'The feast of the last moon before the spring, that's what,' whispered Master Velgian. 'His Highness has guests too. They came into the Arms in the middle of the day. Apparently they've been looking for His Highness for a while.' Velgian spat. 'Can't have been looking all that hard, that's all I can say. They're going to take him back with them though and they might take you and your master too if you're lucky.' Then he smirked. 'If they can find him, of course. Sneaky bastard actually managed to slip out of here without anyone noticing, probably with a bit of help from Syannis. Glad it wasn't on my watch. So now they're going to have their big Feast of the Last Moon and some great announcement, and the person who should be the centre of it all isn't even here.' He snorted in disgust. 'I was going to show off that black powder. Syannis said to bring some if I could. Meant for a prince it was, and instead I'm left with you.'

He nodded towards a large man with wild blond hair, leaning against the wall just inside the door. The man had an impatient look to him. His expression had something of resignation in it too, as though he was used to this sort of thing.

'That's Ser Elmarc Borolan. Story goes that he and the prince were up in the mountains a year back. Lost a lot of friends. No one says how or why. Be on your guard tonight. Right.' He patted Berren on the back. 'Go and get some rest.'

'What?' Berren gaped at the table and then looked at Master Velgian, imploring. Velgian shrugged.

'This isn't for the likes of us, young Berren. We get to stay outside with the dogs and the riff-raff.'

'But!'

'Would you *want* to stay? Forced to stand still as a statue and silent as a shadow for hours on end while the lords and ladies of the city stuff themselves with every conceivable delicacy and ignore you completely, all the while complaining bitterly about how the whole feast is a complete waste of time without His Highness? I'm sure Syannis is expecting you to sit your watch and continue with your instruction in the temple too. No, to bed, young man.' Master Velgian frowned. 'Isn't it tomorrow that the monks of the fire-dragon arrive?'

'Tomorrow is Abyss-Day. The monks would never cross the threshold of a foreign temple on Abyss-Day.' The words came out by themselves, mechanical, exactly the sort of dull useless knowledge that Teacher Sterm drilled into him. He sighed. The food, wherever it was, smelled so *good*.

'Sun-Day then.'

'They might not be here for another week. Teacher Sterm says they won't arrive until the month of Storms is out.' He sighed.

Master Velgian shrugged. 'Then it must be some other group of monks of the fire-dragon who caused such a fuss in Bedlam's Crossing yesterday.'

Berren's mouth fell open. 'Really? They're in Bedlam's Crossing already?' Bedlam's Crossing was the last ferry across the river before the east bank turned into swamps and everglades. On a fast horse, that was less than a day's ride away. 'Wait – how do you know?'

'Every imperial messenger who comes into the city has to go to His Highness first. Some daft old law. Not that His Highness cares, but that's the way of it. Anyone else who happens to be around, they get to hear too.'

'Then they *will* arrive tomorrow!' Berren was hopping from one foot to the other, the feast completely forgotten in his excitement.

'No, you're probably right about them waiting until Sun-Day before they enter the temple. Unless they come *here* first.' Velgian chuckled.

'Here?' Berren squealed, which got him a few glances from some of the other soldiers and the feast guests in the hall. Velgian glared.

'Quiet, boy! No, probably not. There's no love at all between the Sapphire Throne and the Autarch of Torpreah. I think letting dragon-monks and His Highness loose into the same city is quite enough cause for worry, never mind putting some of them in the same room. I very much doubt they'll be coming here.' He chuckled and put an arm around Berren's shoulder and walked him out of the hall.

'Khrozus' Blood, Berren, I remember you when you came up to my shoulder. You're as tall as me already. Now go and sleep.'

Berren went back to his room. He tossed and turned, trying to sleep before he was ready, and it was all the worse for having a head filled with fire-dragon monks. He'd never seen one, probably almost no one in Deephaven had, and he couldn't help but wonder what they'd look like. Eight feet tall with sinewy arms and tree-trunk legs, with fierce and noble faces and wearing red silks, with long curving golden swords and maybe, just maybe, when you looked hard you might see a flicker of flame in their eyes ...

He woke up to Master Sy, kneeling beside him with a candle, gently shaking him. Everywhere was suddenly black and silent. He yawned and stretched and rubbed his eyes and reluctantly sat up.

'Bloody prince gave me the slip,' murmured the thief-taker as they walked. 'He's not here. Keep your eyes open in case, but I wouldn't be surprised if he doesn't come back at all tonight.'

The stairs down into the inner halls were guarded as ever, as were the arches into the moonpool yard and the scent garden. Berren walked through and settled onto his usual bench. There were all sorts of places for sitting in the scent garden. Mostly he moved about to keep boredom at bay, looking for a place where he could comfortably hide from anyone who crept in and still keep a careful watch on the wall with the prince's window. Not that anyone ever *would* come creeping in past all the other guards with their swords and their armour. Besides, anyone with any sense would come over the rooftops. That was the second rule. First thing a Shipwrights' boy learned were the three rules of not getting caught: Go somewhere narrow where big men will be slow. Go somewhere high where heavy men will fall. Go somewhere dark where you can't be seen.

He couldn't do narrow and he couldn't do high, not down here in the garden, but he could at least do dark. He sat on the bench closest to the windows he was watching. He'd grown used to listening to the snores or sometimes the other noises that filtered down. Sometimes he could count how many of the ladies from Reeper Hill the prince had with him.

Master Sy left and then came back again a few minutes later carrying a wooden board piled up with food. 'I hear the feast was a disaster.' He laughed and sat down beside Berren. 'Looks like the food was good enough though. Plenty left over at the end for the likes of us. It's cold but it's still the best food we're likely see for the rest of the year. Enjoy! Velgian and Fennis are practically rolling on the floor, fat as pigs. There's lots more where that came from if you're still hungry. Probably doesn't matter if you slip off for a bit. He's got his cousin up in his room waiting for him anyway.'

They sat and ate together in silence for a while. Berren picked at the food. It was rich; slabs of meat in heavy sauces and not the sort of thing he was used to at all. In the end, he scraped most of the sauces aside. Meat was a luxury, but what was the point if you ended up making yourself sick over it?

When they were done, Master Sy patted Berren on the shoulder and stood up. 'They'll be gone in a few days. You'll miss this.'

Berren snorted. 'Miss getting up in the middle of the night? Not likely.'

'Till the evening then.' Master Sy left. The scent garden fell still and silent and Berren was alone to count the long dull hours of the night, grain by grain.

An hour had passed, maybe two, when sudden loud voices rang out of the tavern halls. Berren had been dozing. He jumped up and scurried to peer around the archway from the scent garden. The full moon was high overhead and it lit up the yard and the moonpool better than any lanterns could have done. The prince came out into the yard with a lady on each arm. 'Good feast was it?' he called. The guards around the doors bowed and murmured something in reply, too quiet for Berren to hear. One of the ladies laughed. The other one was looking nervously about. Berren stayed hidden in his shadows where she couldn't see. He'd assumed the women with the prince were just another pair of ladies from the houses on Reeper Hill but now he wasn't sure. They were dressed too well, too properly.

The prince marched on past, across the yard and into the rooms he called his own. Berren sighed. He went back to his place in the scent garden and began to pick at the last cold leftovers on his plate. From the prince's window overhead, he heard the sound of a door opening and soft laugher. Another hour of moaning and groaning and gasping and sighing to keep him awake – just what he needed!

Another voice broke in, a man's voice, one he hadn't heard before. 'Hello Sharda! I see you're having fun.'

Berren froze. For a moment he wondered who the other voice could be and whether he should raise the alarm; then he remembered what Master Sy had said. The prince's cousin was up there. Berren strained his ears. Whatever the prince said next was too quiet.

'I have news,' said the first voice.

Another pause, maybe some footsteps. 'Good news, I hope. How's ...'

'I have *news*.' The voice was laden with some heavy meaning that Berren couldn't begin to guess. He heard more footsteps; the door opened again, there was another mumbled conversation, this time between the prince and his ladies and then more footsteps and the door closed. Now the prince's voice changed. The lazy drunken rolling words suddenly were gone, turned sharp and brittle as ice. Berren was half up off his seat. He'd been about to watch the prince's ladies as they left in case he caught sight of their faces again, but the prince's tone froze him fast. He sat down again. The talk was too quiet at first, but then came the crash of someone stamping on the floor. 'Of course. What of it?'

A bark of angry laughter and more words that Berren couldn't hear.

'Leave? Why would I do that? They can all get along quite nicely without me. They've all made that perfectly clear and I don't see why I should ...' The prince stopped. The other man's voice dropped to almost a whisper. Berren stood up, moved closer, tilted his heard trying to hear. They were talking too quietly, though. Even when he stood up on his bench, each rustle of leaves smothered the whispered words. Something about the Emperor and an heir and the prince going back to Varr, that was all he could make out.

The prince gave a heavy sigh. He walked to the window and suddenly he was right over Berren's head. 'Why, Elmarc? Why do they want *me*?' He laughed now. 'Me, of all people? I'll be no good for her at all.'

More words that Berren couldn't hear and then there was a long pause. When the prince spoke again, his voice was choked and quiet and Berren couldn't hear either of them any more. Finally there were more footsteps and the door opened. There was a snort. 'You never did anything wrong by me, cousin,' said the voice that wasn't the prince. 'A good few other people maybe, but not by me. I'm all for gathering another band and going back up north and hunting that white-skinned bastard into his grave. Just let's take a sorcerer of our own with us next time, eh?'

Berren heard the door close. After a bit, he saw the tall figure of Ser Elmarc walk out into the yard and away into the bulk of the Watchman's Arms. For the rest of the night, he heard the prince toss and turn and pace the floor and mutter to himself. At dawn, when Master Fennis came down to send Berren on his way, the prince was still awake.

5

A BOWL OF PORRIDGE

The dragon-monks didn't come that day but the news spread like a fire through the temple once Berren let slip they were at Bedlam's Crossing. Even the most demure novices struggled to keep their excitement in check. Berren had the unusual pleasure of sitting quietly at the front of Teacher Sterm's class, watching The Worm's cane flick out at other people for a change.

'They're in the city,' Master Sy told him that evening as they sat in the scent garden. 'I imagine they'll arrive at the temple gates exactly as they open. At dawn.'

Which was when Berren was supposed to be there, except he was always late. This once, though, this once he'd be there when he was supposed to be and he'd see them! Full of himself, he started to tell Master Sy what he'd overheard the night before, all full of questions about what it might mean. He'd just passed the bit where the prince had sent his ladies away when Master Sy put a finger to his mouth and slowly shook his head.

'You didn't hear anything, lad.'

Berren stopped. He frowned, puzzled. 'What?'

'You were dreaming, lad. Nodded off and imagined it.' He gave a pointed look back towards the arch into the moonpool yard. Two soldiers were still on guard. 'I'm sure if Ser Elmarc and His Highness were talking, they wouldn't have been talking loudly enough for anyone to hear them.'

'But …' Master Sy's glare cut him off.

'Don't make the same mistake, boy.'

'What? I don't …'

'Oh for the love of Khrozus!' The thief-taker rolled his eyes. His voice dropped. 'If anyone was standing by an open window having a conversation, they probably didn't mean for anyone else to hear it. That mistake. Don't make *that* mistake, the one where you have a conversation you don't want anyone to hear when you can't see who's actually listening! Emperor Ashahn has sat on the Sapphire Throne for twelve years. His first heir was born on the first day of this year. Heh!' For a moment, he grinned. 'Which reminds me: Kol owes me an emperor.' The grin vanished. 'There are those who don't like the idea that he's founding a dynasty but that has nothing to do with us. We're little people, Berren. In the affairs of princes and kings, little people end up getting squashed.' He sounded bitter.

'Right.' Berren nodded. 'I didn't hear anything then, right?'

'Right.'

'Right.' He'd been looking forward to telling Master Sy about what he'd heard for the whole day. He sighed. Master Sy, though, was looking pleased with himself.

'His Highness will be leaving in a few days, back to Varr for the spring festival. We'll have the Emperor's head in our purses again. I think we might take a day or two of leisure before we go and see what work Justicar Kol has to offer a pair of thief-takers. We'll go down to the old lookout tower on Wrecking Point. You can tell me about everything you didn't hear there.' They sat together in silence for a while longer and then the thief-taker nudged Berren. 'Get some rest, lad. You want to be fresh when your dragon-monks arrive don't you? I'll get Fennis to take over down here a bit earlier tomorrow.'

Fresh? Not much chance of that, not unless he dozed in

a corner of the scent garden though his watch, although he was beginning to wonder if he shouldn't do just that. He'd been doing this stupid job for days and nothing had happened at all. No one had even come in to his little garden, not once, not if you didn't count Master Sy and the other thief-takers. Kelm's Bones! If they really thought someone was going to try and climb in through the prince's window, they'd never had put him there in the first place! For all Master Sy's fine words sometimes, he was still an apprentice and they all still treated him like a child.

And he was still thinking that when Master Sy shook him awake in the middle of the night. He grumped and grumbled and got up, shaking off stupid dreams full of dragon-monks, and shuffled off down the stairs into the back of the Watchman's Arms. A bowl of cold porridge was waiting for him, his breakfast. He sat down and tried to settle somewhere comfortable to doze, but he couldn't stop his mind from wandering. Every now and then he looked up, sure he'd heard something. After a bit he shuffled over to a far corner, hidden behind some stupid bush that was supposed to smell of something nice but smelled to Berren of fish – everything smelled of fish tonight, the city finally overwhelming the scents of the garden. It was a good place to hide though. He couldn't see the yard but he could see the prince's window and in the night shadows, he was invisible. Grumbling to himself, he poked his breakfast with his spoon. It was cold and congealed and his belly still hadn't forgiven him for the night before. He wrinkled his nose and pushed it away.

When he looked up again, there was a face at the arch. He blinked and the face became a whole person, slipping into the shadows around the edge of the scent garden. Someone small, his sort of size. It was too dark to make out anything more.

He stayed very still, holding his breath, straining his

ears, wondering for a moment if he was imagining things. The night was silent. He couldn't hear the usual mumble of conversation from the guards in the yard. A chill ran through him. The soldiers would never have let someone come into the garden, not at this time of night. He couldn't hear them because they weren't there any more. Or because they were dead! Khrozus! No had ever told him what he was supposed to do if someone really *did* slip into the garden. He didn't even have a weapon! Only his old purse-cutting knife Stealer and his practice sword, his waster. A glorified stick. Now what?

He could run, he supposed. Run out into the yard shouting his head off, but what good would that be if there weren't any soldiers out there? Then again, he couldn't see whoever had slipped into the garden now. They'd vanished into the shadows by the arch. They could have crept anywhere. If he ran, he might not even get as far as the other yard. He could see himself, clear as if it was happening right in front of him, racing out of the bushes, opening his mouth to scream his head off and nothing coming out because a knife had whirred out of the shadows and skewered his throat.

Or maybe he *was* imagining it. But he couldn't do nothing! Could he?

One shadow detached itself from the others beneath the prince's windows. Carefully and quickly, it started to climb.

'Hey!' The shout came out before Berren had much time to think about it. His hand closed around the bowl of porridge for want of anything else. He threw it as hard as he could, globs of porridge flying in all directions. He'd been aiming for the shadow's head, but the bowl arced and thumped into the shadow's shoulder instead. It bounced off and smashed straight into the prince's window, shattering the brown glass.

For a moment everything was still again. The climber froze. Berren didn't move. Then a voice called out from inside the Watchman's Arms. The climber jumped down. Berren bolted for the moonpool yard, legs pumping in panic, shouting his lungs out, but the climber was faster, cutting him off. In the moonlight, Berren still couldn't see much. It was someone small with two crossed swords strapped across his back and a hood that cast his face into shadow. The man reached out behind him, drew one of the swords and swung at Berren, vicious and fast. Berren skittered away, drew out his waster. Not that it would stop a good strong blow from even a smallsword, but anything was better than nothing. His shouts for help grew stronger.

The hooded man took another swing. Berren danced away, flicking his waster at the man's face in desperation. He felt the tip of it connect, saw the man flinch and reel away, and then they were apart. Berren bolted for the arch again, out to the moonpool. As he ran, he caught a whiff of something mingling in with the stronger-than-usual city smell of bad fish. Something sharp and acrid. Over his shoulder he caught a glimpse of the swordsman, a silhouette against the sky on top of the far wall. Then he was gone.

Two soldiers ran out of the Watchman's Arms. They had their swords out. They ran past Berren into the centre of the yard and then stopped.

'What is it, boy?'

Berren pointed to the scent garden. 'Someone tried to get into the prince's room!' A third soldier burst out behind him. Berren hardly noticed. He was peering at the ground next to the archway to the garden. On either side, almost lost in the gloom, there were bodies.

Another soldier came running out and then another. The first one dashed into the garden. The second one went to the archway. 'Holy Kelm!'

'The prince!' Two more guardsmen came rushing out

and charged across the yard, almost knocking Berren flat. They ran into the door to the prince's rooms. Berren crept nervously over to the arch. The soldier there was kneeling over one body. Berren crouched down beside the other. The ground was slick with blood. The man's throat had been cut. Berren's hand went to his neck. *Should have had a gorget,* that's what Master Sy would say, as soon as he saw this. *A man standing guard at night should always wear a mail shirt and something around his throat.*

And what Berren would say was that someone creeping around at night should have come over the rooftops, not through the yard where they'd have to do something like this in the first place. His hands were shaking and so was the rest of him, but it didn't stop his eyes straying to the dead soldier's belt. To the sword sheathed there. He felt a surge of envy. If he'd had one of *those*, he could have stopped that man!

A hand shook his shoulder. He gave a little shout of alarm and jumped up. 'Hey, boy! Where did they go?'

There must have been a dozen soldiers out in the yard by now, several of Justicar Kol's thief-takers too. He could see Master Fennis. Shakily, he pointed at the far wall of the scent garden.

'Over the wall,' he mumbled. The soldier's skin was still warm, his blood fresh on the ground. Master Sy came out, bleary and rubbing his eyes, his own blade naked in his hand. His gaze flicked from face to face, hardly noticing Berren. Several soldiers were in the scent garden now. Someone Berren didn't know sat down beside him. The man wore the fine clothes of a rich nobleman. Berren had seen his face with the prince but had no idea who he was. His clothes were crumpled now, as though he'd been sleeping in them.

'What did you see, boy? Quick now!'

Berren started to tell him about what had happened.

He'd got as far as throwing his bowl and running to raise the alarm when the door on the far side of the yard burst open and the prince shambled out.

'What in the name of my great bloody uncle is going on?' he was brandishing Berren's porridge bowl. 'Who threw this through my window?'

Half the eyes in the yard swivelled to stare at Berren. The prince followed them. Berren bowed his head.

'You? Syannis' boy? You threw this?' He pitched back his head and laughed. 'And how many months will you have to work, do you suppose, before you have enough silver crowns in your pocket to pay our host for a new window? If I'm not mistaken, this was made in the glass works over by the Blue Cliffs. Best glass in the realms outside of Varr. Clear and flat. Well, a bit brown actually, but still ... They say the glass-makers there are sorcerers.' He cocked his head. 'How much do you suppose it costs to have a window made out of magic glass?'

Berren stared at his feet. He wasn't sure whether he was supposed to answer or not. 'I don't know,' he mumbled as the silence dragged on. He was tired, so incredibly drained, as though his clothes were made of lead.

'What? You don't know? You don't know what?'

'I don't know what it costs. Sir.'

Suddenly he was being bundled out of the way and Master Sy was kneeling in his place. 'If my apprentice has offended you, Your Highness, it is I who should take the blame, for I was the one who set him to watch outside your window. I will, of course, see that our host is paid for the damage my foolish boy has done. I will also see to it that he practices with furious intent so there can be no doubt in my mind that the next time he hurls an object at a fleeting figure in the dark, Your Highness, it will fly true.'

Berren risked a glance up. The prince had a huge frown on his face. 'Figure in the dark? Master thief-taker, do I detect a twinge of sharpness to your tongue?' He pushed Master Sy away and stood in front of Berren again. 'Get up, boy.'

Berren got to his feet. The prince was looking around now, taking in everything in the yard. His eyes lingered on the bodies and the soldiers in the scent garden.

'You threw it *at* someone?'

Berren nodded. Everyone was looking at him. He didn't know what to say. 'Yes, sir. Someone came in to the garden and started to climb up the vines, sir.'

The prince nodded. He had a little smirk on his lips but his eyes were angry. 'And you saw him and threw a bowl at him?'

'Yes, sir.'

'Usually people address me as Your Highness, boy, but never mind.' He shook his head. 'Why a bowl, of all things?'

'It was all I had, sir. I ... I mean Your Highness.'

For a moment, the prince's gazed flicked towards Master Sy. 'So you, Syannis, master thief-taker, you set your man to watch over me and then you armed him with a bowl?'

'And this!' Berren held up his waster. 'Um, Your Highness.'

'A bowl *and* a stick. A veritable fortress!' His eyes moved on, to one of the soldiers, an old one with a grey beard. 'And you, Lord Tanngris, clearly did not have enough men standing watch in this yard.'

'Ser Rothis and Ser Byrne are both dead, Your Highness,' growled the soldier with the grey beard. 'You are not.'

The prince's smirked drooped. 'And how nice it must be for them to know they died for a good cause. Oh no, wait, they didn't, they died for me. How do you suppose their families will respond, Lord Tanngris? How even nicer it might have been for us all if *no one had died at all.*' He shook his head and snorted. 'Dawn can't be far away and my night is completely disturbed. I am going back to bed. Tanngris, you can keep watch outside my window with as many men as you see fit. We shall leave tomorrow. This city has lost its charm.' He spun away and then turned back and regarded Berren. 'Is there some chance you saved me some unpleasantness, boy? If you did, I'm afraid you've earned yourself few friends and probably more enemies than I can count. Ask for something. It's always good to take a reward. It makes people think that's what you were after all along. Is there something you want?'

Berren looked up. 'I want to learn swords,' he blurted, and then quickly looked down again.

The prince looked at Berren. 'Seems a little late for that to me. Still ...' He looked at Master Sy and then a sly grin spread across his lips. 'Didn't I hear that the Autarch was sending some of his sword-masters here? In preparation for making a little visit himself at exactly the same time as he should have been in Varr to name my niece?' He chuckled. 'As snubs go, that's about as sharp as you can get without stabbing someone. He could at least have claimed poor health.' He nodded. 'Swords, boy. Right. So be it. The monks at the temple shall train you. I'm sure that will delight them. Tanngris, we shall deliver our instructions to the idiots of the sun tomorrow as soon as I can be bothered with getting up.'

With that he was gone. The soldiers and the thief-takers stared after him. Slowly, Syannis shook his head. He gave Berren a hard sad look.

'What have you done, lad? What have you done?'

6

BEWARE THE GIFTS OF PRINCES

On any other day, Berren would never have been at the temple gates for dawn. There wasn't any point for a start, and even with the best reason in the world and no matter how hard he tried, Berren was always five or ten minutes late for everything.

This morning was different. On *this* morning he was standing outside the temple gates ten minutes before the first rays of sun split open the horizon. He had Master Sy beside him and a crowd of jostling onlookers. For most people, this was probably their only chance to see the monks of Torpreah.

They didn't disappoint. As the first sunlight struck the golden spire on the top of the solar temple, a great gong sounded from inside as it did every morning; today, though, it was answered by another gong, every bit as deep and resonant, from across Deephaven Square. At the same precise moment, the beginnings of a procession emerged from the Avenue of the Sun beside the merchants' guild-house. Sixteen men walked in front, straight and proud and dressed in pale yellow robes. Eight men came behind them; they carried a long pole from which hung a gong as large as a horse. After that came mules and wagons but Berren had no eyes for those. He was looking at the monks and nothing else as they walked in perfect slow precision across the square. The sun lit up the dome of the solar temple exactly as they reached the gates. The gong inside sounded again and the doors groaned and opened. A man with a hammer ran up to the gong carried behind the monks and sounded it. Berren saw the eight men carrying it stagger slightly. The noise of it made him flinch. The monks, though, never blinked.

They had marks on their faces. Berren could see that when they were only halfway across Deephaven Square, but it wasn't until they were almost at the gate that he could see what they were. They had the sunburst symbol, a flaming circle tattooed to their face in a brilliant fiery red. They looked fierce and proud.

They were short, too. Short and wiry like him and Master Sy, not heavy and muscle-bound like most of the prince's soldiers at the Watchman's Arms. With a slight shock he realised that the last one was a women, every bit as unreadable as the men. He watched them all go past. They each had two small curved swords strapped across their backs. The light of the sun reached the ground; across the city and the river Arr, the horizon burst into an orange fire. The temple doors fell back and for a moment, a golden light washed over the advancing monks, casting them into silhouette. Berren blinked and rubbed his eyes. From behind they looked a lot like the man he'd seen in the scent garden.

He shook himself. It stood to reason that the killer had been short and carried a sword over his back. Short people were better at climbing and creeping and hiding. And you wouldn't want a great long sword hanging from your belt for quiet work. A smallsword, that's what anyone would take if they thought about it. Strapped across his back to keep it out of the way.

Or across *her* back. For some reason, that thought had never crossed his mind until now. It filled him up with a strange excitement.

'Off you go then, lad.'

Berren followed the monks through the temple gate. He threw Master Sy an idle salute and then ran all the way to the temple and sat down at the back where no one would notice. Other novices crowded in, priests too, and then the monks walked sedately past to stand in the centre of the temple, ringing the altar while the Sunherald of Deephaven himself walked in slow circles around them, droning on about something. Berren even tried to pay attention, but he might as well not have bothered. He was too far away to hear properly and even the words he caught didn't make much sense. The ceremonies were strange and exciting at first, but as they wore on and on all through the morning, Berren's head began to feel heavy. The nights awake in the scent garden caught up with him. Before long he was asleep.

He woke up again to find the temple in silence. The Sunherald was still there and so were the monks, but they were all as still as statues. With a little gasp of horror, Berren saw the sun on the altar. It was nearly midday! He'd been asleep for the whole morning! Oh gods, what if The Worm had seen him? Had he been snoring? What if any of the other teachers had seen him? What if the *monks* had seen him? *Someone* must have seen him! Sooner or later Sterm would find out. Sleeping in temple was just a fraction short of spitting at the altar. Khrozus! He'd be working penances for the whole rest of the year for this!

Everyone was very still. They were all staring at him, or at least that was how it seemed at first. Slowly, though, he realised that they were staring past him, to the great doors behind. He turned around to look.

'Well don't stop just for me,' called a voice from among the silhouettes at the door. Berren knew the voice at once – the prince.

There was a long pause. 'And there ends today's lesson,'

snapped the Sunherald from the altar. Berren's brow furrowed. He checked the angle of the light on the altar again. Not far from midday but not quite there yet.

'Oh, don't tell me you've been preaching away all morning and I happen to have the foul luck to show up just in time for the half-hour recess before you start all over again? Fortunate in a way, I suppose, since we can get right to business without my interrupting anything. Pity, though. I was so looking forward to a good sermoning and my adjutants tell me I'm in something of a hurry now.' The prince began to walk through the temple. He had six men with him; Berren was startled to see that one of them was Master Sy. The thief-taker's face was taut. 'Keep your little dragons handy too, Your Holiness,' laughed the prince as he strode to the altar. 'This concerns them.'

'Novices and initiates, you are dismissed!' The Sunherald started to pace again but with none of the serenity he'd had before. 'There will be prayers at midday and then you will assemble in the practice yard while our honoured guests from Torpreah show us why they carry the reputation that they do.'

Berren watched as most of the priests and the novices and the initiates filed out of the temple. He got up to slip out with the last of them, but Master Sy was there. His fingers twisted around Berren's ear.

'This is all your fault,' he hissed. 'Every bit of it. I hope you're ready for what you've done.'

Berren had no idea what Master Sy meant but he knew better than to say anything. They marched towards the centre of the temple, to the altar and the monks. The altar seemed golden, bathed in the sunlight streaming in through the dome above. Whatever the prince was saying, neither the priest nor the monks were liking it.

'... or not, since it's really quite irrelevant. You will do as I say, and that is that.' The prince's words. He shrugged.

'Well, I suppose you could disobey and then I could have you all shipped off to the mines, strip this little palace of yours bare and turn it into a poorhouse. After the Overlord has subdued the inevitable riots, of course, but then I won't be here to care about *that* little detail.'

Master Sy pushed Berren forward. One of the temple priests rolled his eyes. 'Him?'

'Yes him. The annoying little rude one. Is that about right?'

'You want the Autarch's monks to teach this oafish boy to wield a sword?'

'Oh yes. Although...' The prince leaned forward towards the Sunherald. 'They're *your* monks, aren't they? For as long as they're here?' He turned to the monks and pointed at the nearest, the woman. 'You. You can do it.' Berren's eyes widened and he bit his lip. The monk couldn't have been much older than him. Might even have been the same age. And he was going to be trained by a *girl*?

He glanced at her. You could hardly even tell she was a girl, she was so skinny.

The monk bowed. 'How hard do you wish him trained, Your Highness?' Her face didn't flicker, even as Berren stared at her. Flat chest, narrow hips, all sharp angles and no curves. If she was a girl, she was probably the ugliest girl in the city, he decided. Not that that made things any better.

On the other hand, she *was* a dragon-monk.

The prince blew out his cheeks and stretched his shoulders. 'Oh, as hard as you like, I suppose.'

'Then he will be dead within a week, Your Highness.'

The prince looked Berren up and down and then turned back to the monk with a pained expression on his face. 'Well, maybe not that hard then. I shan't be wanting to hear that this boy got sent to his death by way of a reward. Gods, something like that might even prey on my conscience. Train him hard then, but please, not so hard that he expires.' The prince grinned at Berren. It wasn't a very nice grin. 'Train him hard enough to see whether he really wants it.'

The monk bowed again. 'As Your Highness commands.' It was hard to tell whether she was pleased or angry or simply didn't care one way or the other, although at least all his staring had finally managed to put a bit of colour in her cheeks. The Sunherald was managing to keep his face flat too, but the temple priests were a different matter. Most of them looked ready to explode.

'You cannot … ! Even you, you can't … !'

'What? Spit it out! I can't what? Wander through your city issuing edicts that everyone is forced to obey no matter how random and whimsical they are? But I can, you see. One of the few joys of being a prince.' He frowned and scratched his short black beard. 'Well, one of the few joys apart from the endless parade of wine and willing women, anyway.' He smiled again. 'If you wish to lie awake at night begging your god for a relief against the injustices of the world, consider that your Autarch is busily making a point of snubbing my family and that his monks would not be here for me to impose upon otherwise. Good day.' With that, he turned on his heel and marched out of the temple. His men followed, as did Master Sy, still dragging Berren by the ear. Outside, the prince stopped again. He looked at Master Sy and, fleetingly, at Berren.

'Gentlemen, I thank you for your services. Loathsome duty now beckons. Lord Tanngris will settle our accounts with the Watchman's Arms.' He stopped and stared at Master Sy. 'You. However much I have called you dull, you do not belong here. You are rotting on the inside, and believe me, on that subject I know what I'm talking about. Thief-taking is not for you. Go and do whatever it is you need to do.'

Master Sy bowed. He was trying not to show it, but the prince's words had touched him somewhere raw. His hands were trembling and his skin had turned pale. Berren didn't have time to think about that, though, for the prince was looking at *him* now. His eyes were pale and watery. They had a bit of ice to them. A bit of ice and a bit of anger and a lot of sadness, Berren thought.

'You. Take this, boy.' He pressed something into Berren's hand. 'When your master goes, he's not going to want you with him. You'll probably follow him anyway, whether he likes it or not, but at least let me give you a choice. You may come to Varr. Go to the Kaveneth. Present this and tell them that you have answered my summons. Tell them I say you should be working for Eagle-Beak, if he's still alive. They'll know who you mean.' Whatever he'd put in Berren's hand, the prince closed Berren's fingers over it. 'And don't lose it, eh?'

Before Berren could even look up, the prince had turned and was walking away. Master Sy put a hand on Berren's shoulder. 'Watch him go, lad. That's the last you'll ever see of him, yet his favour will haunt you like a curse. It will be a weight around your neck before this year is up, I promise you.'

Berren opened his fingers to see what the prince had given him. It was gold, like an emperor fresh from the imperial mint but bigger and with a more complicated stamp on it. Not the Emperor's head but a sword and a shield on one side and the imperial standard, a flaming eagle within a triangle, on the other.

'Worth a bit, that,' muttered Master Sy.

Berren nodded. He was staring at the token. He had no idea what it meant but he held it as though it was the most precious thing he'd ever had. He couldn't pocket it for fear of somehow losing it. Maybe a chain, around his neck …

'You could sell it.'

54

He closed his fingers around the token, clutching it tight. Yes, a chain around his neck, that was the only way to be safe.

The thief-taker sighed. He clapped Berren on the shoulder. 'Remember, lad, when this all turns sour, that it all came about because you did the right thing and for the right reasons. Now I'm hungry and my friendships with the priests in this temple have just been royally slaughtered. Ah well, only took ten years to build. Come on: I need a drink, I've got a pocket full of the Prince's silver, Justicar Kol owes me a purse and the most expensive tea-house in the city is right across the square beside the guild-house. So that's where I'm going. You can come with me if you like, or you can stay here for midday prayers if you like the look of your new teacher so much.'

Berren reddened. '*Her?*'

'Don't think I didn't see you looking, and don't think that she didn't either. You're in for some hard hard work, lad.' He chuckled. 'So are you coming or are you staying?'

For a moment Berren hesitated. Not that he wanted to be in the temple for any longer that he had to; but after prayers the monks were going to do their demonstration and that was something he didn't want to miss. He'd get to see his new teacher fight, maybe work out a trick or two so he could show them he wasn't some stupid novice and they'd give him a proper teacher instead of some girl.

Master Sy must have read his mind. 'Oh don't you worry, we'll be back quick enough. I want to see your new teacher show off her skills too. Although *I* simply need to know that she's good enough for my student ... You know, I don't think I'd mind it at all if she ripped your arms off.' He smiled and for once he seemed to mean it. 'Come on, lad. Asking His Highness for sword lessons was foolishness, but it was a brave thing you did. I'll probably never have the money to do this again.' He raised an eyebrow.

55

'Unless your teachers have actually managed to stir a little piety in you?'

Berren vigorously shook his head. 'No chance of *that*!' Still clutching the prince's token, he ran to the temple gates.

7
A CUP OF TEA AND A BAD TASTE

'Myla! Soraya! Lucius!' Halfway across the square, a boy of about seven bolted across the stones. Two girls, somewhat younger, ran after him waving wooden swords. 'Come here!' The girls ran straight in front of Berren, forcing him to lurch sideways, but that just made him collide with the woman running after them instead. They both staggered away, the woman calling out a stream of apologies, Berren too busy checking his purse to hear what she'd said. Old habits died hard. He watched as the woman caught up with first the girls and then the boy, picking them up in her arms one after the other and scolding them soundly while they giggled and laughed. They were rich, you could see that from their clothes. Almost anyone who came up to The Peak was either rich or a novice at the temple.

'Come on, lad!' Master Sy was already a dozen yards ahead. 'No time to dawdle.'

Berren sighed. Here he was, apprenticed to Master Syannis, the best thief-taker in Deephaven. He'd earned his first golden emperor at the age of thirteen. Not been given it, but *earned* it. He was learning letters, even if he hated them, in the great temple of the Sun. He'd earned the gratitude of a prince and he was about to be taught swords by the greatest fighters in the empire. And yet ...

And yet?

And yet sometimes he would have given it all to be a fishmonger's son, quiet and dim and unassuming, amounting to nothing very much and yet oafishly content.

'Come on, come on! They'll ring the bell for midday prayers soon and then we might as well forget about being served in here.' Master Sy pushed open an impressive door of dark carved wood. Berren followed him into a dim room. The air was rich, thick with a hundred different scents and spices – sweet jasmine, bitter liquorice, pungent nutmeg and cloves and cinnamon, all layered over flowers and pipeweed and tea. Even Master Sy paused as though taken aback.

'Right.' The thief-taker pushed on deeper into the tea-house. The room was nearly empty except for a pair of girls about Berren's age who were wearing ... Berren squinted. They were dressed like pageboys except they very obviously weren't. They wore their shirts loose and their breeches tight. As Master Sy approached, they smiled and bowed. Berren stared, hoping they'd bow to him too, but they didn't. He caught Master Sy looking at him, one eyebrow raised.

'The proprietors of the Golden Cup know very well who their patrons are.' The thief-taker wrinkled his nose. 'Fat old men who like to leer.' The two serving girls exchanged a glance and giggled. Master Sy bowed back to them and then asked for a string of things that Berren had never heard of. It was as though he'd suddenly started speaking another language, something completely alien like the tongue of the black-skinned sea-traders. The girls seemed to understand, though; they nodded and hurried away. Berren wistfully watched them go, thinking of them beside the sword-monk who was supposed to be his teacher. See, now *that* was how a girl was supposed to look ...

'Mouth closed, boy.' Master Sy was already sitting down. Berren quickly followed beside him.

'They were ...' He looked for the right word and couldn't find it.

'Lovely?' offered Master Sy. Berren nodded. That would have to do. They were like all the best of the women he'd seen with the prince, the curved beauties from the higher reaches of Reeper Hill, mixed with the honest earthiness of Lilissa. If there was a word for that, he didn't know it.

'Gorgeous,' he sighed.

'The Grim has the pick of all the girls in the city, or at least the poor ones, which amounts to much the same. Rich men come here, and I promise you: every girl The Grim puts to work becomes a mistress to one of them. Sometimes a man in the throes of passion lets slip a little secret or two. Sometimes those secrets somehow make their way back The Grim. Somehow, to some, this comes as a surprise.' He raised an eyebrow and shrugged. 'Rich fools. Deephaven's contribution to the empire.'

'The Grim?' Berren snorted. Last he'd heard, The Grim had been some pirate who'd made his fortune during the civil war before Berren had been born. He'd been a pirate then and the rumours around The Peak were that he was still a pirate now, just a different sort of pirate. Hardly a dirty old man running a tea-house, surely?

'Yes. I hear he chooses them himself.' Master Sy leaned back and spread out his arms. 'The Golden Cup. They say they brew the best tea in the city and bake the best pastries. Master Mardan and Master Fennis both swear these tea-houses will be all the rage soon. Deephaven will be full of them and then Varr and the City of Spires and everywhere else in the empire. I think Master Fennis is even considering throwing in his sword and giving up thief-taking altogether to go and start one in Varr.' He laughed. 'Can't see it myself. You imperials are all too dark and dour and gloomy for something like this. I gather the prince came here soon after he arrived and didn't think much of it at all. I told Fennis he should try his luck further south. Go to Torpreah or Helhex where it's warmer. Varr?' He shook his head, still laughing. 'The place is buried in snow for half the year. What would they do with a house like this?' Then he frowned. 'Keep your eyes open for Kol. He's supposed to be joining us.'

He was interrupted as one of the serving girls came back with a silver tray. She leaned over the table, laying out an array of small silver cups and bowls. Berren tried not to stare. The girl wore her shirt loose. You could see all the way down to ...

For an instant she caught his eye. Hastily, Berren looked away, blushing furiously. The girl smiled very slightly then finished by setting down a plate with a dozen tiny little things that Berren might have called cakes if they'd been about ten times bigger.

'Is there anything else I can give you gentlemen?' she asked, glancing again at Berren. *Yes*, Berren wanted to say, but all the air had been sucked out of him. Master Sy smiled politely.

'Thank you, that will be all.'

The girl left. 'Master, don't you ... ?'

'This isn't Reeper Hill,' said Master Sy sharply. 'They're not ground-floor girls here, and even if they were, the likes of you and I couldn't afford them.'

'But.' But what? He sighed again. Master Sy was frowning. He never liked talking about women.

'Right. While we're waiting for Kol, watch carefully while I show you how this works. Not that you're ever likely to need to know how to pour tea properly, but you might as well learn.'

The thief-taker started doing things with the teapot and the various minuscule bowls of this and that. Berren pretended to pay attention while watching the serving girls out of the corner of his eye. He couldn't stop thinking about the monks, either. As soon as they were done here, he was going to get to see them fight. A demonstration! And then after that, they were going to teach him! The best sword-monks in the whole world and they were going to teach him! *Him!* He couldn't sit still.

Maybe she was actually a boy who happened to *look* a bit like a girl. They wouldn't really make him train with a girl, would they?

'I'll give up, shall I?' grumbled Master Sy. He didn't sound angry. If anything, he was almost smiling, something Berren rarely got to see. 'No, no, you're right. You go ahead and stare at pretty girls. I suppose you deserve it. We did very well out of His Highness's stay here.' The thief-taker patted his pocket. 'I've got a handful of silver crowns for you. Our prince certainly pays better than Justicar Kol ever did, and the justicar, when he bothers to get here, owes me a purse too.' His almost-smile turned into a full grin. 'And with half the city's thief-takers on bodyguard duty for the last few months, I'm sure Kol's got a nice backlog of bounties that need sorting out. He's probably pissing himself thinking that we're all going to retire or else spend the next few months in our cups while the city goes to rats.' The thief-taker lifted his teacup. He closed Berren's fingers around the other cup and lifted Berren's hand into the air between them. Then he touched the two cups together. 'Here's to us then, lad. The best thief-takers in the city. What shall it be this time? There's goods going missing in the sea-docks again.' There were always goods going missing in the sea-docks. Ever since one of the harbour-masters had tried to have them both killed, Master Sy had taken to watching them all. Every one of them had their fingers in something.

Berren shook his head. 'Can we do something else? I'm bored of the docks and they all still think it was one of us who murdered that fat bastard VenDormen.'

'They do.' For a moment, Master Sy smiled again. 'Don't you find that very useful? Makes them all nicely scared of us.'

'Makes them keep their mouths shut too.'

'Some of them.' The thief-taker shrugged. 'There have been barges robbed down at the river docks. Whole cargoes vanishing in the night.'

'Mudlarks,' sniffed Berren. 'Kol just wants an excuse to send you over there with some of his soldiers to burn them out again.'

'Probably.'

'What about whoever it was who tried to break into the prince's rooms, eh? Isn't there a reward up for that?'

Master Sy snorted. 'Won't be from Kol. He doesn't usually worry too much about people getting murdered. Things getting stolen, that's more his interest. There's been some curious stuff showing up in the night markets of late. A few wagoners getting a little too rich. Velgian tells me they even had Taki black powder. Maybe we'll start there.'

'But no one else even saw what happened!' Berren had a picture clear in his mind. A silhouette in the scent garden of the Watchman's Arms. Short with two swords slung across his back, almost exactly like a sword-monk.

'Lad, that's trouble of the worst sort. Best you keep out of it.' Which was the thief-taker's way of saying he was already thinking about it. 'I tell you what interests me: someone broke into the courthouse a while back. Killed two guards and stole some papers. Kol's paying well to get whoever did it. Very well.'

Berren shrugged. He was just the apprentice, after all. He wasn't sure he cared what they did. He'd be stuck in the temple learning letters and swords for however long the sword-monks were here anyway. Master Sy could go and do what he liked.

Learning swords from a girl. He shuddered.

The thief-taker wasn't smiling now. If anything he was looking angry. Outside, across the square in the Temple of the Sun, the noon bells started to ring, calling the faithful to prayer. 'No.' Master Sy shook his head. 'Best leave that one well alone.'

Berren shrugged again.'What if it was a monk?' he asked, eyeing the serving girls as they walked past.

'Then you'd be dead and the prince too most likely. Might as well ask if it was one of ours. A bad thief-taker.'

'Don't they all go bad, sooner or later?' That's what Master Sy used to tell him. *Don't trust any of the others. Too much temptation.*

The thief-taker glared at him. 'Go on then, lad, who was it?'

'Can't be Master Mardan or Master Fennis. Too tall, both of them.'

'Velgian's worse with a blade than with those fearful rhymes of his.' The thief-taker laughed. 'Did you know he got mugged? He was down near the river docks on his way back from the River Gate the day after your little set-to at the Watchman's Arms and he got jumped, right outside the House of Cats and Gulls. Couple of mudlarks. One of them thumped him in the face, the other one cut his purse and they left him there, sitting on his arse in the slime with nothing but a bloody nose to show for it.' Master Sy shook his head. 'Some thief-taker, eh? Tiarth isn't in the city at the moment. I suppose there's plenty of others though. Plenty of snuffers too.' The Golden Cup was growing noisy. Even though the temple bells were still pealing, men were coming through the doors in a steady stream. Fat men, mostly, all of them dressed in rich clothes. For a moment, Berren forgot about Master Sy. He stared open-mouthed as one of them groped the serving girls and laughed to his friends. The girls put on a good show of being amused. Whether they meant it or not, Berren couldn't tell.

'Money, lad,' hissed the thief-taker. 'The guild-house is right next door. A few pious fellows go out across the square to the temple for midday prayers. Most of them come in here for Grim's sweetmeats. They have riches, lad, more than you can dream. They can make you into a prince of the city or they can swat you away without even blinking. These are the ones who pay Justicar Kol, these men. We take their coin. Everyone does, one way or the other, even your precious prince. Watch them closely by all means, but do it with care.'

Master Sy finished his tea and poured himself another. For a few minutes they watched the growing crowd in silence together. Now and then the thief-taker would point out a face and whisper a name. As the Golden Cup grew full, one of the serving girls slipped over and whispered in Master Sy's ear. The thief-taker nodded. A moment after she went, he got to his feet.

'Come on, lad. I don't know what's happened to Kol, but we don't want to be late for your monks.'

Berren frowned. He knew exactly how long noon prayers took and it was longer than this. He glanced down at the pastries still left on the table.

'In your pockets, lad.' They didn't even go out the same way they'd come in; they slipped out the back as though they were servants.

'She asked us to leave, didn't she?'

Master Sy didn't answer, but once they were outside, he stopped. The look on his face when he turned was enough to make Berren take a step back.

'The Golden Cup isn't for us, lad. It's for fat f—' He took a deep breath. The anger fell into slow retreat. He seemed to reach for some different words but couldn't find any.

Eventually he simply shook his head. 'Not for the likes of us. That's all there is to it. Come on, lad. I don't think we'll be coming back.'

8

DRAGON-MONKS

They walked around the back of the Golden Cup, through the alleys until they were on the edge of Deephaven Square again. Master Sy stopped near the temple gates where a man was selling sweet pancakes laced with honeyberries, yellow and round like the midday sun. Suncakes. The thief-taker bought a couple for each of them, took a mouthful and gave a satisfied belch. 'Don't suppose you ever get out from your lessons during the day, but these are the best suncakes in the city. Expensive, but the best.'

Berren, who skipped prayers to eat one whenever he could afford it, said nothing. He licked the crumbs off his lips and followed Master Sy through the gates. The priests and the novices were still at their devotions but the monks were outside. They'd drawn a circle in the sand and had started to practice, stretching their arms and their legs between frenzied bouts of sparring with sticks. Berren walked up to the line in the sand and plonked himself down to watch, munching away on his second suncake. He'd never seen anyone doing the things these sword-monks could do, and this was just practice! He'd never met anyone who could bend their legs so far for a start, and when they went on to handsprings and backflips, his jaw dropped. It was as though they were bouncing right back up off the ground! He drew a breath between his teeth.

'Wow!'

'Impressed?' Master Sy sounded anything but. 'Acrobats do this in Four Winds Square every festival.'

Berren nodded. He'd seen them too. But acrobats didn't have swords.

After a few minutes, the monks seemed to notice they were being watched. Two of them stopped, the girl and the oldest of the monks, the one who'd been standing and watching the others. The girl stared at Berren with open animosity. Berren stared back. With her hair cropped short, a sunburst tattooed across her face, she might as well have been a boy. Even the tight yellow shirts the monks wore didn't help.

The older one cocked his head at Master Sy.

'I am the elder dragon here,' he said. His tones were flat and formal, empty of either friendship or hostility. He glanced briefly at Berren. 'Has this boy been trained at all?'

Master Sy bristled. 'He's had some lessons, yes. Mostly on stance and grip and basic technique.' Berren wrinkled his nose and glanced at the sky. *A few. Nowhere near enough.*

'Can he hold a sword?'

The thief-taker stood up and beckoned Berren to do the same. When they were both on their feet, he put his own sword into Berren's hands. 'Show them your guard.'

Obediently, Berren took up a defensive stance. He gritted his teeth and curled his toes as the girl shook her head and rolled her eyes. The elder dragon inspected Berren thoroughly. He put a gentle palm on Berren's shoulder. Then, without seeming to move at all, he pushed Berren over as easily as if he'd flicked a leaf into the air.

'Who taught him to stand like this?' Berren's shoulder felt as though he'd been kicked by a horse. He could hardly move his arm; he cradled it as he struggled to get back to his feet. The elder dragon had been *touching* him. How could he hit so hard from so close?

67

'Actually, I did,' frowned Master Sy. 'I'd appreciate it if you didn't break him.'

The elder dragon gave a bow. 'Of course.' He waved a hand and beckoned the girl forward. The more Berren looked at her, the more he thought of the silhouette he'd seen in the scent garden. *That* could have been a girl, he supposed, if it had been a girl that looked like a boy ...

'This is Tasahre. Tasahre is the youngest of my students. I am considering having her train your apprentice. Her skills are adequate.' As though the Prince himself hadn't singled her out! Why did he have to point at *her*? Because she'd been the closest when he'd happened to think about it? Berren clenched his teeth.

The elder dragon nodded to himself. 'The experience will do her good.' His voice was carefully neutral; Tasahre, however, looked anything but indifferent. She glared venomously at Berren. Berren glared back.

Master Sy frowned. 'She and Berren must be almost the same age.'

'Tasahre has been with the order since she was three years old. She has been holding a sword since she was six. She is not one of my better swords, but I am confident that any shortcomings in her technique will be unimportant in this case. I imagine she would have been your boy's equal at about the age of ten, yours by the age of twelve.'

Master Sy snorted. 'That's a hard claim to credit.'

The elder dragon took a step to the side, beckoning the thief-taker to cross the ring in the sand. 'You may see for yourself if you like.'

For a long time, Master Sy didn't move. Tasahre watched him, muscles tense like a coiled snake waiting to strike.

'The boy is yours, after all. It is right and proper that you should test his teacher.'

'Oh, I'm quite sure it's not your little sword-monk who's

being tested.' Master Sy stared back at Tasahre. The elder dragon smiled blandly.

'It will also be useful to Tasahre to see the style of her pupil's previous teacher. This way she will see the flaws that have been brought to his training and she will know what corrections must first be made before any bad ways become habit. Assuming it is not all too late for that. As you observed, they are almost the same age. In many ways, your boy is far too old to learn.' Berren's stomach tightened. His heart beat faster. He was going to show her! It wasn't as though Master Sy hadn't taught him anything at all!

'I've always been told there's not much point in teaching a man what to do with a sword until he's at least strong enough to hold it properly.'

'Interesting.' For the first time, the elder dragon allowed some emotion to show: he looked very slightly intrigued. 'Your own teacher came from Caladir or Brons then?'

'Kalda, actually.' Master Sy sounded annoyed. 'You won't have heard of it. Small school on the fringes of the Dominion. They took their instructors from the sun-king's court where they could. Oh, and she did a lot of real fighting. On battlefields, you understand. Killing people. We used to have a lot of that.'

'Ah.' The elder dragon nodded solemnly as if that explained everything. Then he beckoned again. In the background, the doors to the temple were swinging open. Midday prayers were over. Finally Master Sy nodded. He took back his sword and crossed the line in the sand, walking slowly, keeping his back to the sword-monks with his blade in his hand. Tasahre didn't move, although her eyes left Berren and followed the thief-taker instead. The novices were coming out of the temple. They weren't allowed to run, and the sight of them walking as fast as they possibly could would have made Berren laugh, except … Except something was in the air, some sense of expectation and it made him uneasy. Master Sy was twirling his sword, loosening his arm. They weren't using practise weapons either and Berren knew exactly how sharp Master Sy kept his steel.

The thief-taker turned around and drew up into a neutral guard. Tasahre didn't move. More and more priests and novices were streaming out of the temple now. They sat at the edge of the ring in the sand, watching, full of anticipation. Berren stared too.

Tasahre turned to face Master Sy with slow precision. She had her back to Berren now. She half-crouched. For a moment everything was still; then she sprang and Berren had never seen anything like it. Some twenty feet separated her from the thief-taker and she covered nearly all of it in a single leap. She landed in front of him, both swords out, one blade sweeping through the air where Master Sy's head should have been. Berren gasped. She didn't even try to pull the attack! The thief-taker shimmied sideways at the last possible instant. He ducked the sword coming at his head and his own flicked towards the girl's kidneys, so fast that Berren barely even saw it. The sword-monk did, though. She twisted aside, parried with her second blade and swung again. She was fast, cat-quick and every bit as agile.

'Stop!' called the older monk. Immediately, Tasahre jumped away from Master Sy. She held her swords in guard and didn't move. The thief-taker watched her, wary.

The elder dragon walked across the sand. He prised first one sword and then the other out of Tasahre's fingers and replaced them with a single wooden practice sword. 'There,' he said. 'Two swords is how we learn, but your opponent has only one. Now you will have to adapt your style to your circumstances. Begin.'

She came at the thief-taker slower this time, circling around him, edging closer. They exchanged a flurry of blows, all thrusts and parries, no sweeping cuts this time. They were both so quick that Berren had no idea who was winning, if anyone was winning at all. He saw Master Sy wince. A moment later, Tasahre stepped back and threw down her wooden sword.

The thief-taker bowed. 'You have touched me twice. You fight well.'

'You are holding back!' she said.

'I don't want to hurt you.'

All the sword-monks flinched at that. The elder dragon moved quickly to put himself between Tasahre and Master Sy. There was an exchange of words, too quiet and quick for Berren to follow; then the elder dragon took up another practice sword and handed it to the thief-taker. He gave the steel one to Berren.

'Begin!'

This time the sword-monk flew at Master Sy. The air rang with the sound of wood striking wood as she battered him slowly backwards. Every second, one sword or the other seemed to come within a whisker of striking home. Berren had seen Master Sy do this before though, let himself be pushed back; he waited, holding his breath for the time when the thief-taker would step sideways instead of backwards, flick his wrist and end the fight.

He did exactly that. Except Tasahre's waster was somehow in the way. She blocked his lunge. For a moment they were so close they were almost touching. Quick as a snake, the sword-monk punched Master Sy in the face with her other hand, squarely on the nose. The thief-taker staggered back, blood streaming down his face, and the sword-monk went straight after him. She came low, lunging at his hips; Master Sy twisted away but there was a desperation to the way he moved this time. The sword-monk scooped up a handful of sand as she rose and threw it at his face. As he turned and raised his guard to protect his eyes, the practice sword caught him a thumping blow in the ribs. A clear win. Master Sy staggered again. His guard dropped.

The sword-monk didn't stop. She dropped almost to the ground and cracked the waster hard against Master Sy's leg, just above the knee. Berren winced. Somehow he didn't go down, but Tasahre was up again, leaping into the air. She kicked, one foot thrust out, straight into the thief-taker's chest. He flew backwards, his leg collapsed and now he was down.

Tasahre stepped away. She bowed, once to Master Sy, now gasping in the sand, once to the elder dragon, and once to the assembled priests. Then, quietly and calmly, although she was still shaking from the fight, she took her place with the other sword-monks. The elder dragon waited until she was seated and then went to look at Master Sy. He knelt down and poked at the thief-taker's leg, then put his hand on the thief-taker's knee. Master Sy let out a cry of pain. The monk said something too quiet for anyone but the thief-taker to hear, got up and walked away. He gestured as he did, and immediately, two more sword-monks jumped to their feet. They ran to Master Sy, lifted him up between them and dragged him to Berren.

'Master?'

The thief-taker steadied himself on Berren's shoulders. His face was tight with pain. 'You will have to help me,' he said, his teeth clenched together, 'to get home.'

9
A DEATH IN THE FAMILY

The monks started on something else but Berren had lost interest. Master Sy could barely walk. He could hop, but his injured leg couldn't bear weight at all, not without the thief-taker clenching up in agony. Berren found himself a handcart but the thief-taker shook his head. No, it wouldn't do for the city's most feared thief-taker to be seen pushed about in a cart.

So they walked, Master Sy's arm around Berren's shoulders, three good legs between them. Afternoon bells rippled out from The Peak, chasing after them, and by the time they reached Four Winds Square, Berren's legs ached and his arms were burning. People turned to stare as they passed. A man being half-carried across the city might have been common enough down by the waterfront or the sea-docks, but not up here. People knew him too, knew Master Sy. Now and then, eyes would stop and stare at them and then hurry away, muttering *thief-taker* under their breath.

Finally they were across and into the narrow web of streets and alleys and the little yard where the thief-taker lived. A small gang of weavers from nearby Clothmakers' squeezed around them. They were familiar faces, even if Berren had no names to put to them. They filed past in silence, a nod here and there to the thief-taker, even one to Berren. After they passed they clustered together again. Berren could almost hear them whispering.

'Should I get Teacher Garrient?' he asked as he opened the thief-taker's door. Garrient was the moon-priest who'd been the thief-taker's friend from almost the moment Master Sy had set foot in Deephaven. He'd helped them before when Berren had taken a blow to the head from a mudlark over in Siltside, and on other occasions besides.

The thief-taker shook his head. He hopped into his front room, in through the little narrow door where tall men like Master Mardan had to stoop, slumped into his chair and pulled up his breeches. The skin above the side of his knee was an angry red; in the middle was a mark, pale white skin like an old scar. It was the sign of a sunburst.

'There's nothing he can do.'

'What?' Berren didn't understand. 'What about … ?' He wasn't sure whether to say it. *What about the witch-doctor who lives in the House of Cats and Gulls that you pretend not to know much about?* Something ran deep there. Much as his master tried to hide it, he and the witch-doctor were bound by something, some dark secret they'd each brought with them to Deephaven. 'What about Master Kuy?'

'No! You stay away from him!' For a moment the thief-taker looked wild. Then he winced in pain. 'No. Kuy couldn't break a seal of the sun. Much as he might wish otherwise.'

Berren stood. He ought to find something to do. At times like this, he'd learned, the best thing to do was simply to keep out of the thief-taker's way. But he couldn't keep himself from blurting out: 'Why did you let that stupid monk win?'

'What?'

'Why did you let that monk win? Why?'

Deep furrows folded Master Sy's brow. '*Let* her win? I didn't let her win, boy.'

'You did! You didn't fight properly!'

'Boy!'

'You *let* her … A *girl*!'

Crippled leg or not, Master Sy was out of his chair in a heartbeat. He grabbed Berren's shirt and shook him, then staggered and nearly lost his balance. 'I didn't *let* her, boy,' he shouted, inches from Berren's face. 'She was *better* than me!' He let go. Took a deep breath and flopped back down. 'I'm sorry. But she was. A lot better.'

Berren glared. 'She smashed your leg!'

Master Sy looked at his knee. 'Yes, and she would have left me a cripple, too, but it will heal soon enough. Her teacher promised me that much. The mark of the sun will see to that.' He wrinkled his nose. 'Smells of dust in here.'

Berren didn't answer. Until last night, the house had hardly been lived in for the best part of a twelvenight. He went into the kitchen to fetch a jug of water. It tasted of dirt and copper. When he came back, the thief-taker was snoring.

He was still snoring that evening when Berren gave up and went to bed, snored through most of the night while Berren tossed and turned and dreamed and was still snoring in the morning while Berren ate his breakfast and went out to buy himself some candied fruits. Berren took his time, meandering around the city while he ate his treats. Along Weaver's Row and Moon Street, down the Godsway to the river docks, skirting the dead-fish stink that hung around the House of Cats and Gulls. He walked along the Waterfront with its hustle and bustle of sailors and traders and market stands, then grudgingly out through the River Gate on to the jetties at Sweetwater to bring back buckets of fresh water to drink.

Midday prayer bells rang across the city as he walked back up the Godsway and slowly home. If Master Sy was still sleeping, he swore he'd stuff him in a handcart and wheel him to Teacher Garrient, no matter what his master had said.

He paused as he went through the door. The house was silent. The thief-taker was still in his chair. He didn't look as though he'd moved since Berren had left him, but his eyes were open.

'You're missing your lessons,' he murmured as Berren came close. Then he looked around, as though he was in a stranger's house and not his own. There wasn't much to the thief-taker's parlour – a table, three crude wooden chairs, a fireplace and that was it – but Master Sy seemed suddenly intent on inspecting every corner as though checking to see all his walls were still where he remembered. He stopped and stared at a crack in the plaster, then frowned and moved on.

'I was ... !' Missed *lessons?* Furious indignation boiled up Berren's throat, into his mouth, all ready to be hurled across the room. Master Sy raised a hand.

'With the sword-monks, lad. That's what I meant. I think they practice every day.'

Berren's anger faded. Sword-monks. The prince had given him what he wanted, what he'd always wanted. He ought to be excited but he wasn't. Anxious, that was more like it, after what they'd done to his master. Scared even, perhaps a little downhearted.

'They'll hurt you too. That's they way they train. They won't break you though.'

If it was down to taking a beating every day then Sterm the Worm and his cane could do that already. Tasahre. He'd caught her name and he'd caught the evil look in her eye before she'd done her best to cripple Master Sy. She was horrible. She was a monster.

The thief-taker gave Berren a long hard look. 'You know what, lad? I'm hungry. Famished.' He tossed a silver crown across the room, straight into Berren's hands. 'Go and get us some ...'

Which was as far as he got before the door flew open

76

and there was Justicar Kol. In one hand he held a loaf of bread. In the other he was brandishing a pair of sausages and a rolled up sheet of paper which he waved at Master Sy as though it was a sword. 'What in the name of Kelm's sweet-scented crap have you two done?' He frowned, gave Master Sy a hard look and then stared at the thief-taker's knee. Where Tasahre had struck there was now a bruise, black and livid purple and the size of a man's hand, from the bottom of the thief-taker's knee to halfway up his thigh. 'What happened to you? Kicked by a mule?'

'By a monk.'

Kol blinked. Berren shrugged. Not all that long ago he'd been terrified by Kol, the bald former thief-taker who now set the bounties. Now, out of his official robes, he was short and nondescript and not frightening at all. The sausages, though …

'Impressive,' muttered the thief-taker, looking at Berren. He grinned. 'Put them on the table, Kol.'

'Hungry?' The justicar brusquely shoved Berren aside and sat down at the thief-taker's table. 'Yes, they said you'd be hungry. Make the most of it because it looks like we're all going to starve this summer.'

The thief-taker sent Berren into the kitchen for a pot of old dripping and a knife. They sat down at the table. Master Sy broke the justicar's bread and then he and Berren tore into their unexpected lunch.

'They said you'd be hungry,' said the justicar again. He looked at Berren. 'So the story I hear is that you saved our glorious prince's life. Then the Autarch snubs the Emperor, our prince uses you to humiliate the Autarch's monks, the monks can't do anything about it so they take it out on your master? Nice.' Kol put a hand on Master Sy's shoulder and grinned at him. 'Actually, I did hear you got into a fight with a girl. They didn't tell me the bit about her breaking you so good. Knee was it, Syannis?' He peered hard at the bruise and then poked it.

'Ouch!'

'Hey! Look what you got given!' Kol looked back at Berren. 'Got a funny mark on his skin that didn't used to be there, eh? Slept for exactly a day straight. Hence me showing up now and not this morning, and bringing lunch with me. I reckon, if you were to get your lazy self up out of that chair, master thief-taker, you'd find that leg of yours is working perfectly well again by now. A bit stiff and sore perhaps but nothing more. You know how many times I've seen that mark? Every day.' The justicar rolled up his sleeve, up past the elbow. He pointed to a little white mark on the skin there, amid a mass of scarring. At first it seemed a blemish, like a star, but when Berren looked closer he saw that it was a sunburst like Master Sy's. Older and harder to make out, but there was no mistaking what it was. That was something you forgot about Kol, until he chose to remind you from time to time, that he used to be a thief-taker too. 'Got that before your master ever came to Deephaven. They don't do it for just anyone, either. That's a healing mark that is. Monk got a bit carried away then, did she? Not a good omen for you, Berren, eh?' He made a face.

'I know what the seal is, Kol,' grumbled Master Sy.

'Double-edged sword, that mark. Very doubled-edged. Means they can come to you for a service and they don't tend to ask for small things. Still, better than not being able to walk, eh?'

The thief-taker paused from his bread and sausage to stretch out his leg. He frowned, looked surprised for a moment, then went back to eating. Kol rolled his eyes.

'Tell you what, why don't I read this *very important* proclamation aloud, since you're all so busy stuffing your faces with my food. Spare me the pain of watching you chew.'

Master Sy paused for a moment. 'You owe me a purse, Kol, for wet-nursing your prince. And that emperor for our little bet about an heir, I might add.'

The justicar ignored him. He hesitated. Something hung in the air around him, something waiting yet reluctant to come out. Berren fingered at the pouch around his neck, the safest place he could think of to keep the prince's token. Kol caught his eye.

'You won't be going anywhere while these monks are still here to teach you swords, eh? Pity.'

'I'd sell that,' said Master Sy quietly. 'Sell it and forget you had it. There's nothing but pain and misery in something like that. You don't believe me, you go and ask Kasmin. If you can find him.'

For a long second, no one said anything. The silence around the justicar grew thick and dense. Kol bowed his head. 'Ah. See. That's part of what I came here to tell you. Kasmin is dead.'

10

COLOURS TO THE MAST

Silence hung in the thief-taker's parlour. Outside, a wind rattled the shutters, but otherwise all was still. There was no one out in the yard today.

Kasmin had been Master Sy's oldest friend. Almost the last reminder of the life he'd once had, long before he sailed into Deephaven with nothing but the clothes on his back and the sword at his hip. They'd been thief-takers together for a while, working for Kol back when Kol had some hair, or that's how Master Sy always put it.

'How?' Master Sy's question cracked the air like a whip.

'Crossbow. They found him a few mornings back. Shot twice. In the spine and in the back of the head.'

'How many is a "few" mornings back, Kol?'

The justicar squirmed. 'Eight.'

'And you didn't tell me?'

'I didn't know for four of them.'

'And then you still didn't tell me?'

Kol cocked his head. 'I'd have come yesterday, but you were sleeping.'

'Kol!' That was Master Sy's dangerous voice. The one he used right before his sword came out.

The justicar took a deep breath. 'You were working for His Highness. If I'd told you, you'd have gone looking for whoever did it. Just like that. Dropped everything. Made both of us look like arses.'

'Who did it?'

'I don't know.'

'Oh, why am I asking? Like you care who murders who down in The Maze.' Abruptly the thief-taker stood up. He winced as he put weight on his bruised knee. 'Don't pretend he somehow matters.'

'He was one of us once, Syannis.'

'Get out!'

'I can't.' He unfurled the piece of paper he'd brought. It smelled slightly of sausages. 'Read it!'

'Get out, Kol. I have business.'

'Syannis, you're not a thief-taker any more. Read it.'

Master Sy growled. His fists were clenched and his knuckles were white, resting on the hilt of his sword. Kol took a deep breath. He rolled the paper up again. 'All right, read it later. I'll tell you instead. As of yesterday afternoon, those monks are my thief-takers. Whether I like it or not. The Sunherald has decreed it. I'd say that's mostly thanks to you two, by the way. Just so you know why the rest of them hate you now.'

The thief-taker spat. 'And what's the Overlord say? It's his city, not the Autarch's.'

The justicar looked furtively about, as if there might have been some fourth person in the thief-taker's tiny living room that he somehow hadn't noticed. 'Look, the Overlord is the Emperor's man in name, but he's his own man first. There's close as anything a civil war brewing, same one as has been coming ever since Khrozus knocked old Talsin off the Sapphire Throne. The Path never accepted Khrozus, they never accepted his son, they have a lot of sway with the guild of merchants and the guild of merchants are the ones with the money. So the Overlord's been sitting very carefully on the fence for some time now and I can promise you it's going to take a lot more than a few irate thief-takers to push him off it. The Overlord says we do our jobs and keep the peace. Monks or thief-takers, it's all the same to him.'

'And you, Kol?'

The justicar shrugged. 'Replace my thief-takers with swords-monks? It's an honest justicar's wet dream, Syannis. Incorruptible maniacs with no concern for their own well-being, the power to smell lies and taste sorcery? Who scorn gold and despise greed and do it all in the service of a god who doesn't care which sea-house gets the better of the others each month? Gods, Syannis, they're even free. Like I said, an honest justicar's dream. I give it six months before the merchant houses realise just how much they don't want people like that poking around in their affairs and make the Overlord get rid of them. Until then, though ...' He shrugged and dropped a purse on the table. 'What I owe you, wager and all. There's enough there to keep you through to winter if you're frugal with it and we'll be back the way we were well before then.' He backed away from the table and stood in the doorway of the thief-taker's house. 'If you choose to spend your time chasing after whoever your lad saw in the Watchman's Arms, or anyone else for that matter, don't look for any help from me. If I were you, I'd keep very quiet. In fact, if I were you I'd get out of the city for a while. They're watching. In particular, they're watching you.'

'Get. Out.'

Kol shrugged. 'I'm sorry about Kasmin. He was a good thief-taker once. Not a great one, but at least he was honest. I've set my new helpers after his killer. There's simply not much else I can do. When there's news I'll let you know.'

He left. Berren watched him go but the justicar hadn't even made it to the end of the yard before he turned and came back, shaking his head. 'Look, I know enough to know that if anyone wanted Kasmin, there's a good chance they're after you as well. A justicar doesn't get to have too many friends, so I'd prefer not to lose any more. Keep an eye open, Syannis. Make sure someone's got your back.'

For a long time after the justicar had gone, Master Sy sat exactly where he was, still as a becalmed ship, not blinking, not even seeming to breathe. Then he walked to the door, swirled on his cloak and strode out into the yard, limping very slightly.

'Have you been looking?' he muttered.

Berren hurried after him. 'What is it, master?'

'I promised you an emperor if you ever saw a flag. Four white ships on a red field. Shot twice? In the head and in the back? Looks like that's one piece of gold I'll get to keep.' He spat on the cobbles. 'Just as well, since apparently I can't afford an emperor right now.'

'I look every day, master. Well most days. It's not there. Not that one.'

'Really? Well let's see. Get that purse before someone steals it!'

Berren bolted back to the house. He swept up Justicar Kol's purse from the table and looked inside. Thirty or forty silver crowns glittered back at him and one golden emperor. Food and firewood until autumn if they were careful. He tied the purse onto his belt and stuffed it inside his trousers, then ran back out again after his master. For a man with an injured leg, the thief-taker could still manage a turn of speed when he wanted and he was already almost at Four Winds Square by the time Berren caught up again. One hand tapped his chest where Prince Sharda's gold sigil hung around his neck. It was becoming a habit, checking it was still there.

'Maybe you shouldn't sell that after all.'

'Master, what's going on?'

The thief-taker didn't answer. He pushed on as fast as he could, across the square until they reached the two enormous curved bronze swords that rose up out of the stones to mark the entrance to the Avenue of Emperors. The swords were carved with ancient runes in the language of the sun. One solemnly declared the values of honesty, openness and compassion. The other promised bloody dismemberment to thieves and liars. Walking under them always made Berren's skin tingle – they were supposed to be enchanted – and it took him a second or two to realise that Master Sy had stopped. Not only stopped talking but stopped walking as well.

The Avenue of Emperors ran right across the city, from the river docks on one side to the sea-docks on the other. It ran more or less in a straight line. From high up, near the bronze swords it gave a good view of the harbour. At this time of day, before the afternoon rains, the air was bright and clear.

Something about the ships had struck his master dumb, but however much Berren peered among them, he couldn't see anything unusual.

'What is it, master?'

'I told you when we first met that a man had once stolen something from me. You asked me what had happened to him.'

'You said nothing.'

'Nothing. Yes. Can you make out any of the flags from here?'

Berren shook his head. The ships were far too far away. You had to be right down in the docks, preferably on the waterfront, before even the sharpest eyes could make out the colours flown out in Deephaven harbour. What a clever head did was take a look from up here to see if there were any new ships anchored in the bay and then go and ask one of the harbour boys who were forever running up and down the Avenue of Emperors with messages for their rich masters. The harbour boys always knew who'd set anchor and who was about to sail and a whole encyclopaedia more about what ships were carrying and where they were bound. They were always willing to share if a penny or two came their way.

'I'll go ask if you like,' Berren offered.

Master Sy shook his head. 'I want to see for myself.'

They walked on down the avenue, past the statues of the various emperors of Aria. Master Sy had tried to make Berren learn their names but they'd never really taken. He knew Khrozus the Great, or possibly Khrozus the Butcher or Khrozus the Bloody, depending on who was doing the talking. He knew Talsin, the deliberately broken statue near the top of the avenue. He knew Thortis, the first Emperor of Aria, up next to the bronze swords opposite the current Emperor, Ashahn the Wise. Wise until someone toppled him and renamed him Ashahn the Stupid, at least.

They had to push their way through the thickening traffic pressing down the hill towards the harbour. The crowds began to buffet him. What he really wanted, Berren decided, was one of those new farscope things from the glass-makers in Varr. Not that he'd ever seen one, but Master Fennis had. The prince had brought one with him and they'd all gone up to The Peak one day and climbed the Overlord's tower. The prince had passed it around. Master Fennis said that it made everything all wobbly looking, but that you could see all the way to the City of Spires. That would have done nicely, Berren thought. He could have scrambled up the statue of some old emperor no one remembered any more, sat on his shoulders and stared out to sea.

'This way.' The thief-taker grabbed Berren's arm and dragged him off into a narrow street that delved into the back-shadows of the Courts District. They emerged on the Kingsway, another wide road leading down to the sea, but the Kingsway didn't lead directly to the docks so the traffic here was never quite so bad. This was a part of the city Berren didn't know. Assayers'. Not a place he had much reason to visit. You could still see the harbour clearly enough though.

They reached the bottom of the hill and Master Sy caught Berren's arm a second time. He stopped outside a ramshackle building of heavy stone that looked as though it had once had some thoughts about growing into a castle but had changed its mind, fallen asleep and drifted slowly into ruin. The thief-taker pointed up. Leaning out over the street at a slight angle was a narrow stone tower. The old Harbour Watchtower. It looked as though it was about to fall down, but then it had looked like that for some fifty years.

The thief-taker banged on the heavy wooden door to the tower. After a long wait, it creaked open.

'Haven't seen you here for a while,' grumbled an old voice from the shadows inside.

'Haven't needed to be here.' Master Sy wrinkled up his face and sniffed the air. 'I can smell it. Even from here.' Then he snorted and shook his head. 'You want to be a bit more careful about that.'

Berren sniffed. There was a sharpness to the air but it wasn't a smell he could place.

'You here to bring trouble?' asked the shadows. Master Sy shook his head.

'I'm told the city doesn't need my services just now. Seems to be getting on fine as things are. I'm only here to take in the view if that's all right with you boys.' He smiled grimly. 'You might want to keep your eyes open for any sword-monks coming this way though.'

'Sword-monks, eh? Never heard of them.'

'Oh, you will. You can't miss them. Bright yellow with the sun tattooed on their face. Got sharp noses too, sharper than mine by a yard. By the time you see them they'll have smelled you out. You might want to think about that. They won't take kindly at all to what you make down in your cellars there.'

'Just the tower?'

Master Sy nodded and the door opened wider. 'Go on then. You know the way. Take your time. You see any of them sword-wotsits of yours, be sure to yell about it.'

The thief-taker stepped inside. Cautiously, Berren followed. The smell was stronger now. 'What do they–' He didn't get any further before a sharp kick on the ankle made him squeak and hop in pain.

'Manners, boy. You should know better than to be asking questions until we're back outside. Just use your nose and keep your mouth shut until we're at the top of the tower.' He stopped and opened a rickety door that led onto a spiral staircase. The steps were steep and narrow and not quite straight. They were long, too. By the time they got to the top, even Master Sy was out of breath. His knee was bothering him.

'Master?' Berren reached out a hand. The thief-taker batted him away.

'I tell you, once we're done here, I intend to have myself some fun with these sword-monks.'

At the top of the stairs stood another old door, battered and warped. Shafts of sunlight pierced its cracks, casting brilliant lines across the walls and floor. The thief-taker pushed it open and stepped carefully outside. An old wooden walkway ringed the top of the tower. Wind tore in off the sea, strong and tugging at his clothes; Berren almost lost his balance, but that wasn't the wind. The wood under his feet tilted with the tower, almost wilfully trying to pitch him off to the street below.

'Careful.' Master Sy was laughing. He walked around the platform to the other side, where a half-rotted wooden ladder took them the last few yards to the tower's flat top. At least here there was a low parapet, even if the mortar was crumbling and whole stones came loose in Berren's hands.

'It's not as high as Garrient's moon-tower.' Master Sy had to almost shout to make himself heard over the wind. Berren made a face. Behind them to the east rose The Peak, the rich heart of the city and home to the merchant princes whose towers and temples clustered around Deephaven Square. From there, Deephaven's wealth trickled reluctantly out into everyone else's pockets. Somewhere on the other side were the river docks, clustered around the mouth of the Ar, the greatest waterway in the world. The rest of the city, where everyone else lived, sprawled inland. A string of fishing villages spread further up the coast; the banks of the river towards Varr sprouted thickets of inns, warehouses and other lodgings for those who aspired to riches but had yet to find them. All these had grown so close together that it was hard to say where one ended and the next began.

And then there was the harbour, the almost circular sheltered, deep-water cove that gave the city its name. Ships from across the oceans anchored here. It was the largest, greatest, richest port in the empire, probably in the world.

'Does it ever stop making you wonder?' mused Master Sy. 'All this wealth, all this gold. All from carrying stuff across the mile that separates the river and the sea. Just for carting things up a little hill and down the other side.'

Berren shrugged. He rarely wondered about things like that. What *he* wondered about were the women from the Watchman's Arms, frolicking in the moonpool with their clothes clinging to their skin and hiding nothing. Or the ones from the Golden Cup. Or vicious flat-chested Tasahre who'd leapt and sabre-danced her way through Master Sy's guard. Who clearly and obviously despised Berren in every look she'd given him.

And who, for some reason, kept butting into his thoughts. He clenched his fists.

'Berren? Berren?' Master Sy snapped his fingers in front of Berren's face. Berren jumped.

Yes. That. 'Er, no. Not really.' Sometimes he wondered how he could become immensely wealthy in a very short space of time. That was about as close as he got.

'Well. You seem to think you have good eyes. See any red flags out there?'

'Red?' Berren peered. Even the closest ships were hundreds of yards away and there were so many masts all rolling back and forth between each other that getting a good look at any flags at all was a matter of luck.

'Yellow flags are the ships of the sun-king. Black flags are the Taiytakei. White flags are—'

'The Emperor's, but I won't see many of those. I know.' Berren squinted across the water. The black-flagged Taiytakei ships generally clustered together at the northern end of the harbour, furthest away from where Berren sat. The yellow flags of the sun-king were at the southern end. Between them were dozens of other ships, mostly smaller ones. Most flew white flags, with a smattering of other colours. 'What are red ones?' Had he ever seen a ship decked out in red? He couldn't remember one.

'The merchant princes of Kalda,' said the thief-taker quietly. He was pointing. 'There. What's that?'

Master Sy's finger was aimed straight at the nearest cluster of ships, the yellow flags of the sun-king. Among them, a darker flag flew.

'Dunno.' Berren shrugged. The flag was too far away to tell what colour it was except that it was dark. 'Could be a Taki ship in the wrong place?'

Master Sy shook his head. 'They keep to their own. Dark red, lad. That's the colour of the sea-princes of Kalda and the Free Cities. Not that they're free at all. No, they pay their tithes to the sun-king in Caladir just like everyone else across the Sea of Storms. A ship of theirs will come this far maybe once a year. You'll always find their ships and the sun-king's together, because only the sun-king's Taki navigators know the way. That's it, lad. That ship.' He was squinting, his finger shaking. 'Four white ships? Is that the design? Is that it?' His voice was hoarse.

Berren squinted as well. Four white ships on red. He'd been looking for those colours for nearly two years. He couldn't have missed them, could he? Not now … The flags kept flapping though, making it almost impossible to tell. 'Doesn't look like it.' Then, for a moment, Berren saw it clearly. 'No,' he said, quite sure of himself. 'Not four ships. Just one. Or maybe an upside-down tree. But not four.'

The thief-taker lowered his hand. His fingers curled and his fist clenched. He was still shaking, quivering with anger. 'Or an upside-down axe? Double-headed?'

'Could be.' Berren tried to get a better look, but the wind was fickle and the flag danced back and forth, never still for long enough to be clear.

'Could be.' Master Sy growled. Repressed fury crackled from every word. 'Good enough, lad. Good enough. Was it white?'

'Looked it.'

'The Headsman.' The thief-taker nodded to himself, as if that made perfect sense. Berren had never heard of such a man.

'The what?'

'The Headsman. Still sailing then.' He was still nodding as he got to his feet. 'Bolt in the back of the head, one in the spine. That'd be him all right. Well we'll see about that.'

Berren got up too, swaying slightly as the pitch of the tower-top caught him out again. 'Master? See about what? Master?'

But Master Sy was already climbing down the ladder and he didn't hear. When Berren caught his eye, the thief-taker seemed to be very far away. His lips were drawn back, the teeth behind them clenched.

11
HUNTING FOR CROWS

The thief-taker took the stairs fast and never mind his gammy knee. Berren hurried after him, but it wasn't until they got back out into the street that Master Sy stopped. He took the justicar's purse from Berren, then frowned. He weighed it in his hand. 'There's more silver in there than we had coming to us, that's for sure. Why? Charity?'

Berren snorted. 'Charity? From Kol?'

'Quite.' Master Sy began to walk again, slowly this time, further on towards the edge of the docks.

For a moment as they crossed the Kingsway outside the old tower, Berren caught sight of someone staring at him, eyes wide, almost in shock. The thief-taker must have seen it too, but they were eyes across a crowded street and by the time Berren had pushed his way to where they'd been, the man was gone. The furrows on Master Sy's brow could have been put there by a plough.

'Eyes open, Berren. Wide open. Someone's not happy to see us.'

They reached the edge of the docks where the Kingsway opened up into a huge crescent of cobbles with the sea and the harbour walls on one side and giant warehouses arrayed along the other. Sailors swaggered back and forth, some of them bleary-eyed from a sleepless night in one of the drinking holes that filled the darker alleys beyond. A line of burly men had formed a human chain, picking up sacks and crates from boats drawn up against the edge of the harbour and passing them along to a milling collection of carts. Further along the waterfront, another chain was passing supplies across the dockside from a warehouse out onto a cluster of jetties. A party of black-skinned Taiytakei traders in their rainbow robes and their bright feathers walked serenely out from the Avenue of Emperors, discreetly escorted by half a dozen snuffers to keep the worst of the riff-raff at bay. A squad of imperial soldiers lounged around a covered wagon. Yellow- and silver-robed priests of the sun and the moon walked side by side, the faithful and the desperate following in their wake like the tail of a comet. Gangs of rough men, press gangs, lurked by the dockside flophouses like sand-spiders waiting to pounce. Boys ran weaving between them all, carrying news and messages or else simply mischief. Berren smiled to himself. He could never quite shake the feeling of coming home whenever he visited the docks.

'The Headsman,' said Master Sy gruffly, walking purposefully into the crowd, eyes still darting everywhere. 'When I knew him, he was one of Radek's captains. He was a vicious bastard. If he's here, could be that Radek won't be far behind.' He stopped to buy a pair of bread rolls stuffed with pickled fish. A mirthless smile flashed across his face. 'We'll have to be careful about this sort of thing. Kol's money won't keep us in pickled herring forever.'

At the entrance to the Kingsway they sat down on the sea wall. Across the way, the tall bulk of a warehouse cast the road into shadow. Berren took a mouthful of pickled herring while Master Sy stared out to sea. Chiming bells and the rattle of ropes against masts wafted across the waves, mingling with the wash of shouts and curses and heave-ho-ing from the docks. The air smelled of salt and fish. Seagulls circled out over the water, swooping in among the ships but steering clear of the shore. A small army of ragged boys with slingshots and empty stomachs infested the waterfront. The seagulls had learned the hard way to be mindful.

'Yes,' murmured Master Sy after he'd been staring for a few minutes. 'That's the Headsman. That's his flag.'

Berren cast his eyes around the docks. Between the wind blowing in off the sea and shadow of the warehouse, he was starting to feel cold. The party of Taiytakei traders had reached the carts that were being loaded from the sea. The imperial soldiers were still lounging around their wagon. The priests had stopped by the human chain on the far side of the docks and were milling around trying to find a way to pass.

'The kingdom I come from is a long way away from here. Kasmin, a few others, they came too, in drips and drops over the years. I suppose we thought Deephaven was so far away that no one would ever catch up with us.' He took a deep breath. 'And yet here he is. The Headsman.' Master Sy chewed on his bun. Berren had a head full of questions, but he'd come to know his master. The thief-taker would talk or he wouldn't and asking questions never made much difference.

The thief-taker let out a big sigh. 'It was a small place, our kingdom. Poor and not particularly important. Little more than a small town with a few fields around it. Not much worth taking. Oh, we used to have wars all the time, us and our stupid petty neighbours, but not like this one. Not like when the merchant princes of Kalda came with their mercenary army. After they were done with raping our women and killing our men and selling our children to the slavers, eventually some of them had to settle down to the business of being kings and breaking the backs of our people for the long term. Meridian was his name, the one who made himself king. He left it to his cousin Radek to hunt the rest of us down. Years it went on. Years and years until one by one we broke. The Headsman was the most bloodthirsty captain he owned.' He clucked and stroked his chin. 'And now here he is. Kasmin's dead and Kol's laid it on thick as grease on a soap-maker's hands and wound me up like a Taiytakei doll. Perhaps we–'

Out of the corner of his eye, Berren caught a glimpse of movement up on one of the rooftops. He looked up and saw a man looking straight back down at him – straight back down at him along the length of an arrow and a drawn-back bow …

Master Sy had seen it too. He shoved Berren hard in the back. Berren lurched off the wall and staggered into the street. The thief-taker had hold of his arm, dragging him further. They ran to the wall of the warehouse and pressed themselves against it. Master Sy hurried around to the dockside entrance where a pair of doors large enough for a cart hung open. He glanced up at the roof one more time then dived inside, drawing a shout from the two bored men who were paid to guard the door. They were just starting to move after him when Berren dashed between them.

'Hey! You!'

The warehouses around Deephaven's sea docks were vast. Inside the gates they each had a yard, an open space where carts could load and unload and turn around. After that they were all different. Some – the ones belonging to the greater city princes – were simple, large open spaces filled with a lattice of massive beams and planks and ropes and cranes. Others, the ones shared between many merchants like this one, were little villages of alleys and storerooms and walls within walls. In the yard two carts sat ready, almost loaded. Half a dozen teamsters were lifting crates from a pile on the floor. Master Sy raced past them, still limping slightly. On the far side of the yard was a platform with ropes and pulleys for lifting crates up to the higher levels.

Beside it, a narrow wooden staircase zigged and zagged all the way to the roof. The thief-taker arrowed for it; before he could get there, Berren raced ahead.

'Berren!' The thief-taker's shout was admonishing but Berren paid no attention. He'd seen Master Sy at the top of the old watchtower, hobbling after climbing so many steps and here were almost as many again. The thief-taker would practically be hopping by the time he got to the top and the archer would be gone if he wasn't already.

Amid the bones of the roof a wooden gallery hung out over the yard below. Passages disappeared deeper into the upper gloom of the warehouse. Berren ignored both. What interested him were the large open windows that let air and light into the main yard. They had shutters, locked and barred from the inside at night to keep out thieves, but while there was daylight they were open. He ran to the nearest one, looked out and up.

'Berren!' Master Sy's tone was more urgent this time. He was about halfway up the stairs. Berren ignored him, leaned out of the window and then stood up on the stone sill. Up outside, a walkway ran around the roof, the edge in easy reach. He took hold with both hands and then jumped. For a moment he was hanging, legs dangling free some forty feet over the Kingsway, high enough to be dashed to bits if he fell. Then he had one leg lifted up and then the other and he was rolling onto the roof and onto his feet.

The bowman wasn't there. As quickly as he could, Berren crept up the roof, keeping low and quiet. The bowman wasn't on the side overlooking the docks either. Nor was he on the second side that overlooked the Kingsway as it turned up the slope towards Deephaven Square.

A flash of movement caught Berren's eye two warehouses along, a figure creeping across the rooftops. Berren skittered down the other side of the roof. There were alleys down below that ran from the docks to the Kingsway, thin dark damp places keeping one warehouse apart from the next and narrow enough to jump if you were brave enough. Berren leapt over to the next warehouse, scurried around to the docks' side away from the man with the bow and jumped a second alley. If the man hadn't moved, they were on the same rooftop. He hesitated there for a moment and then crept up the sloping roof to the top and looked down the other side.

The bowman was in front of him, a little way towards the docks, looking down. Berren edged closer. As quietly as he could, he took a few steps down the slope of the roof.

His foot trod on something wet and slimy and shot out from underneath him. He fell, landed on his backside and started to slide.

The man looked round. Berren couldn't stop himself. He rolled sideways; before the archer could raise his bow, Berren slammed into him, kicking the man's legs away and then throwing himself flat, spreading his arms, fingers digging at the tiles to stop himself falling. The man flipped up into the air and came down almost between two rooftops. He dropped his bow and grabbed hold of Berren. For a moment Berren thought they were both going to slide over the edge together. They ground to a halt though, with Berren's legs dangling over the cobbles below. The bow clattered off the walls and down. The archer had a grip on Berren's belt with one hand, on the edge of the roof with the other. He started to haul himself back, dragging Berren further, yelling curses in some heavy accent that Berren couldn't understand. Berren kicked at him, once, twice, as panic raced through him. The man was pulling him down! He kicked again and again as he clung to the roof-tiles.

The man let go of Berren's belt and lunged for the edge of the roof. His fingers clawed for purchase and then they were gone. There was a scream and then a thud. There weren't any footsteps. Berren peered down. In the gloom of the alley, the bowman lay sprawled, motionless, on the cobbles.

12

PEOPLE COME TO SANDOR TO FORGET

It took a while to get back down to the alley. A gang of boys scattered as Berren and the thief-taker approached. Berren started to give chase but quickly stopped. Even if he caught one of them, so what? The body was still there, half stripped. The bow was gone, boots, belt, purse, everything short of his shirt and breeches, and Berren didn't doubt that they'd have gone too if he and the thief-taker had taken another minute to climb down from the warehouse roof. Master Sy crouched down beside the body and turned him over. The bowman had landed badly. One leg was snapped, the bone sticking out through his shin. His head had hit the stones hard. There wasn't all that much blood but the man was quite dead.

'Do you know him?' asked Berren. Master Sy shook his head. 'He was shouting. I couldn't understand what he was saying.'

The thief-taker nodded. 'I heard. He's from the Free Cities.' He shook his head then tore open the man's shirt. At the far end of the alley, Berren caught sight of eyes, watching them. Dock boys, waiting greedily for whatever they could steal.

Master Sy ripped one arm off the shirt. On the dead man's skin up near his shoulder was a tattoo of an axe, the same as the one on the flag Berren had seen from the watchtower.

'One of the Headsman's.' The thief-taker sounded grim. He straightened then took a penny out of his purse and threw it down to the end of the alley. A boy scurried from behind the corner, snatched the coin almost as it landed, and dived back for cover. 'So he really is here in Deephaven. There will be others, I don't doubt. This the fellow who eyed you back on Kingsway?'

'No.' The man who'd stared at him across the street as they came out of the old watchtower had had different clothes. 'That one had a beard.' Had a heavier build too.

Master Sy shook his head. His words were bitter. 'He was waiting for us. So either the fellow you saw got word up to him mighty quick or else he knew we were coming. He knew who we were, too.' He growled. 'Kol needs to know about this.'

He threw another penny down the alley. 'Hey lads, I know you're there. This fellow's dead and whatever he had, he's not needing any more. What I want is to know where he was staying. Might be that one of you with your sharp eyes has seen him before, coming and going from a tavern or an inn or a flophouse. Got a silver crown for anyone who can take me to where he slept.'

A young boy stepped out from the far end of the alley. He kept his distance. Another boy, a little older, stepped out and pushed the first one aside. The older came up to the thief-taker.

'Please sir, I can show you, sir.'

'You know who I am?'

The boy shook his head. 'It's no bother to me, sir.'

'I'm a thief-taker, boy. You know what that means?'

This time when the boy shook his head, he was wide-eyed. Berren thought he might run.

'Means I keep my promises and I eat thieves for breakfast. You really know where this man used to rest his head?'

The boy gulped. He glanced back into the shadows. The younger boy nodded.

'Right then. You show me. You and your little friend.'

Out in the docks, the boy led them towards the Avenue of Emperors. The imperial soldiers were still there, slouched beside their covered wagon. One corner had lifted up. Underneath, Berren could see kegs, all packed together. As he passed the wagon, he was sure he caught a whiff of Master Velgian's black powder, sharp and acrid and strangely familiar.

Master Sy's limp was getting worse; he was wincing with almost every step now. The boys led them up the Avenue of Emperors and in among the fancy lodgings for ship's captains and the merchants and traders who owned them, places like the Captain's Rest. Berren had been there once, back when the thief-taker had been hunting pirates and their elusive master. It was like a palace; but the boy didn't take them there. Instead he went the other way off the Avenue, into the fringes of The Maze, the alleys where the press gangs worked and no militia dared enter. The boy went on in, weaving deeper among the narrow streets until they stopped at a place that was part flophouse, part Moongrass den.

'Are you sure this is the place you want to be taking me, boy?' asked Master Sy mildly. Berren knew exactly what he was thinking. There were plenty of places in the Maze where all that waited inside was a good mugging or else a sap round the back of the head and waking up five miles out to sea. Both the gangs and the muggers often sent boys out into the docks to try and lure people in.

The younger boy nodded. 'Seen him come here, mister.'

The older one held out his hand. 'Give us a crown then.'

Master Sy smiled at them both. 'You come inside with us. If it turns out you were telling the truth, you'll get your

100

crown. If not, well, there might be a crown for me instead when I take you to a sweathouse.'

The older boy paled. The younger one didn't seem concerned. He shrugged. 'I seen him come here,' he said again.

'Good.' Master Sy didn't wait for any more. He pushed open the door and they all reeled as the reek of Moongrass poured out like warm treacle. Fingers of it wrapped themselves around Berren's head, worming their way inside his skull. He coughed and staggered. Past the door, a dingy hall was filled with tables. The windows were shuttered. Half a dozen scrawny men dressed in little more than rags looked up and stared, all gaunt faces and hollow eyes in the gloomy light of a few cheap candles. None of them moved. Berren wasn't sure how much they even noticed. They looked, but what did they see? Already he was starting to feel light-headed.

Another man emerged from the gloom as Master Sy stepped inside. This one looked like the others, but he wore a scarf over his face and his eyes had a purpose to them. He looked the thief-taker up and down and then silently held out a hand.

Master Sy shook his head. 'I'm not here for your smoke.'

The man nodded. The scarf covered his nose and mouth and made his expression hard to decipher. He mumbled something that Berren couldn't understand. For some reason, the scarf had caught Berren's eye. There was something about its torn and fraying edges that was immensely fascinating. He wondered what it had been before it was a scarf. A shirt, maybe?

'No. I'm looking for someone,' said Master Sy.

The man frowned. He started trying to push them out of the door. Berren put his hand on his waster; to his surprise though, Master Sy let the man lead them back out onto the street. The cool crisp spring air made his skin tingle all over, like a hug of fresh water. He shivered. The city smells had never seemed so rich. Fish. Always fish.

The man carefully closed the door and pulled down his scarf. Berren gasped. The man's chin and mouth were a mass of scars.

'People come to Sandor to forget.' His speech was as broken as his face. 'Not to look.'

'Man with an axe tattooed on the top of his arm. Scar on his neck, two on his face. Short black hair. Foreigner. Spee lah thees eh.' The thief-taker's accent was so perfect that it startled Berren out of his reverie of smells. Master Sy opened a hand to show a silver crown. The scarred man nodded.

'More than one like that,' he mumbled.

'Doesn't matter to me. They all came from the same place. Where are they staying? Any of them.'

The scarred man looked hungrily at the silver in the thief-taker's palm. He hesitated and then his shoulders slumped. He snatched for the coin but Master Sy's fingers closed before he could take it. The scarred man shrugged. 'Little Caladir. The Two Cranes.'

Master Sy cocked his head. 'That's a way away. Like their Moongrass did they?'

'They came to sell, not to smoke.'

The thief-taker opened his hand. The coin vanished. The man pulled his scarf back over his face and a cloud of smoke billowed into the street as he opened his door and closed it again. Master Sy tossed another crown to the younger of the two boys. The boy yelped for joy and ran; the older one dithered for a moment, looked at Master Sy, saw he wasn't going to get anything and gave chase.

'Should have split it between them,' muttered Master Sy.

Berren didn't say anything. He'd been both of those boys.

Splitting it wouldn't make any difference. Sooner or later the older one would catch the younger one and then the crown would be his, and that was simply the way of things. 'What's the Two Cranes?' he asked instead. His head was clearing now, the fuzziness slowly fading. Which was sad, in a way, because the fuzziness had felt nice. That's what everyone said about a touch of Moongrass. Nice. The trouble started when a touch became a headful and you completely forgot who you were.

'A place where the sun-king's sailors stay, the ones who can afford it. The sort of place we might find the Headsman.'

'So are we going there now?'

The thief-taker glanced up at the sky. Then he shook his head. 'No. We're going home and getting you ready for your sword-monk lessons tomorrow.'

Berren stared pointedly at the thief-taker's leg. 'All the way back up the Avenue?'

Master Sy winced. 'All the way, lad. No hurry now. We know where he is and we know he knows we're here. This needs some thinking.'

Berren gave his master a steady look. Thinking. He was coming to learn what that meant. It meant pacing up and down all day – or rocking back and forth in his chair. It meant shouting at Berren about little things that didn't really matter. And in the end ... in the end ...

Master Sy nodded. He smiled and patted his sword-hilt, almost as though he was reading Berren's mind. 'Getting dark soon. Press gangs will be about. Don't want to wake up and find myself a skag on some ship.'

However true that was on the surface, they both knew that in the two years Berren had been Master Sy's apprentice, the thief-taker hadn't once shown himself in the least bit bothered by such things. What he meant was that this was *his* business, and his alone.

And that was all right, because standing out here in the afterglow of a touch of Moongrass, Berren realised he had some business of his own now. That black powder smell he'd picked up from the wagon beside the imperial soldiers in the docks – mix that with a bad dose of rotting fish, and *that* was the whiff of something sharp he'd sniffed off the assassin in the Watchman's Rest!

He was going to find out who it was.

✣ PART TWO ✣
THE HEADSMAN

13
SWORDS, STEEL AND A PRESS OF SKIN

The afternoon sun shone on the temple yard, hot and hard like the earth under Berren's feet. Sweat dripped off his face and spattered around his feet. The other monks hardly seemed troubled at all, either by the heat or by the effort of holding a sword straight out in front of them for hours on end. Their shoulders, Berren decided, must have been made of iron; or else they had some sort of magic that made their swords lighter. They'd been doing this to him for days.

First thing in the morning they went for a simple run, down to the sea-docks and back. The monks took it easy enough down the hill and then sprinted for the entire mile back up again, leaving Berren wheezing and gasping in their wake. As soon as they got back they started jumping. Jumping on the spot, long jumps, high jumps, hurdles and things that Berren couldn't even begin to work out how to do – backflips, handsprings, things that would have made an acrobat gasp – the monks almost seemed to bounce for fun. Eventually, when his legs had given up, they made him lie down and lift weights instead. The monks lifted each other. The worst of it wasn't that they were all so much better than he was, it was that none of them said anything. They never spoke a word of praise or disdain, only the bare basic instructions.

A couple of hours of lessons with Sterm the Worm and

his cane were almost a relief after that. Then he was back out into the practice field, this time for stretching, bending himself into shapes that a normal person simply wasn't supposed to make. Every time he thought he'd contorted himself into as position that couldn't possibly get more painful, Tasahre would come over and kick his feet further apart, or sit on some part of him or rearrange him into some other shape that hurt ten times more. She rarely said anything either and her face was always a mask, but he could feel the malice in the sharpness of her movements. The monks, Berren was sure, hated him.

On Sun-Days and Moon-Days, that was all they did before their midday prayers, an hour of standing, sitting or lying in positions that made them look as though they'd had to break several bones to get there, then half an hour to either run and eat some food or else lie in a heap waiting for the pain to go away, your choice. After prayers, Berren had Sterm again and the relief of sitting in the shade of a cool cell with nothing being stretched, torn, ripped or otherwise abused. On Tower-Days and Mage-Days, the monks cut their stretching short and went running again instead, only this time they didn't run in the streets but along the rooftops down among the warehouses by the docks. They climbed walls, leaped alleys and danced from roof to roof. At least when they did this Berren could keep up. He knew the city better than the monks and he'd been up to these places before with Master Sy. Between hard high alley walls, whispers had nowhere to escape save for eager ears listening from above, and no one thought to look up at night. He came to like Tower-Days and Mage-Days. Council-Days were the worst, when the monks all vanished and he was left with Sterm right through the middle of the day.

And then, on every day except Abyss-Day, in the heat of the late afternoon, he did this: standing stock still, holding a waster straight out in front of him with Tasahre standing across the small fighting circle she'd drawn in the dirt, staring right back at him. Today she was balancing an hour-glass on the end of her sword to make the exercise a little harder for herself – and to remind Berren that, although it might feel like he'd stood there for hours, although it might feel like his shoulder was slowly turning to molten lead, they had in fact been doing this for five minutes and he had another five to go.

She had the hourglass balanced on the flat of her blade and she wasn't shaking at all. He hated her.

On the first day, he'd lasted four minutes before his arm had simply given up. On the second day it had been five. Today it was seven. He'd hated it at first, the realisation of how useless he was. But now he counted the seconds, and if he counted one more than the day before, that seemed like a victory.

Tasahre stayed completely still for the last three minutes then smoothly let the hourglass go. 'Guard,' she said, and nothing else. She spent a minute or two fiddling with Berren's stance, twisting his arm and and wrist, kicking his feet until he was standing in guard the way she wanted. They went through the same thing every day, practising simple blows, a cut or thrust, a parry and a riposte, the sort of thing he'd been doing with Master Sy for the last year. It was humiliating. Tasahre could have done it blindfold. Now and then she stopped and told Berren all the things he was doing wrong. Sometimes she'd stand right behind him, her legs pressed against his, chest against his back, hands on his wrists, pushing and moulding him into the stance she wanted. The sensation was odd and strangely intimate.

For those hours in the late afternoon they worked alone, Berren and Tasahre. The other monks paired up around them and simply pretended he didn't exist. The elder dragon sometimes stopped to watch, but he was watch-ing Tasahre, not Berren. He was watching how well she adjusted to the unwanted burden she'd been given. In the odd moment when he wasn't busy resenting being taught by a girl his own age, he almost felt sorry for her, although he'd have felt a lot *more* sorry for her if she didn't crack his ribs with her waster whenever his attention wandered.

For the last hour of the evening the monks all sat in a circle, taking it in turns to fight one another. Everyone fought everyone else, one bout only, and Berren was no exception. While the others fought with light padding and steel swords, Berren fought with his waster. Most of them simply batted him aside, clocked him on the head and withdrew before he even knew what was happening. One or two made a point of hitting him in a particularly exotic way, but after the first few days they grew tired of show-ing off and dispatched him with the same disdain as the others. Tasahre let him come to her and simply battered his attacks away without moving from where she stood until they both agreed he'd had enough. Still, he enjoyed watching the monks fight each other. He began to see who favoured what approach, which combinations, who was a sliver quicker and who was a fraction stronger. Tasahre, he saw, was usually beaten by most of the monks. Usually but not always.

At the end of each day he staggered back to the thief-taker's house as the sun set. He chewed through whatever crusts of bread were left and drained the bowl of lukewarm gruel that the thief-taker had left for him, barely noticing what was in it, and then went to bed. Usually the thief-taker wasn't there; even when he was, Berren was asleep before he could ask what Master Sy had been up to. He was exhausted, every single day. As he fell asleep, though, he found himself thinking of the scent garden over and over again, of the silhouette he'd seen clambering over the wall and of the strange black-powder smell the assassin had carried with him.

On Abyss-Day, the temple classes were closed, the monks spent their time at prayer and in meditation, and Berren finally got some rest. Abyss-Day was the day that thieves and snuffers claimed as their own. It was the day of delving into the deep, the day of blindness and ruin. No one did business on Abyss-Day; even most of the market and harbour traders stayed at home. It was the day of mischief and mayhem, before the light and truth that Sun-Day would bring; for Berren, though, Abyss-Day was the blessed relief of a lie-in in the morning, a few hours of dozing and stretching and moaning about how much all his muscles hurt, and then, when his stomach finally took charge, of eating. He eased himself down the rickety stairs and into the kitchen, lured by the smell of bread that wafted through the thief-taker's house. There was fruit, too – Master Sy always liked his fruit if he could get anything fresh.

'Morning, Berren.' The thief-taker was sitting in a chair in his parlour, feet up on the table, massaging his knee.

'Master.' Berren helped himself to an entire loaf of bread. He sat down on the floor across the parlour and tore into it until his stomach stopped growling. Then he looked up and smiled brightly. 'So?'

'So?' Master Sy smiled and shook his head. 'So I'm fast losing my appetite for long stairways.'

'I was thinking of that fellow on the roof with the bow. So is it right then? The man we're looking for is in the Two Cranes?'

'The man *I'm* looking for, lad. And yes, he is.'

'And?'

'Watching and waiting, lad.' The thief-taker shook his head. 'Watching and waiting.' Which was the thief-taker's way of saying he was up to *something*, but Berren knew better than to press his luck with questions.

'Was me that caught him,' he muttered. 'You remember

that, master. When there's more than watching and wait-ing to be done, I want to help.'

Master Sy smiled. 'I'll do that. For now you can help by keeping well out of the way. Not something to mess with, this one.'

'I'm not a boy any more, master.'

'Maybe not, Berren. When there's more than watching and waiting to be done, you can be a part of it. But for now there isn't, so you stick with your sword-monks. Was you that tipped him over the edge so we couldn't ask him any questions, you just remember that too.'

Berren finished his loaf of bread and wandered back to the kitchen looking for more. He came back with a couple of apples. They were soft and mushy and not crunchy at all. He made a face.

'Late harvest from up north.' The thief-taker shrugged. 'They've been kept half-frozen in an outhouse for the winter and then sat on a wagon for a week and a ship for another. They're not exactly fresh, but then what do you expect for apples in spring? Was thinking of boiling them up and making a paste but I suppose I'll not bother now.' He watched as Berren devoured the apples, core and all, and then sat, looking around the room as if searching for more. 'You're not still hungry are you?' He shook his head. 'They not feed you at the temple?'

'Not much, no.'

The thief-taker got up. He winced as he put weight on his knee. 'Here, then.' He threw his purse to Berren. 'Go feed yourself. There's not much in it. I'm off to bed. Up all night watching the Two Cranes. Don't forget to go and get water.'

A squeak of protest got as far as Berren's mouth. He swallowed it back down and looked into the purse instead. A handful of pennies and that was all, not even a single crown. And he'd been looking forward to spending the day with his master, wandering the city, telling him all about the monks in the temple and asking questions, lots and lots of questions.

'Said there wasn't much.'

'Master?'

'Lad?'

'I was thinking ...' How to ask without sounding like an idiot?

'Usually a good way to start that, yes.'

'Well, as well as the man with the bow, I was thinking about the assassin who wanted to kill Prince Sharda.'

The thief-taker shook his head. 'Drop it, lad. It's not a place you want to go.'

'But–!'

'No, no.' Master Sy waved his hands dismissively. 'I know that look on your face. That's the hunter's eye, that is. You've got scent of something and now you want to track it down. You're thinking we should go after whoever it was, right?'

'Well ...'

'Thought so. The answer's no, it's a bad idea and we're not going anywhere near it. Another time I might humour you for something to do, but I've got my business to attend to and you're not to go near that one on your own.'

'But–!'

Master Sy sat down again. 'Think, lad! First thing, there's no money in it. If you found out who it was, then what? Who's going to pay you for that?'

'The Justicar?'

The thief-taker roared with laughter. 'Kol? Why? It's thieves he's after, anyone who pricks the skin of the merchant guilds enough for them to notice, that's all. He's theirs. The only time he'll care about a murder is when it's one of those fat pigs we saw in the Golden Cup.' The thief-taker leaned towards Berren. 'I'll tell you who'd pay you for that: whoever did it. They'd pay you handsomely to keep you quiet and then they'd have you killed. What sort of person, do you think, tries to have an imperial prince murdered?'

Berren's eyes lit up. 'Someone in the temple! Everyone knows the priests there don't like the Emperor and his house one little bit. And it was the night the sword-monks came. What if it was one of them?'

'No! *Think*, boy! If there's one thing I've tried to teach you, it's that you look for the money. Never mind who it was you whacked on the nose – although whether you think you'd ever manage to do that to a sword-monk is maybe something you should ponder while you're training with them – whose purse were they taking, that's the question! Some priest?' He laughed and shook his head. 'There's Talsin's heirs, they're none too pleased with who's on the throne. Maybe the Overlord himself. You think the sort of man who pays a snuffer to murder a prince is going to let an urchin from Shipwrights' bring him down? And then yes, there's the assassin himself. He killed two men. Slit their throats. He's a cold snuffer, that one. Did you know ... no, how would you? The soldiers at the Watchman's Arms were poisoned, quite a few of them. Not a killing poison, but a sleeping draught to make them dopey, and that means that whoever he was, he was in the Arms earlier that night. Chances are it was one of the prince's own men who did it. You going to go to Varr to look for him? Drop it, Berren. You stopped a murder, you got your reward. Leave it at that.'

Berren was shaking his head. 'The soldiers he had were all big. The man I saw was our sort of size.'

Master Sy groaned. '*Leave* it, Berren. You chase after that snuffer, he'll kill you the moment he gets a sniff of you. Stick to your lessons and keep your head down.' Master Sy stood up once more. 'Live to fight another day, eh? Just this once.' He creaked his way up the stairs and went to his room and closed the door. Before long, the house shook softly with his snoring.

Live to fight another day? For what? Berren mulled that one over. Like Master Sy always said: *I'm not a thief-taker for Kol's silver, I'm a thief-taker because I don't like thieves.*

He got up and headed off for The Eight. On his way out, he thumbed his nose at the thief-taker's snores.

14

MORE THAN A PASSING INTEREST

He went looking for the justicar, but it turned out that Kol wasn't in The Eight that day and Berren eventually went back to the temple at dawn on Sun-Day with no idea where else to go. For the rest of that week he spent his days with Tasahre, watching the other monks, singling them out one by one, reading how they moved, how they fought, and, where he could, what they looked like from behind leaping up a wall. They were the right build, short and lithe southerners. Some of them went missing now and then – he saw that now. He asked, but Tasahre shook her head. That was business of the order and not his concern, she told him, and so he didn't bother asking the others; still, as the week drew on, he watched. Different monks disappeared each day, usually just one or two of them but sometimes half a dozen. They were always missing in the morning and at midday but back for the afternoon. When he approached any of them, they simply walked away. None of them would talk to him, not even a word of greeting. The only time he got close to most of them was late in the afternoon in the fighting circle, and then only for as long as it took for them to bash him on the head with the flat of a sword, bow and walk away.

Whoever had been in the scent garden, they'd gone away with a bloodied nose. He would have remembered if one of the monks had had a swollen face, wouldn't he? And

Master Sy was right, he couldn't imagine ever catching one of them so off-guard. The black-powder smell bothered him too. Did monks use black powder? He hadn't seen any. Maybe he was wrong and it had been someone else, but that thought only made him even more determined. The Eight was on his way home from the temple, near enough. Kol was never there but he found Master Fennis and Master Velgian and asked them both to put a word in for him.

The days passed. The city fell into the madness of the Spring Festival – even Master Sy took a few nights off from watching the Two Cranes or whatever it was he did and took Berren down to the Abyss-Day celebrations at the docks – and then blearily nursed its hangover. The month of Rebirth gave way to the month of Floods and the river began to swell, living up to the name of the season hundreds of miles away around the City of Spires. Berren might have slowly forgotten his assassin, except that every day as he practised with Tasahre, he kept seeing in her shape a flicker of the silhouette he'd seen leaping the wall of the Watchman's Arms.

It was about a month since he'd started with the sword-monks when he came out of the temple in the evening to find Master Sy slouched by the gates waiting for him, arms folded over his chest and looking cross.

'The Eight,' he said shortly. 'Kol wants to talk to you. Apparently you've been asking questions.' He almost frog-marched Berren across Deephaven Square and down the Avenue of the Sun. 'Told you to leave it be, didn't I?' They reached Four Winds Square, marched past the courthouse and down the narrow street that ran beside it, past the bronze octopus fountain and into the ivy-covered frame of The Eight. Kol was sitting there at his usual table and he had most of his thief-takers around him. As Berren and Master Sy came in, Kol gave them both a hard look.

'Finally. Sit. Have a drink.'

'Got anything to eat?' asked Berren, who was starving as usual after a day with the sword-monks. The justicar rolled his eyes. He looked around, waved at someone, pointed at Berren and snapped his fingers. As Berren and Master Sy sat down, Kol leaned in towards his thief-takers. He glared at Berren.

'Life's hard with our usual source of bread and shelter having been taken away, eh?'

'Technically you never lost yours,' muttered Master Fennis.

'Not that his purse would tell you that,' sniggered Master Mardan.

'Shut it, you pair! I have a proposition. There's no bounty, but you lot had better pay attention, because if you don't we might have those sword-monks here for a lot longer than I thought and frankly they're not half bad when it comes to thief-taking, even if their methods take some getting used to. Now listen: you all worked for me at the Watchman's Arms ...'

Fennis jingled his purse. 'Best money I've seen for years.'

'Well when His Highness finally buggered off back where he came from, it was to be named guardian of the Emperor's heir, and *she's* still sucking at her mother's tit. Do you know what all of that means? No, thought not. It means that if anything happens to the Emperor, someone else gets to sit on the throne until his daughter hits sixteen. As of the spring festival, that'll be Prince Sharda and not the Emperor's brother like it would have been before.' He looked straight at Berren. 'Berren here thinks we should be looking for who it was who tried to kill him. He's probably an idiot, but it narks me that it happened on my watch. So I'm in. My question is: are you? Think about it, my boys, because we're not talking about thief-taking any more, we're talking about something wholly different.'

Thief-takers Fennis and Mardan nodded enthusiastically. Master Sy shook his head.

'Too dangerous. Not interested.' He wasn't the only one either. Master Velgian looked positively terrified.

'I think it's a terrible idea,' he said.

'You have no idea what you're dealing with, Kol.' Master Sy closed his eyes. 'I could tell you everything I told my apprentice, but you, of all people, should know better. So what is it, exactly, you think we're going to get out of this?'

'Worst that can happen, we discredit these bloody sword-monks and they go home. Best that happens, we get showered with gold until we're drowning in it, that's what I think is going to happen. You beg to differ?' As he was talking, a boy came to the table and set a bowl of stew down in front of Berren. Berren started shovelling it into his mouth as fast as he could.

'Sword-monks!' Velgian was shaking his head frantically. 'Not good, Kol! I'm not going against sword-monks!'

Orimel the Witch-Breaker sniffed. He peered at Berren's stew. 'Smells good,' he said. He spoke with an air of thoughtful quiet if he spoke at all, and so when he *did* speak, the other thief-takers, even the Justicar, usually stopped and listened. 'The assassin – *an* assassin – tried again in Varr. He was caught that time. I've heard many things. On Sun-Day it was the Emperor's brother, on Moon-Day one of the sons of the Lord of Neja, on Mage-Day a fire-mage, then a black-skinned Taiytakei mystic or one of the pale-skinned fey folk they say live far to the north. I've heard that the assassin is dead, that he is free, that he escaped, that he has been cut into a hundred pieces with a sorcerer questioning each and every one. Very little of what I have heard can be true, but an assassin has unquestionably been caught.'

'Same one?' Kol raised an eyebrow.

Orimel held up his palms. 'Who can say, Justicar?'

Kol glowered. 'Well then. Who's in and who's out? If you're out, piss off.'

Velgian couldn't get out of his chair fast enough. Beside Berren, Master Sy got to his feet. 'Come on, lad. This is a fool's game and I've got fish of my own to catch.'

'Oh no you don't!' Kol banged the table. 'You can go, but not him, not until he's told us everything he knows. Besides, maybe he wants in, eh, Berren?' Kol grinned. The justicar had never been good at that, at least not in any way that didn't make him look like he wanted to eat someone, preferably while they were still alive. But he was right. Berren wanted to stay. He wanted it badly.

Master Sy snorted in disgust. 'You're fools, both of you. Fennis, I thought you were chucking this in and heading off to Torpreah to start a tea house?'

'Varr, Syannis. In Varr.'

'Idiot.' With a last shake of his head, Master Sy stalked out of The Eight. Kol waited for him to go.

'Stew good, lad?'

Berren belched loudly.

'Have another then. But you can start by telling us exactly what it was you saw that night. Everything, boy. Don't miss anything out.'

Talking about it, having the justicar and a few of the thief-takers actually listening to him for once, that was exciting. He went through it all as it happened, how he'd been there and seen the man slip in and how he'd fought him off and then afterwards, the two soldiers dead on the ground, their throats slit.

'Should have worn a gorget,' muttered Master Fennis.

When he was done, Kol made him go through it all again, this time picking apart the bits that were exactly as they had happened and the parts that Berren had added to make the story more exciting. At the end he nodded, although he was frowning fiercely. 'Bloodied nose. Small fellow. Funny smell. Swords like a sword-monk but rubbish at swordplay?'

'Hey! He was fast!'

Kol tried not to smirk. 'You cracked him one. All right, *mediocre* swordsman then.' he was back to frowning now. 'Well, you're the one who knows them. Was it really a sword-monk?'

Berren shrugged. The more he saw of them, the more he doubted it. 'I thought so at first. But none of them ever had a bloody nose.' He tried to remember watching them march into the temple, the very morning after it had happened. Would he have noticed something like that, under their tattoos? He wasn't sure he would.

Kol rolled his shoulders. He looked bored now. 'I'll ask about. You keep an eye on them for me, boy. Right. Probably a snuffer pretending he was a monk. Pity.' He glanced at Mardan and Fennis. 'You two can piss off now. Go get drunk or something. Find me snuffers. A short bloke who's got a mean streak but can't actually do much with a sword.'

'Why, I do believe I'm looking at one now!' Master Mardan smiled back at the justicar. He was getting up though, and so were the others.

'Gods, Mardan, any funnier and people might mistake you for the clown you are.' Berren started to rise too, but Kol glared at him. 'Not you, boy. Got more questions for you.' When Mardan and Fennis and Orimel were gone, Kol got up. He came over to Berren and sat down in the chair beside him, where Master Sy had been before he left. 'Your master. What's he up to? Why's he not biting on this?'

Berren shrugged. 'Don't know. Said it was too dangerous. Said there was no prize in it and I'd just get myself killed and he had something else to be getting on with.'

'Aye.' Kol looked troubled. 'Well, he might have a point

or two there. But what's this other thing he's got to be getting on with?'

'I …' Berren bit his lip. 'Maybe I shouldn't say.'

'He's after whoever killed Kasmin, right?' Berren tried not to say anything but his face must have spoken for him. Kol nodded. 'Thought so. Been doing some digging around that myself. Not sure he should be the one telling you about getting their fingers burned. He's stalking a sea-captain from Kalda who calls himself the Headsman, right?' Again, Berren's face must have given him away. 'Kelm's Teeth, boy, remind me not to trust you with any of *my* secrets – it's like reading a bloody book. Anyway, that warehouse where you had your little fracas, I looked into that. The Headsman's renting a part of it. You know who else rents a space there? Saffran Kuy. The warlock.'

'The witch-doctor from the House of Cats and Gulls?' For a moment, Berren couldn't contain himself.

'Call him that if you want. Not my cup of tea, even if Syannis gets along with him somehow. You know what the Headsman's got up there?'

Berren shook his head.

'Neither do I. When you find out, make sure I get to hear about it. I don't care which one of you tells me, but one of you better had. Got it?'

Berren nodded quickly and almost jumped out of his chair. 'I'd better go. It's late. Swords in the morning. Supposed to be at temple for dawn still.' At the door, Berren paused. 'That purse you left for us. There was more in it than was owed. So what's Master Sy doing for *you*?'

For a long time the justicar sat and stared at Berren. Then he took a deep breath. 'I've known Syannis for ten years, Berren, and I knew Kasmin for longer. I know you all think I'm a heartless bastard who wouldn't part with a single penny unless there was something in it for me, and for three hundred and eleven days of the year you might well be right. That was the three hundred and twelfth. Staying alive, that's what he's doing for me. Now get lost before I ask for it back.'

15
A TIGER BY THE TAIL

Berren ran outside, past the fountain and up the street into Four Winds Square. He was already yawning. Good food and plenty of it, a day full of hard work and he was ready for bed and a good night's sleep. There'd be a few sharp words from Master Sy on messing with matters that didn't concern him when he got home, no doubt.

He was two streets away from the thief-taker's house when a silhouette stepped out of an alley in front of him. Berren skittered to a stop on the wet stones of the street. He froze there for a second. The silhouette was of a shortish man with two swords over his back. The man who'd murdered two imperial guardsmen, who'd had the audacity to try and take the life of the imperial prince himself. Now he was standing in the street, only a dozen paces away.

The assassin slowly drew his swords, one in each hand. For that first moment, Berren was sure he was about to die.

'I know who you are, Berren.'

The moment passed. Other thoughts followed: that it was dark but still long short of midnight and others might come this way at any moment; that he'd beaten this man once before, in the scent garden; that he wasn't far from home and Master Sy; and then a last thought came along, slower than the others yet more pressing. Why step out in front of him? Why be seen at all? Why not a shadow in the dark with a short curved knife and a throat-slitting flick of the wrist and away into the night, unseen? So he held his ground.

The assassin growled. 'There's no purse to killing you, boy. Do you *want* to live?' The man's face was lost in the shadow of a deep hood. 'If you *do* want to live, put your justicar off my scent. I'll be watching both of you. If you don't, the next time I see you, I'll kill you. Do you understand? Now run!' The assassin's voice was thick and guttural, a bit like the archer from the warehouse roof. Berren took two steps backwards and then stopped.

'No.' He drew out his waster. This wasn't right at all. 'Who are you?'

'Your death, curse you boy!' The assassin hesitated an instant before he charged, both swords raised. Berren knew he ought to run, that Master Sy would tell him he was mad to stand fast; but he'd fought against sword-monks now; he'd beaten this man once before, and there was something ... something *wrong* about the way this assassin held his swords, something about the way the assassin came at him that wasn't right, as though it was all a bluff. The swords whirled at Berren's face but with no real skill; Berren jumped sideways and poked his waster at the man's head as he went past. He missed, but the wooden tip caught the cloth of the man's cloak and pulled back his hood, and now Berren could see who it was.

'Master Velgian?' He stopped, stunned. It all made sense! Velgian being mugged and getting a bloody nose – that hadn't ever happened, it had been Berren's waster that marked him! And the smell, the black-powder smell in the scent garden and the look on Velgian's face when Kol had said he meant to go after the assassin! But why? Velgian, of all of them, a killer?

The poet thief-taker turned and stopped and looked at Berren with sad eyes. 'Why couldn't you just run, lad? Why couldn't you leave it be?'

Berren glanced up and down the street but there was no one else in sight.

'Path of fire! You were supposed to be asleep! I didn't want to hurt you. I liked you. Sun knows there was enough sleeping draft in your breakfast to fell a horse! I could have killed you like I killed the others, but I would have let you be. Why did you have to chose that one night not to be hungry, eh?'

Berren knew exactly. Too excited about seeing the sword-monks the next day, too full of left-overs from the feast of the night before. 'Why did you do it, Master Velgian?'

'Why do you think, boy? For the purse and the fistful of golden emperors inside it, that's why. Damn your eyes! I didn't want it to come to this, but now what choice have I got?' He took a deep breath. The way he held himself changed. 'I'm sorry, lad, but it's you or me now.' He came at Berren again and now all the bluff was gone and Berren knew for sure that if he tried to fight, this time he'd die. He turned and bolted and Velgian was right on his heels.

'I promise not to tell!' yelled Berren over his shoulder.

'And I wish I could believe you!'

He sprinted into the little yard outside Master Sy's door. 'Master Sy! Master thief-taker! Help!' He reached the door and kicked it as he passed but it stayed shut and then he had to keep running because Velgian was right there and he couldn't even stop to open his own door. 'Master! Velgian! It's Velgian!' He darted down a little alley instead, the one that went round to Master Sy's back yard; he bounded up onto the back of an old empty chest the thief-taker kept by his back door and then up onto Master Sy's kitchen and on to his roof. If *that* didn't get Master Sy's attention, nothing would.

'A pox on you, boy!' shrieked Velgian behind him.

From Master Sy's roof there was only one way to go, but Berren knew the rooftops here as well as he knew the streets. They were his home as much as anywhere and even in the dark he knew exactly which way to go – straight over the top, double back across the alley, around the side of the yard …

'Give it up, boy!' Velgian wasn't dropping back. He was a thief-taker too, after all.

Being up on the rooftops made him think of the archer who'd fallen off the warehouse. He changed direction sharply. One rooftop to the next and then the big leap, right across the street, the one place you could do it but you had to get the jump just right and land in exactly the right place. Berren flew across the gap, caught the edge of the roof on the far side with his toes, let his momentum carry him forward and then grabbed onto the roof with both hands, pulling himself up and scrabbling with his feet. It was a hard jump to make, even if you knew the trick to it. He scrambled up the roof and looked back. Velgian had skittered to a halt on the other side of the jump. He still had his swords drawn.

'Berren!'

'Don't! You'll fall, Master Velgian. You will.' Now that he'd led the poet thief-taker here to his little trap, escape was enough. Then home, Master Sy, the justicar, he could tell them all he was right …

Velgian started to run, still with his swords out, straight at the gap. It was a good jump and he almost made it. His foot caught the roof and he pitched forward just as Berren had done, only Velgian wasn't ready for it. His hands were full. It was all over in an instant. His foot slipped off, he dropped both his swords, clawed at the roof and then he was gone, over the edge.

No, not quite. When Berren inched closer, he saw Velgian still hanging by his fingertips.

'Master Velgian!' The roof was steep, like all the roofs in this part of the city. 'Whose purse, Master Velgian?'

127

'You going to help me up, boy?' Velgian's fingers were slowly slipping. Berren offered him his hand and then withdrew it. The roof was too steep, his own footing too precarious. If Velgian wanted to be helped, Berren could help him, but what Velgian really wanted was to take Berren over the edge with him – he could see it in the thief-taker's eyes. Nothing to lose any more.

'Thought not. Got some sense there.'

'Whose purse, Master Velgian? Whose gold bought you?'

Velgian's arms were shaking. 'Are you listening, boy? You tell Syannis one thing for me. You tell him that Saffran Kuy is not the friend he thinks. You tell him that, Berren. Do that for me. Tell him ...'

The edge of the roof snapped under his fingers. It was only twenty feet down to the ground, but Velgian landed flat on his back. He bounced and lay still. By the time Berren got down, Velgian was dead. His neck was broken.

They were in sight of the thief-taker's house. Berren dragged Velgian to the door and pulled him inside. Master Sy wasn't there, presumably off watching the Two Cranes again or whatever it was he did, but Berren could hardly go to bed and leave a body in his parlour for the thief-taker to find when he came back. In the end he curled up in the thief-taker's chair and fell asleep there, waiting for his master to come home.

It wasn't Master Sy who nudged him awake barely moments after his eyes had closed, though, but the Justicar.

'Wake up, boy.' He was poking Berren with a finger. 'Wake up. And then tell me, right now, what the bloody Khrozus Master Velgian is doing dead on the floor.'

For a moment Berren wondered if he should run, but he was too tired and what was the point? He didn't understand why Velgian, of all of them, would have done something like this.

128

'He fell,' he said, and then slowly and carefully went through everything that had happened, trying to put it all together in his head as he did, as if that might bring some sense to it. When he was done, he was no better off than when he started.

'Velgian?' Kol rubbed his face, struggling with disbelief. Berren nodded. He could see quite clearly now how the poet thief-taker must have been the man in the scent garden. Everything about him was right, right size, not the best swordsman, moved the right way, everything. But why? Why would he do it? Even Kol seemed bemused.

'For a purse filled with the Emperor's head like he said, I suppose.' Kol took a deep breath and frowned as though he still didn't really believe it. He gave Berren a strange look. 'There are ways to get to the truth, even now,' he said. 'Does he have any family to claim the body?'

They looked at each other. As far as Berren knew, Velgian had come to Deephaven from somewhere far to the east. He'd come alone, and if you believed his boasts in The Eight, he'd had a string of lovers as long as your arm. But in the end he always struck Berren as a lonely man. 'I don't think so. Don't you know?'

Kol shrugged. 'You thief-takers keep yourselves to yourselves. If he had anyone, he never spoke of them to me. Right then. You're not going anywhere for the next few weeks are you, Berren? No, let me say it another way – you stay where I can see you. You and Syannis both. Now I'm going to have to go and haul some of my men out of their cups, which isn't going to please any of us. So he'd better still be here when I come back.'

'He was trying to say something when he fell. Something about the witch-doctor.'

A dark look crossed Kol's face. 'Was he now? Well like I said, there's people in this city who can do something about that. If they can be persuaded.'

He went away and came back half an hour later with a pair of militia-men and a handcart. They lifted Velgian into it and wheeled him away. Kol watched them go.

'Something I need to talk about with your master. Got some news for him about what's keeping him at the Two Cranes. So I'll be staying around for a bit.' He gave Berren another odd look, sort of angry and sad at the same time. 'None of your business what it is unless he says otherwise though. If I were you, I'd piss off to bed and get some sleep.' He settled into Master Sy's chair. 'Yeh, that's what I'd do if I were you, and I'd quietly forget that any of this ever happened. Velgian, eh? Poor bastard. Your master's right. Meddle with the affairs of kings, look what happens.'

It was only as Berren huddled under his blanket on his mattress of straw that he realised Kol hadn't been talking about Master Velgian at the end.

16
KEYS

On the last Moon-Day of the month of Floods, Master Sy was waiting for him when he came home. Velgian was long gone, forgotten, it seemed, by everyone except Berren. Kol was back to his tight-lipped self and the thief-taker remained wrapped in his own plots and schemes. Today, as Berren came in from another week at the temple, Master Sy was sitting at his little table with two enormous dried spiced sausages sat on plates in front of him and a loaf of bread between them.

'Monks working you hard as ever?' He was smiling. Berren nodded. The aches and pains weren't as bad as they'd been when he'd started but he was still exhausted when he came home.

'It's the same every day, though. Just the same things, over and over and over again. And still with a waster.' When was someone going to let him hold a real sword, that's what he wanted to know. When he was old and grey and shaky and could barely even pick it up any more? He sat down, picked up one of the sausages and sniffed at it. A Mirrormere Hot, stuffed with pork and a vicious mix of spices. His favourite. He grinned and cocked his head.

Master Sy smiled. 'Tuck in.'

Cured pork didn't come cheap in a city that lived largely off fish. Berren smiled back. 'You want something.'

'Monks teaching you anything useful yet?'

He shrugged. 'I suppose.' He didn't dare say anything else, not to Master Sy. Tasahre might not be what he'd been hoping for, but he'd learned enough from the thief-taker over these last two years to know how lucky he was and when to keep his mouth shut.

'Treating your teacher with respect, I hope.'

'Of course, master.' He didn't have much choice in that, either. Tasahre could probably kick him right through the temple walls if she wanted to. Or worse, she could simply stop teaching him. Yeh, and she gave him shivers when she did that thing of standing right up against him to get the angles in his arms and legs right. But it was best not to think about that.

'Seen anything odd?'

Berren shook his head. 'At the temple? Not much. They're a bit here and there. They go off into the city sometimes but I don't know what they get up to.' He bit off the end of his sausage and started to chew; then he raised an eyebrow. 'They're a bit like you, master.' His mouth was starting to tingle with the heat of the spices. He tore off a lump of bread. 'So has Kol found someone to conjure up Master Velgian's spirit and ask him why he did it yet?'

'Speak of the dead with respect, lad.' The thief-taker watched Berren for a while, chewing on his sausage. The whole inside of Berren's mouth was burning nicely now. 'Good one is it?'

Berren nodded, reaching for the jug of goat's milk.

'I can tell. You're bright red and sweating.' The thief-taker sniffed and took a bite of his own. He stood up and walked to the door. 'Abyss-Day tomorrow. No lessons. You said you wanted to be a part of what I'm doing, well tonight there's more than watching and waiting to be done. You got enough strength to do some thief-taking?'

'Yeh! 'Course!'

132

'Right, come on then.' The thief-taker got up. 'Bring your sausage with you.'

Berren stuffed his cheeks with a last mouthful of bread and hurried into the yard outside. He chased after Master Sy along the dim twilight of alleys and passageways that wound down the hill into The Maze. 'Master, how much would it cost to have a sword of my own?'

The thief-taker threw back his head and laughed. 'Berren, you have no idea what you're asking. I couldn't afford steel for you even if I wanted to, not until your sword-monk friends have pissed off the city princes enough to get themselves thrown out and we're back to having paid work. Even a bad sword costs more than most men will ever see.' He looked up at the sky. Stars twinkled down between tufts of cloud. 'Dry tonight, I reckon.'

Berren was looking at Master Sy's short steel sword, trying not to feel envious. 'Was just asking. I'll start saving my crowns then.'

'You need emperors for a good sword, lad, and several of them. Still, maybe you can do some sword-smith a favour, eh? Get yourself a bargain.'

'Yeh.' Berren nodded again. He thought about how long it would take to get that sort of money. Years, probably. He turned away so the thief-taker wouldn't see his face and followed as they walked into the evening. Master Sy talked on about this and that, a bit about swords but mostly about what he'd been doing and about the Headsman. Berren nodded and grunted and pretended to listen but his mind was far away. He was thinking about Velgian and what he'd done, and he was thinking about swords. He was thinking about how to get one. *For the purse and the fistful of golden emperors inside it, that's why ...*

By the time they reached the Two Cranes, Berren had his mind back where it was supposed to be. Master Sy slipped into the twilight shadows of an alley a few dozen yards from the hostel's entrance. There were guards watching the street, snuffers with swords looking out for any riff-raff who might cause trouble for their wealthy guests. When the doors opened, the air spilled out from inside. It smelled of perfume and spices and wine and carried the sounds of laughter.

There was a sword-monk too. Berren didn't see at first, not until Master Sy pointed. And then Berren had to look again. He gasped.

'Tasahre!' He was certain it was her. Now and then he caught a glimpse of movement as she lurked in shadows of her own.

'Yes. They've been watching me,' murmured Master Sy. 'Making a right nuisance of themselves actually.' The thief-taker grunted. 'You know how I spend my nights, lad? I hide out here watching people come and go. Quiet as a mouse, stealthy as a shadow, me. Then some idiot comes along dressed in bright yellow and props himself up against a wall where he thinks nobody can see him and now every-one in the Two Cranes thinks they've got a sword-monk after them. Fun to see how many have got the wind up them but it's still a nuisance. Moon-Day nights I get her. Today she can make herself useful.' Master Sy lowered his voice. 'When the Headsman comes out, I need you to stay here, out of sight. I'll tell you what to do. And do *not* let her see you!'

'But–'

The thief-taker put a finger to Berren's lips. He grinned and looked slightly sheepish. 'That night you and Master Velgian had your coming together, Kol was coming to see me anyway. He was coming to tell me that the Headsman's got something up with the harbour-masters in the House of Records up near Reeper Gate. I've been watching long enough to know the Headsman spends a lot of time up there and he's keeping some curious company. The House of Records is about the safest place I can think of for him to keep something short of leaving it on his own ship. It costs money and it can't be anything big he's got there, but whatever it is, it's well guarded. It has a very good lock on it too, judging by the keys he keeps on his belt.'

'You want me to–' Pick his pocket? Was that it?

'What I want you to do right now, boy, is stay very quiet and still and use your eyes.'

For a long time they watched in silence. People came and went, mostly small clusters of men in rich clothes and always with one or two snuffers nearby. The sounds from inside the Two Cranes grew louder as the night drew on. The warm late-spring air finally began to cool and a dampness started to rise out of the streets from the afternoon rains.

'There!' Master Sy crouched beside Berren as six men came out of the Two Cranes. Two snuffers walked in front, lean and wiry with eyes that darted from side to side and fingers never far from the hilts of their swords. A few paces behind came two men in long dark cloaks and fancy hats. They were laughing together. One of them was short and so fat he was almost round, with an equally round fat face and an eyepatch. Here and there, curls of light hair escaped from under his hat. He looked old. Not *old* old, not grey and hobbling old, but older than Master Sy.

The second man was taller, younger. He walked with a cane and he had a loud voice with a heavy accent that cut the air. When he laughed at the fat one's jokes, it was more a braying honk than proper laughter. Behind them both came another pair of snuffers, long and lanky this time. These ones carried short straight swords, like the one Master Sy had.

The thief-taker rested his hand on Berren's shoulder, cautioning him to be still. The six men walked past the mouth of the alley. The snuffer in front glanced straight at Berren but saw nothing but shadows. For a few seconds after they passed, Master Sy stared as though he was lost in some faraway place. When he came back, it was with a snap.

'Boy, do you see the fat fool with the eyepatch?' The men were already on the fringes of the docks, mingling with the crowds there. Berren squinted.

'Yes, master. I do.'

'That's the Headsman. Best you remember his face. Did you see the keys on his belt?' The thief-taker's lip curled. He waved something under Berren's nose, a bunch of keys. 'Look what I got. Borrowed. Copied. Put back again. All without anyone knowing. See, you're not the only one who knows a trick or two.' He pulled Berren back, deeper into the shadows, whispering. 'And so we come to why I'm bribing you with a particularly fine piece of sausage tonight. It was a good one wasn't it?'

'It was very nice.'

'A favourite of yours, am I right?'

Berren nodded.

'I want to see what's the other side of this key. What about you?'

Of course he wanted to come! But still, he hesitated. 'What do I have to do, master?'

The thief-taker scowled. 'I need a pair of eyes to keep watch. If it goes wrong, I need someone who can take a message to Justicar Kol and tell them whatever we found. And I might need someone to ... I might need a diversion.'

Someone to run, he meant, and be chased. Berren sniffed. 'You and your gammy leg.' The thief-taker's leg had never quite recovered. If you didn't know him, you'd never notice most of the time, but he couldn't run the way he used to. Berren had seen him wince on the stairs once or twice too. He saw the thief-taker's face darken and wished he hadn't said anything. 'Yeh,' he said quickly. 'Whatever I can do, master.' He arched his back, stretching his spine and beamed. 'Afterwards, I want you to teach me something,' he said. 'Something I can use in a fight.'

For what seemed like an age the thief-taker didn't even blink. Then, very slowly, he nodded. 'Something you can use in a fight.' He raised an eyebrow. Berren nodded vigorously then stopped as the thief-taker waved him away. 'Lad, eventually you'll learn that I, too, have a sense of humour, so I'll pretend that was a joke and laugh about it, shall I? Ha. Ha ha. Heh. There. Are we done now?'

'But ma—'

The thief-taker growled. 'Listen, boy, I've been teaching you how to fight since the day you came to me. I've been teaching you how to stand, how to move, how to hold a weapon. I've been teaching the muscles in your arm how to be strong—' He stopped, and then hissed. 'Berren, knives and swords *kill* people. So who, exactly, do you want to kill? Velgian? You saw what happened to him – is that how you want to end?'

'I—'

'Of course, mostly what knives and swords kill are idiot novices who think that having one makes them invincible. Right up until someone with a good stout stick gets inside their guard and knocks them down. And then, because they're up against someone with a sword, and because that scares the living sun out of them, they make sure as Khrozus that you *stay* down.' He sighed and shook his head.

Berren stared glumly into nothing. His shoulders slumped. 'I just want to beat Tasahre. Just once.' He gritted his teeth. When disappointment came knocking, what did a sword-master do? They didn't wail and moan and cry, that was for sure. They fought back. He looked up again, fingering the gold token around his neck. There was always Varr, always the prince ...

The thief-taker was looking at him through narrow eyes. It took Berren a moment to realise that Master Sy was laughing, shaking his head and laughing.

'And that's all is it? You want me to teach you something to beat a sword-monk? Nothing difficult then.'

Berren nodded.

'You want to show that upstart girl what a thief-taker can do, eh?'

Berren nodded again.

'That upstart girl over there who can't hide in shadows for shit? The one who almost broke my leg?' Master Sy had a gleam in his eye now. 'Well now then, why didn't you say? *That's* different.' He stood up, tightened his overcoat and shook his head, still muttering to himself. 'Wants to show off to a sword-monk? Oh Berren, you have no idea.' He laughed then patted Berren's shoulder and peered out of the alley. 'Well well. Now you're talking about a very particular fight, and so we shall see what we can do. Tomorrow. Abyss-Day. When we're done with our business tonight, I'll teach you something that no sword-monk has ever faced. My promise.'

17

THE HOUSE OF RECORDS

The thief-taker led the way to the docks. Most of the buildings that faced the sea were great wooden frames walled up with bricks, little more than shells for storing the mountains of kegs, barrels, crates, sacks and chests that flowed in and out of the city. The thief-taker walked on past all of those up to the Wrecking Point end of the harbour near the Reeper Gate. There was a huge stone building here, almost like a castle with tall walls and windows that were high above the ground and barred tight enough that not even a boy-thief could slip between them. The gate was open but there were guards on it, the Emperor's guards no less, with their swords and the burning eagle on their chest. An archway ran past the gate and the guards, into darkness between black walls of shadow.

'Been here before?' asked Master Sy. He jangled his stolen keys.

Berren shook his head. There were no ships anchored at this end of the bay, no crowds of drunken sailors or grumbling labourers here. It wasn't the sort of place where raggedy dock-boys were welcome, and in his time with Master Hatchet he'd learned to avoid the Emperor's guards.

'First time for everything then.' Master Sy slapped him on the shoulder. 'The Emperor's House of Records. Although I doubt the Emperor himself has the first idea that he has such a thing.' He walked towards the gates, brazenly in the open. The soldiers stiffened but then relaxed again.

'Master thief-taker,' nodded one. Syannis stopped in front of them, in the lamplight pooled in front of the gate. He turned and took his time to look back over the docks.

'Busy night?'

'Quiet. You got business here?'

'Yes.' Berren had never heard a lie slip well off his master's tongue, but he was hearing it now. Selling silk and honey, old Hatchet would have said. 'Questions for our harbour-masters. A few answers too.'

'They'll be out and in their cups by now.' The guards exchanged a laugh as they stood aside. The thief-taker lingered for a few moments longer and then walked on between them, down a vaulted passage that led into a large open square. They paused there, in the shadows. Berren looked around, taking it all in. The buildings here weren't like the rest of the docks. They were smaller and made of stone, with chimneys and windows that made them look like people actually lived in them. Some of them even had lanterns burning over the doors and snuffers slouching outside them. The snuffers up here were supposed to be even worse than the ones on Reeper Hill.

'These houses belong to the factors for the merchant princes,' murmured Master Sy as he scanned the darkness. 'The Headsman comes up here every morning. He goes to the House of Records. That's where the harbour-masters keep all the logs of which ships are in the harbour, when they arrived, when they're leaving, that sort of thing. They keep their manifests there too, but they also have strong-rooms with iron doors and the best locks in the city. There for anyone who can afford them.'

Berren screwed his face up. 'Master?'

'The Headsman's keeping something in there. Something too precious to keep with him at the Two Cranes but not something he can keep on his ship. I want to know what it is.'

A realisation bloomed in Berren's head. 'If you knew what was on each of the ships, you'd know which ones were worth stealing from ...'

Master Sy was laughing. 'You're about two years late, lad.'

'Eh?'

'VenDormen.'

Berren shuddered. VenDormen was the man who'd tried to have them killed, a harbour-master who'd been running a gang of pirates on the quiet.

'He was selling secrets from the House of Records. So now you see why only the harbour-masters and the most trusted officers of the merchant guild have a key. Yet my one-eyed friend has one too. And now so do I. Did he steal his? Did someone give it to him? If they did, who? And why? Tonight we find some answers.'

Berren scratched his nose. 'So we're ... we *are* looking for pirates again. Are we?'

He knew at once that he was wrong. For a moment he thought Master Sy would get angry with him, but all the thief-taker did was shake his head. 'No, Berren, I have an idea there's more to this than simple theft.' He laughed. 'Mind you, there might not be. The Headsman wasn't much more than a pirate when I knew him last. Could be money in this. You might get a few coppers or even a crown or two for catching a pickpocket. But merchants *hate* pirates. Catch Raider Yammek, and there's a reward of a hundred emperors to be had.'

'A hundred!' Berren felt himself go cold. 'That's enough to ...'

'Quite.' Master Sy put a finger to his lips and dropped to a crouch. 'Enough to buy a really *good* sword. Now, do you see that each door has a coat of arms over it?'

Berren nodded, not daring to speak.

'Those are the coats of arms of the merchant houses. They shelter behind the Emperor's swords. But that one there ...' Master Sy pointed to a dark corner of the square. 'Through that arch and down the end of another alley is the House of Records itself. Down there you'll find the arms of the Overlord of Deepwater. Do you think you can get there without anyone seeing you?'

Berren nodded again.

'Take the keys. One of them will fit the lock. I'll keep these snuffers busy. Best if you don't let them see you. Once you're in the alley it should be dark enough, but you need to be quiet, lad. Stay close to the door when you're inside. Stay quiet and wait for me. I won't be long.'

'But won't they see *you*, master?'

'Why yes, I think they will.' He bared his teeth. 'Got to make sure the Headsman finds out what I'm up to somehow, eh lad? But best if they think it's only me. Just in case.'

'But the guards on the gate! They already saw me!'

The thief-taker shook his head. 'Imagine you're the Headsman. Imagine you have the choice of bribing a few of the Emperor's men or a few snuffers. Which would you choose?' The answer to that was obvious – snuffers were swords for hire and people paid them for their eyes all the time. The Emperor's soldiers, they were a different matter.

Master Sy smiled. 'Exactly. He won't even think of it. Now: once we're inside, you keep quiet and you keep out of the way. Someone will come, one of the Headsman's henchmen. They'll bring snuffers of their own and I don't know how many. Whatever you see tonight, you keep it to yourself. If anything happens to me, you tell Kol and no one else, no matter what it is or what happens or who asks you. Got that?'

Berren nodded. This was the sort of thing Master Hatchet might once have told him to do, only with vastly more ambition. He set his sights on the door. In his head, he worked his way back to where he stood, darting from shadow to shadow. Another thrill of excitement shuddered inside him – this was more like thieving than thief-taking, and it was the most fun he'd had in ... Probably since he'd stolen away on that boat to Siltside.

He took one last careful look at the snuffers guarding the various doorways. They looked bored and sleepy. None of them were alert or on the lookout. Then he moved, slipping around the fringes of the lamplight, careful to stay in the shadows, closer and closer until he reached the darkness of the alley. No one stopped him. No one shouted after him. He heard Master Sy talking to a snuffer somewhere and then he slipped down the alley. It was short, just leading to another door that was almost lost in the night. He looked up at the coat of arms above him – a dark triangle on a pale field. In the starlight, he couldn't see the eagle but he didn't need to. These weren't simply the arms of the city Overlord, they were the arms of the Emperor himself! He fingered the golden token around his neck and smiled. Would the prince who'd given it to him approve? Probably not, but he wasn't entirely sure.

His fingers felt around the edges of the door until they found the lock. As quickly as he could, he went through the keys until he found the one that fitted. Then he opened the door and slipped inside, tip-toeing quickly, room to room, checking to be sure he was alone. There were two large downstairs rooms at the front, four small ones on the first floor, four more on the second. They were all empty. A single passage led into the back of the house, pitch black stone walls lined with strong heavy doors. Each one carried a coat of arms. Berren traced them with his fingers. He could picture them – the symbols of the city merchant houses. The doors were all locked. He wondered whether to try some more of the keys, then thought better of it.

A moment later, Master Sy was at the door. He was limping again.

'Well done!' he said. Berren swelled with pride. 'Good work.'

'I looked. There's no one else here. Didn't see much though. Just lots of paper.'

'With writing on. Yes. I hope after tonight you'll see why I wanted you to learn letters.' The thief-taker was whispering even though the house was empty. He quietly closed the door behind him. Berren was trembling with excitement.

'What now, master? Are we here to take something?'

'Secrets, that's what we're after. One of those snuffers couldn't wait to run off as soon as he saw me. He'll go to the Two Cranes. How long to get there, do you reckon, at a run?'

'Five minutes, maybe?'

'And then he's going to look for the Headsman, but we already know the Headsman isn't there, so that'll slow him down a bit. Say another couple of minutes and then another five for the Headsman's snuffers to get here.' The thief-taker stretched and massaged his knee. 'Might as well take a quick look at whatever there is for us to see while we're waiting.' He strode into the first of the downstairs rooms, the biggest in the house, with a large table and a dozen chairs laid around it.

'We're going to wait for them?' Berren gulped.

'Don't know how else we're going to find out which strongbox is the right one, and even if we did find it on our own, I doubt we've got the keys to *that*.' Master Sy picked up a piece of paper and a quill. 'Here, make yourself useful. I want you to search for something.' He wrote some letters down and gave Berren the paper. 'If you see anything with this name, you bring it to me.' Berren looked at the paper

and screwed up his eyes in concentration. *Radek of Kalda.*
'And make a mess. When the harbour-masters come in
tomorrow, I want them to know that *someone* was here,
even if they don't know who it was.'

'But they'll know that from the guards!'

The thief-taker smiled nastily. 'Yes, lad. They will.'

They moved from room to room. Master Sy tore open
drawers and scattered papers across the floor. Berren followed. After a few minutes, the thief-taker stopped.

'Give me the keys,' he snapped. Berren tossed them to
him. He paused, listening out but there was nothing to hear.
'Go upstairs. Hide. Stay there and stay out of sight. I'll be
down the back. And listen: you hear anyone come in, you
don't move a muscle, lad. You leave the rest to me.' Master
Sy vanished into the darkness. Berren heard the keys jingle
for a few seconds after he was gone, then nothing. He crept
up the stairs and set about searching for a good place to
hide, but in the dark, everywhere seemed as good as everywhere else. Idly, he picked up a few papers that lay on a
desk. They came in different types, he realised, after he'd
tried to read a few. Some of them even had the Emperor's
seal on the bottom! There were lists of which ships were in
the harbour. For each ship, there were lists of what cargo
the ship had brought and what cargo it was taking away.
He had to go to a window and hold the papers up to the
moonlight to even read them at all. It was hard work and it
took so much of his attention that he almost didn't hear the
door at the front of the house open.

'We should get the watch,' murmured a voice from
downstairs. Berren froze. *Gods! That was quick!* He crept
to a corner by the windows where he could hide in a little
alcove behind an old heavy desk.

'Oh no. If he's here, I don't want the watch being
around.'

Berren crouched down and huddled back as deep into the shadows as he could go.

'Just him, right? Him and maybe his boy.'

'Right bloody mess he's made, that's for sure.'

'Never mind that,' snapped a new voice. Berren stifled a gasp. Was that the man with the cane and the grating laugh? Could that be right? There couldn't be many voices like that in Deephaven, not in the whole world! But they'd seen him leaving the Two Cranes! He wasn't supposed to be here! 'I don't give a fox's beard about all this crap. He's been here and if we're lucky then he's *still* here and you can do what I pay you for.' There was some shuffling and then the creak of footfalls on the stairs. 'You! Go on! Check upstairs! You! You come with me. I want to see if he's found the strongbox.'

Strongbox? Berren's ears pricked up.

The door to the room where Berren was hiding eased silently open. Berren crouched down, pressing himself even further back into the shadows. The man with the cane had snuffers with him and all Berren had was his stupid wooden waster. His heart beat faster, climbing up his throat. He could run, that's what he could do. He could run for the door and away like the wind. His legs tensed ...

The thief-taker slipped into the room and eased the door shut behind him. Berren caught a glimpse of him in the frail light that filtered in through the windows. The feet on the stairs reached the top. In silence, Master Sy crept behind the door. He opened his coat and drew the stubby sword he carried.

'Who's here?' called the snuffer at the top of the stairs. 'I know there's someone here. I can smell you. Show yourself or it'll be the worse for you.'

Master Sy took a tiny step closer to the door.

'The watch is on its way. Show yourself now!' The voice dropped. 'Look, I don't care what it is between you and them foreigners. We can come to some arrangement. I'll say you were already gone. But, by Khrozus, if you don't show yourselves right now, I'm going to kill you.'

Berren's heart jumped. He'd seen these snuffers and knew how they were armed, with long curved cavalry swords left over from the civil war or with short straight blades like Master Sy. The ones he'd seen with the Headsman had worn padded jackets, maybe even lined with mail ...

He looked towards the door but Master Sy hadn't moved. He was still standing motionless, his sword held at the ready.

'No one down here,' shouted a voice from downstairs. Berren heard a second pair of boots climbing the stairs. 'Someone's been in the room but they didn't find the box. I say he's already been and gone.'

'Well someone's up here,' said the first snuffer. He must have been right outside the door. 'I can feel it.'

'I still say we should go out and get the Emperor's men.'

'And how do we explain what *we're* doing here, eh? Khrozus! What a festival of shit this is!'

'Kelm's Teeth! Look at this mess.'

'If he's here then you're going to find him,' bellowed the man with the cane. 'You find him right now and you kill him. If he's gone then you still find him and you still kill him. You dogs clear about that? The Headsman's going to have a fit.'

Footfalls sounded on the hall outside. Berren saw Master Sy ready his sword. He was holding it in front of his face now, the blade horizontal, pointing at the door. His other hand reached out ...

18

THE FACE OF THE ENEMY

The door flew open. For a moment it blocked Berren's sight. Master Sy disappeared from view. The door began to swing to. Outside in the hall, two shouts and one clash of steel rang out. Then there was silence.

The door stopped, half-open. Something was in the way, stopping it from fully closing. Berren hardly dared to breathe. And then he heard his name. It was Master Sy's voice, a low whisper.

'Berren?'

Berren went to the door and pulled it open again. What stopped it from closing was a pair of boots. One of the snuffers was lying there, flat on his back. The thief-taker's sword had ripped his throat out and there was blood everywhere. Berren gawped in awe. He wished he'd been standing somewhere else when the door had flown open so he could have seen what Master Sy had done.

Out in the hall, by the top of the stairs, a second snuffer lay still. Master Sy was standing over him.

'Come here.'

Berren ran over. The second soldier had his throat slit open as well.

'You want me to teach you to fight?' whispered the thief-taker.

Berren nodded, almost salivating at the prospect.

'Then take a long look, because this is how it ends.' He

ran down the stairs, favouring his good leg, leaving Berren behind to stare at the bodies and wonder.

When Berren was done staring at the bodies, he ran his hands through their pockets and helped himself to their purses. He'd been right about the jackets and they had good boots and good clothes too, and if he'd been with Master Hatchet there was no question: he'd have stripped both the snuffers of as much as he could carry.

There was a shout from below, another clash of steel and a strangled cry: 'You? You're dead!' That was the man with the cane. Whatever Master Sy's reply, it was too quiet to reach up the stairs. Berren took a sword from one of the snuffers. The usual old cavalry swords were too long for Berren's arms, but this ... this was perfect. A sword like Master Sy's. The man's belt was too big and he couldn't get the scabbard free, but he didn't care. Simply holding a real steel blade made him feel six feet taller. Made him feel like he was a man, not a boy any more.

Another yell came from below and another clash of blades. Berren bounded down. In the gloom of the hallway he saw the man with the cane, his back to the front door. He had a sword, but his hand was shaking. Between him and Berren stood Master Sy, his long coat hanging loose. He had a sword too and *his* was as steady as a rock. Two more snuffers lay slumped in the passageway, dead or well on their way.

'No, no.' The man with the cane was shaking his head. 'No!' He looked from side to side as though some miracle might save his life. He reached one hand behind him, fumbling for the door. Master Sy took a step forward; the man skittered sideways.

'Deephaven is a long way from Kalda. What does the Headsman want here? What does Radek want?'

'We should have killed you in Forgenver.' The man was almost crying with frustration and fear and rage.

Quick as a snake, Master Sy lunged. The man with the cane darted back for the door. He turned the first blow away but he wasn't quick enough for the second. Master Sy's blade caught his hand, cutting it in two. The man's sword, three of his fingers and a ragged piece of flesh fell to the floor. The man screamed.

'Age making you slow is it?' growled Master Sy. 'I remember you. Radek's Weasel, we used to call you. Made you the Headsman's nose-picker did he? Never did your own dirty work if I remember, but you were quick. Not so quick now, eh?'

The man fell to his knees. He clutched his ruined hand. Blood ran steadily down his shirt. He was weeping now.

'The temple. What business has the Headsman got with priests? Why does he keep bringing them here?'

Priests? Berren suddenly forgot about his new sword. Priests? Master Sy hadn't said anything about priests or temples. Did he mean *his* temple?

'Nothing! I don't know anything about that! He doesn't tell us!'

'That's very hard to believe. *Very* hard to believe.'

'It's true!' The man's voice grew shrill. 'But he's been to see the grey wizard too! They got their own thing going. I can tell you all—'

'You're a liar!' Berren couldn't see Master Sy's face, couldn't see much of anything in the gloom of the hall, but he heard the rage biting into every word. The thief-taker took a step forward and raised his sword.

'Don't! Don't!' The man's cane lay on the floor near Berren's feet. It gleamed golden in the moonlight. 'There's things you don't know. It's all different now. Listen to me! Gold! Sackfuls of it. Plenty enough to share. You could be a part of it!'

'With you?' A high-pitched tone of disbelief crept into the thief-taker's voice. 'Be a part of something with you

150

and the Headsman and Radek? After what they did?'

'Listen, damn you! You kill me, your life won't be worth shit.' He glanced at Berren. 'You kill me, you're dead, prince. Dead. Both of you are dead.'

The thief-taker leaned forwards and spat in the man's face. 'Even now you can't help but show yourself for the turd that floats to the top of the sewer.' He drew his sword back, ready to strike. 'Besides, you said I was dead already.'

'Radek knows you're here! The Headsman already sent word! Kill me and you're a dead man! But listen to me! It's the black powder. Everything's changed!'

'Not for me!' The thief-taker screamed something else, something that sounded like a name but was so contorted with fury that it came out as an animal sound. Then he drove the short blade of his sword down through the soft flesh between the man's neck and his collar bone, with all his strength behind it. The Weasel lurched, gurgled, rolled his eyes and then fell forward, the weight of him tearing the sword out of Master Sy's hand.

'Boy,' he hissed without looking round, 'go find somewhere else to be.'

Berren backed away and crept up the stairs to the dead snuffers. For something to do he finished taking the sword-belt off the lanky one and put it on. He fumbled his sword back into its scabbard. Then he stood, imagining how he looked. The belt was definitely too big and the scabbard dragged on the floor however he tried to wear it. He could still take the sword, though, couldn't he? No one else needed it.

Slowly, he drew it out of its scabbard again. This turned out to be a lot harder than it looked.

'You want to start with something lighter,' said Master Sy from the top of the stairs. He was leaning against the wall, watching. 'It's too heavy for you,' he said.

'Can I keep it?'

He could see the answer in Master Sy's face at once. There were a hundred good reasons why he shouldn't.

'I'll grow,' he said quickly. 'I'll get stronger.'

And then, to his surprise, Master Sy nodded. 'Maybe you can trade it for one you can actually hold.'

'They said something about a strongbox.' He kept seeing the man with the cane die, kept hearing what he'd said. It wasn't that it troubled him. Rather, it had thrilled him just as the time he'd seen Master Sy kill three men in an alley over a purse that had turned out to be filled with nothing but rusty iron and a few pennies. But priests? Black powder? A grey wizard? What did it all mean?

'So he did.'

They went downstairs. Master Sy ran his hands over the dead body by the door. When he stood up, he had another key in his hand and a gleam in his eye. He led Berren back to the stone passage with the heavy doors. One of them was open now and the thief-taker moved slowly inside. The room beyond was pitch black, with no windows. They felt their way around, blind in the darkness. Pushed up against the far wall was a wooden chest bound in metal. It was too big and heavy for even two men to lift and carry away. Master Sy fumbled with the key he'd taken from the dead man with the cane. There was a click. Berren reached to open it.

'Careful.' Together they lifted the lid. Berren was sure it would be laden with gold and treasure, but when he reached inside, all he felt were bundles of parchment. Underneath those were round cases, hard and leathery, the sort you might use to store a map. Then his fingers finally closed on something hard and metallic. He couldn't see what it was in the darkness but it felt like a buckle for a belt or a cloak. He imagined it to be silver or even gold, maybe even covered in gems! He slipped it into his pocket.

'Come!'

At the far end of the strongroom passage there was another door. It was a heavy thing bound in iron, impossible to see in the dark until you walked right into it. Master Sy fiddled with his ring of stolen keys once more until he found the one that opened it. Berren sighed with relief – he could see his feet again. Shadows were one thing; shadows were for hiding and watching and he liked shadows. But full pitch dark where a man couldn't even see where he was treading, that was a different matter.

He stepped out. They must have been in one of the myriad alleys that ran around the back of the docks and Reeper Hill, one that he didn't know. He looked for the moon but it had dipped below the warehouses. The door, he saw, had no keyhole and no handle on the outside. In fact, from the outside, you'd barely know it was a door at all.

'Stay here. I won't be long.' Master Sy trotted away down the alley. He was limping again, quite badly. When he came back, he was pushing an enormous handcart. A tarpaulin lay bundled up inside.

'You'll have to help me,' he said. 'We're going to move the bodies.'

'The bodies? Why, master?' No one had seen the killings. 'What if the watch stop us?'

Master Sy went inside. Berren followed.

'Khrozus Blood! What a mess!' The thief-taker started to laugh.

Three men dead on the floor downstairs, two more upstairs, blood everywhere and papers strewn about the place. 'The soldiers and the snuffers – they *saw* us, master! They're going to know!'

'They saw Weasel and his men too.' The thief-taker rounded on Berren. 'Listen, lad: When the harbour-masters find this, they're going to have fits. And yes, they're going to know who was here, and yes, they're going to want us all strung up – you, me, the Headsman, the lot of us.' He pointed at the bodies. 'One way or the other, we have to disappear now, lad. We leave them all behind us, everyone knows how it turned out. We *all* vanish, no one knows but us.' The thief-taker shook his head. 'With a bit of luck, people will think we're dead. Maybe the Headsman might start wondering about Weasel and his snuffers, and how much can he trust them? Uncertainty makes for fear, Berren, and fear is always the thief-taker's friend.' He cracked his knuckles. 'We can get Kol doing our work for us – your monks would string the Headsman up as quick as look at him. What business has he got at a temple though?' He looked at the bodies again and sucked air between his teeth. 'Kol could take the bodies to his catacombs and then try and get a priest to talk to them, but …' The thief-taker was frowning furiously. 'Or Kuy could do it. I dare say he's not the only one. But these ones don't know anything. Except about us.' He rubbed his hands. 'No, they've all got to go.'

Kuy! He meant *Saffran* Kuy, the witch-doctor from the House of Cats and Gulls. 'So it's true then? The witch-doctor can really make dead people talk?' He'd never seen the witch-doctor in the flesh, but that was what the city whispers had always said: if the dead had secrets to spill, take them to the witch-doctor.

'He really can. Now be quiet and get to work. We need to be up to Wrecking Point and back before it gets light.'

Whatever past Master Sy and the witch-doctor shared, the thief-taker kept it to himself. As best Berren could make out, they'd both come from the same place, a long time ago, both running from the same enemies. He shrugged and bowed his head, wise enough to know when there wasn't any point in arguing, and got on with the job of dragging two corpses, bumping them down the stairs and out to the back door. He helped heave them into the handcart on top of the ones from downstairs; then Master Sy dragged the last corpse from the front door of the House of Records out to the back. It took both of them with all their strength to lift him in as well. When they were done, Berren's hands were sticky with blood. It was on his shirt too.

'This won't do,' growled Master Sy. 'This won't do at all.' Berren ran around, arranging the tarpaulin on top of the cart. Master Sy circled a few paces away, pointing out where a hand or a boot or a lock of hair had broken free and was hanging out for all to see. All the while, Berren's heart pounded. What if the watch came by? It was the middle of the night and the alley was dark and deserted, but still, this was the docks! And if not the militias, there were plenty of other gangs all ready to be full of trouble.

But no men came, no drunken sailors who'd lost their way, no shady men with cloaks and daggers and hoods to hide their faces, no gangs with padded jackets and big sticks. When the bodies were properly hidden, Berren and Master Sy went back to the strongbox. They scooped up the piles of paper and map-cases and went back to the cart. With five bodies, it took both of them to push it into motion.

'Master, why are we doing this? What if someone stops us?'

'Why would they?'

'Because it's the middle of the night!'

Master Sy shrugged. 'But this is the docks. Is it that unusual to see a respectable citizen and his apprentice pushing a heavy cart up towards the Wrecking Point road in the middle of the night?'

Berren rather thought that yes, it was quite unusual indeed, but he held his tongue, and whatever Master Sy thought, the thief-taker kept to the alleys and the back-streets nonetheless. They pushed their cart into the warren of Reeper Hill, up steep narrow little roads that were never quite deserted, not even in the middle of the night. Here and there shadows lurked in doorways to let them pass, or else saw them coming and flitted a different way, out of their path.

When they reached the top they were both gasping for breath. The higgledy-piggledy houses of Reeper Hill fell away until there was nothing but the long crescent of broken cliff-top that was Wrecking Point. There was a road and then a path along the top, one that ran all the way to an old watchtower that no one used any more, except you couldn't get there unless you brought a bridge with you because of the great cracks that ran right across the rock. No one came out to Wrecking Point at night. Not for anything good.

The path stopped abruptly. A chasm as wide as a man barred their way. Sheer walls of black stone fell forty feet down into the sea. The path picked up again on the other side, but only for those agile enough to jump the gap. The rest of Wrecking Point was an island.

Berren slumped against the handcart. He was drenched with sweat. The thief-taker already had the tarpaulin off, but it took both of them to lift out a body. Master Sy seemed all ready to simply hurl it off the edge into the water below; Berren had other ideas – he set to work on the man's boots.

'What are you doing?'

'Good boots, master. Good armour, too. They'd be worth something. We might as well take it as not, master, especially if there's no work to be had for the rest of the year. They don't need them any more.'

'Where I come from, looting the dead is a wicked thing to do.'

'Bu–'

'Besides, where will you sell them? The boots, perhaps, could go to someone like your old friend Hatchet. But the sword? The armour? They're stolen. They're bloody. Are you going to go wagoning in the night market? What if someone remembers your face? Think, lad! These aren't chances you should be taking. There's no need for it. The Headsman doesn't know anything about you, might not even know you exist. Keep it that way. From tonight, we're dead.'

With a heave, they tossed the first body over the edge and onto the rocks below.

'The tide's on the rise,' said Master Sy. His limp was bad now. 'With luck it'll take the bodies out to sea. If fortune truly smiles on us, that's the last anyone will ever hear of them.' They tossed a second body over.

'Won't anyone go looking for them, master?'

The thief-taker laughed. 'They were never there. The Headsman's not going to admit he had his men in the House of Records in the middle of the night. You heard his man. I'm not sure they had any better right to be there than we did.' Another body dropped into the sea with a splash.

'What about him, though? The Headsman?' asked Berren when they were done.

'People like him don't throw themselves on the mercy of the watch. They pay people like me to find the thieves who stole from them and bring them to justice. Which to those sort means a killing, long and bloody.'

'People like you?'

'Snuffers, lad. And thief-takers. People who hunt men. The Headsman knows I'm here, but he's known that for a while now. He's not going to know what happened tonight, perhaps not even where, but when five of his men don't come back he's going to know it was me. And we're going to make sure it stays right where it is, between the two of us. Him and me. Don't want anyone else near this, especially not you. There'll be a price on my head after tonight, simple as that, and then there'll be a reckoning. He'll come for me, he'll buy snuffers, but this is *my* city, lad, not his.

Come on. And bring that. No sense in leaving a perfectly good handcart behind.'

Without another word, he began the long walk home. The cart seemed light as anything, now it was empty, and they made much better time. Still, as they walked, Berren couldn't help glancing back over his shoulder now and then. His head was full of things to think about. He had a sword. He'd seen the thief-taker cross a line, and do it without blinking. They were outlaws now, both of them.

And the witch-doctor down by the docks could talk to the dead.

19

BURYING THE TRUTH

Berren slept soundly. When he woke up, brilliant lines of sunlight shone through the gaps in his shutters, lighting up unexpected corners of his little room. It was late. The night's exertions had finished him and, by the looks of things, Master Sy hadn't banged on his door before dawn as he usually did.

On the floor, the sword from the night before gleamed. Berren rolled off his straw mattress, sat up and pulled it from its sheath. He didn't know much about weapons but the edge seemed straight enough. He ran his fingers over the steel. It felt slightly oily. There were two little notches in the cutting blade, but still, it was his now. He'd dreamed for years that he might own such a thing. With a sword hanging from your belt, people treated you with respect. Other gangs of boys didn't throw stones at you and the watch didn't beat you black and blue simply because they could. A sword made you a man.

A jolt of panic hit him. He was late! He should be at the temple, should have been there hours ago ... Then he remembered: This was Abyss-Day, the day of the dead and the damned and the dark and no lessons. He sighed and smiled and rolled back onto his bed and stared at the blade of his sword. It had belonged to someone else until last night, a snuffer whose name Berren would never know. Having a sword hadn't saved *him* ...

He dressed himself. He supposed his master was sleeping late too, but even so he'd best get up and get on with his chores. Master Sy had been in a strange mood as they'd made their way home. He didn't say much at the best of times, but a gloom and a silence had settled over him as they'd walked away from the docks. He was like that whenever the past came up, when he saw anything to remind him of the life he'd had before he'd come to Deephaven. Or maybe he'd been like that because his leg had been hurting like buggery again and he could barely even walk by the time they'd crossed the city. Maybe it meant they hadn't found what they were looking for.

Which made Berren remember the strongbox. He rolled onto the floor and reached under his straw bedding. The clasp he'd found was still there. That was his – no reason for Master Sy to know anything about it. He looked at it and felt a pang of disappointment. It was plain silver, carved into the shape of something that looked like a cross between a helm and a crown and not worth nearly as much as he'd hoped. He shoved it back under the straw, jumped to his feet and charged out of his room.

'Master! Master!' There was no answer. He ran through the house but Master Sy wasn't there. His boots were gone, though, so Master Sy was gone too.

In the parlour, the map-cases from the strongbox were all opened and empty. Pieces of paper and parchment were scattered everywhere. A few were ripped or screwed up into crumpled balls. Berren started to tidy them up; while he was doing that, he read a few. It was hard work, but even when he could make out the words, they didn't make any sense. There were lists of names and places and none of it meant anything. He chewed on a piece of yesterday's bread and sipped at some water.

Ah well. Usually when Master Sy woke him up, his first duty was to go and get fresh bread for the day. Then, on

160

Abyss-Day, he had his chores. Cleaning Master Sy's boots for a start – couldn't do that if his master was off wearing them though, could he? – but then there was fetching water and a hundred and one other things and he'd cop a clip round the ear if he forgot anything. He didn't much mind most of his chores, but if there was one he could have been rid of, it was getting water. It was a long way and it meant going past the House of Cats and Gulls and through the River Gate and then paying a penny to get back, and Berren had better things to do with his pennies.

The House of Cats and Gulls made him think of the witch-doctor who lived there, Saffran Kuy. No one quite seemed to know how long he'd been there or how he'd arrived. From the stories Berren had heard, one day there had been a warehouse, the next, a witch-doctor. People scattered fish outside his door and it stank, stank strong enough to bring tears to your eyes. Even with the wind behind you, you always knew you were getting close from the porters with scarves wrapped over their faces and how the cobbles grew slimy underfoot. The guards on the River Gate wore scarves too; they swore and cursed at the witch-doctor for the smell but none of them ever lifted a finger to drive him away. Every Abyss-Day as he passed the witch-doctor's house, Berren wondered how many of the stories he'd heard were true.

The witch-doctor could talk to the dead. Master Sy had said that, and he'd said it with certainty as though he'd seen it, and that made him think of Velgian. What was it that the poet thief-taker had wanted Master Sy to know, right there at the end before he fell? Justicar Kol had taken the body to the catacombs, but maybe the witch-doctor had a way to know? He shivered. Whatever it was that his master and Saffran Kuy shared, it wasn't enough to make him go knocking on the door of the House of Cats and Gulls, that was for sure! Saffran Kuy is not the friend he thinks!

The man with the cane had said something before Master Sy killed him, too; something about the Headsman and a grey wizard? Grey was the colour of the dead. So did *he* mean the witch-doctor too? Maybe Master Sy had gone there then, to warn him?

The sun was already high and there might not be any more bread to be had for the day. He'd get some fruit, too, just in case. He went into Master Sy's room to look for the thief-taker's purse. Everything in the thief-taker's room was as it always was. There was a bed, a wooden rack for hanging clothes, a table and nothing else. On the table sat a semi-circle of short, squat candles that hadn't moved for as long as Berren could remember, the usual quill, pile of papers, bundle of old letters tied in ribbon, and the box, the plain wooden box almost as long as Berren's arm. They were all there, arranged exactly the way they always were. The thief-taker's purse was where it always was too, hanging from one end of the wooden clothes-rack. Berren opened it and took out a few pennies, plenty for bread and fruit.

He shivered. It was the box. He'd never seen the thief-taker open it, but he'd opened it himself once. Inside was a knife, with a hilt made of gold and strange patterns shimmering in its blade. There was something wrong with it. Whenever he went near, it always seemed to call to him. It was worth a fortune, maybe it was as simple as that, but he'd touched it the once and he'd never touch it again.

He shook the feeling off, went for bread and fruit and then treated himself to a handful of roasted nuts. After that, he idled his way down Moon Street, past the temple there and on to the river, about halfway along the wide-open expanse of cobbles that ran alongside it. A sprawling mass of wooden jetties reached out into the water like the skeletal remains of some vast sea creature. The Rich Docks there were every bit as busy as the sea-docks, but they had more rhythm to them. In the sea harbour, the comings and goings of the great ships were driven by the tides. Down at the river, the movements of the barges were driven by the tides too, but also by the rise and fall of the sun. Lightermen preferred to sail the river in daylight, so the river docks were a night place; as the morning tide rose, whatever the hour, a flotilla launched itself at the river and the jetties emptied; as the afternoon waned, the traffic coming the other way, down from Varr and the City of Spires, arrived to fill them up again. At this time of day with the sun high up in the sky, there weren't many boats, but that didn't make much difference. There was always some sort of market set out along the riverside and it was heaving as ever. Back when he'd been a cutpurse and a thief, this had been his favourite place. He still liked the press of the crowd, and if ever that got too much, well, you could always move on down towards the River Gate and wrap a scarf around your face against the smell. No one went down by the River Gate unless they had to. Unfortunately, to get water, he was one of those who did.

By the time he got back, midday had come and gone. The first thing he noticed as he carried his buckets to the kitchen was that the rotting stink smell from down by the witch-doctor's place had followed him home.

'Master?' The thief-taker's boots were by the door. They were in need of a clean.

The stairs creaked as the thief-taker came down from his room. He looked tired and drawn as though he hadn't slept since the fight in the House of Records.

'I was wondering where you were, lad.' He yawned and sat at the table. Berren put down the bread and the fruit.

'Chores, master. I went out to get food and water. Master?' The thief-taker had that gloom about him again.

'I went through the papers we stole after you went to sleep. The Headsman's manifest says he came here with a cargo of black tea. Well I know Kalda, and shipping black

163

tea from there to here makes about as much sense as wearing your boots on your head and your hat on your hands. So whatever he's carrying isn't just an excuse, it's a lie, and that means I'm right, there's more to this than I thought. Weasel said something about black powder. Black powder, black tea. Same thing, do you think?' Master Sy shook his head. 'I went to the temple this morning,' he said, without looking up. 'You'll stay there and live with the novices for a bit. Until this is done.'

Berren opened his mouth, but the thief-taker cut him off.

'They'll teach you manners and letters, they'll teach you right from wrong and they'll keep you safe until the Headsman is dead. And the monks will teach you swords. That's what you wanted isn't it?'

'Master ... !' No, no! Not living in the temple like some priest boy, that was *never* what he wanted. Lessons in letters if that's what it took to learn swords, but never any more ... And how long was *until this is done*?

'Berren, what's between me and the Headsman has nothing to do with thief-taking and not much to do with right or wrong. There's no part in this for you. I need you somewhere safe.' The thief-taker frowned. 'Don't want you hurt for no good reason. And remember, lad: people may know you were there last night, but no one knows you were inside the House of Records. Keep it that way. No one can touch you as long as you stay inside the temple. It belongs to the heralds of the sun and no one short of the Overlord himself can tell them what they must do. Outside its walls, though, I can't keep you safe, not any more.' For a moment the thief-taker looked sad. 'It won't be for long. I promise.'

Yeh. And this time say it like you mean it. Lies came off Berren's tongue like honey from a honeycomb, but from the thief-taker they were mostly awkward and obvious and this one was no exception. Berren just stood and stared. He'd been all ready to ask about the witch-doctor and Velgian and whether there was any way to find out what he knew; now he couldn't think of anything except the last words that the prince had said to him: *when he goes, he's not going to want you with him.*

'I don't ...' He didn't know what to say.

'Before long, the Headsman's going to be lying in a gutter and this will all be over. A week or two, no more, I promise you.' Master Sy shrugged and got to his feet. 'Anyway, that's the way it's going to be, however much you don't like it. I'm sorry, Berren. I didn't think last night. Didn't think nearly enough about the consequences.' He sighed, and Berren wasn't sure whether to believe him or whether this had always been on the thief-taker's mind, right from the start, a way to keep him out of the way.

'I don't–' he started again, but the look on his master's face cut him short. There was no quarter to be had here.

The thief-taker forced a smile and put a hand on his shoulder. 'I know, Berren, I know. Maybe I should never have taken you. But you asked for it and I did, and even if I hadn't, it's the only way I can look after you. Now pack your things.'

Berren glared and went back upstairs, up to the room that was his. He'd grown used to that, sleeping alone and having his own space, his own air. It wouldn't be the same in the temple. The novices there slept in tight little dormitories, all on top of each other like back when he'd been with Master Hatchet. He didn't have much – two nice sets of clothes and a clean set of shoes that Master Sy had bought him, some other tattered clothes that he might have been proud of when he'd been living with Master Hatchet, and that was it. He had his purse with a few dozen pennies, a small handful of precious silver crowns and one golden emperor, hoarded for the best part of two years now. He had the sword he'd taken from the dead soldier. Would the priests let him keep that? He imagined they wouldn't. What else did he have?

There was the token around his neck and the Headsman's silver clasp. He put that in his pocket.

Did he want to be a priest? No. Did he want to learn more letters? No. Did he want to learn any of the things Sterm the Worm would teach him? No. But he *did* want to stay with the sword-monks and learn to fight. He wanted that very much, and Master Sy had promised it wasn't for long ...

He fingered the gold token on the chain around his neck. What else could he do? If he ran, he'd run to Varr, that was obvious. To the court of the Imperial Prince. But he could do that whenever he wanted. Maybe Master Sy would be right, maybe this business with the Headsman *would* be over soon and everything *would* be back the way it had been before. Maybe.

'If it helps, I've got a present for you,' called the thief-taker from the parlour. 'Should keep you amused while you're stuck in the temple.'

'Master?' A present?' Berren poked his head out of his room.

The thief-taker was at the bottom of the stairs. He forced a smile. 'Yeh, a present. Come with me and bring that sword of yours.'

'What? Where we going?'

'Wrecking Point. Make sure those bodies have gone. And it's a good place for what I have in mind. Out of sight where no one will see.' Master Sy stood there, waiting for him. 'I promised I'd show you a trick or two to take down those sword-monks, didn't I?' he said. 'And I always keep a promise.' As Berren came down the stairs, the thief-taker threw him a waster. 'Until dusk, I'm going to teach you swords. My way. And it's going to hurt.'

166

20

A SWORD-MONK LEARNS A LESSON

'Y ou're late.' Tasahre held her sword perfectly still. Berren matched her. Now and then they both glanced at the sky. The seasons were changing. The clouds above warned of afternoon summer rains come early.

The sword-monk's face was bruised. She had an ugly brown and purple splodge on her left cheek where some-one had punched her. Berren knew better than to ask how she'd come by it.

'Yes. I'm living in the temple now. I had things to do.' Which was another way of saying that he'd nodded to his master as he'd left and and the thief-taker had nodded back, just like on any other day, and then he'd made his way slowly across the city, taking in the dawn sights and the sun, ambling at his own pace to The Peak and the new life that was waiting for him. It felt like he was being sent to prison. He stared hard at the bruise on Tasahre's face. Maybe he could make her feel conscious of it.

'I have heard.' Tasahre didn't blink. If she noticed him staring, it didn't show. 'The temple does you and your master a great honour. I hope you both deserve it.'

'Master Sy has many friends among the priests here. He's done a lot for them.' Not that Berren knew exactly *what* the thief-taker had done. Whatever it was, it had obviously been enough to survive Prince Sharda forcing them to teach

Berren, despite his master's grumbles.

They looked at each other across the circle in the dirt. Eight minutes gone. Tasahre still had the hourglass balanced on the flat of her blade, still held it perfectly still. Berren had a waster again. His precious sword had stayed at Wrecking Point. There were hiding places galore up there. At the end of the path where they'd tipped the bodies only the night before, he and Master Sy had finally practised, steel against steel. As night-time fell, they'd looked over the edge one last time. The sea and the tides had done their job and there was no sign of the men they'd killed. He'd held the blade he'd taken from the dead snuffer and looked at it for a while; then he'd clambered among the rocks away from the path, wrapped it carefully in a sheet that Master Sy had brought for him and slid it between a pair of boulders. He'd covered it with sand and earth and taken a good look at where he was. It would be a while, he knew, before he could go back. At least until then, it was somewhere safe. Until he needed it. And for one glorious day, he'd been a true swordsman ...

'This is something to do with the people who drove your master here, is it not?'

Berren stared at the bruise.

'I've heard his story. An unusual one. Do you believe what he tells you?'

Mute, Berren nodded. He glanced hopefully at the hourglass. Eight and a half minutes. He could already feel the first twitches in the muscles that ran along the top of his shoulder. 'He told me bits.' There had to be a way to distract her, didn't there?

Tasahre raised her eyebrows the tiniest fraction. 'The priests have told me that your master is the bastard son of a king from a province on the far reaches of the sun-king's dominion. They say that a cabal of death-mages fleeing from the sun-king's witch-breakers took up residence there and that the king was foolish enough to welcome them, for whatever reason. I am told that the princes of the great city of Kalda raised an army, broke the cabal and scattered them. I know that in war, tragedies fall upon the innocent and the guilty alike.'

Berren's arm was shaking. Half a minute to go. Anger, that would do him. The thief-taker's anger, the rage that simmered beneath the surface whenever he talked about the past. *They were an invading army. Imagine you'd been here in the civil war, Berren. Imagine you were Pelean's brother, seeing him crucified over Pelean's Gate, listening to his screams. Then you'll see what happened in Tethis as I see it ...* The shaking reached his blade, but his arm still held it level and there were only a few more grains left to go.

Tasahre blinked. 'How did he come to be a thief-taker? It seems an unusual choice. Do you know?'

No, he didn't, he didn't have a clue, that was the simple answer. But Berren couldn't even shake his head now. His shoulder screamed at him. The last grain of sand tumbled to the bottom of the hourglass. Gritting his teeth, he kept his sword exactly where it was. Tasahre stayed quite still for a few seconds more, then flipped the hourglass into the air and caught it as she sheathed her steel.

'Well done.' She almost smiled.

Berren let his sword down slowly. What he wanted was to hug his arm to his chest and hop in circles wailing and moaning until his shoulder forgave him, but he wasn't going to let her have that.

'Guard.' She walked around him in a circle and adjusted the angles of his wrist and his elbow.

'He wasn't the only one who came here, though,' said Berren. 'I know that much.'

Tasahre stood in front of him. She picked up a waster and they settled into the usual routine of slow cuts and thrusts to start with, all easily parried.

'He had a friend, a real friend, called Kasmin. He came to Deephaven a year or two earlier. He was a thief-taker too and then he used to run an alehouse in The Maze. Someone killed him, just before you came.' Berren watched her closely for any sign that she recognised the name but her face gave nothing away.

'Your justicar told us this. They, too, were friends once it seems. I'm sorry for your master's loss,' she said as they stood apart for a moment. 'Who is the Headsman?'

The question caught him off-guard. 'Master Sy's going to kill him.' The words blurted out without him thinking. Tasahre cocked her head as Berren cursed himself. *He* was supposed to be catching *her* out, not the other way around!

'The elder dragon tells us that great swordsmen never kill. They do not need to. Their presence is enough.' She frowned, as if she didn't quite understand how that could work. Berren had seen it, though. It was the same thing that Master Sy always said, that a good thief-taker never needed to draw his blade, that the thieves should always be too scared to do anything except what the thief-taker wanted them to do. Yes, he'd seen plenty of that over the years. He'd seen Master Sy at work and the fear that followed him.

On the other hand, he'd seen Master Sy kill men too. They set to work again, faster now.

'Is it true that a sun-priest can talk to the spirits of the dead?' Velgian. He was thinking of Velgian again, dead and desiccating in the city catacombs. 'They caught the man who tried to kill Prince Sharda.'

Again her face gave nothing away. 'Yes.' She cocked her head. 'This was some weeks ago was it not? And your justicar wishes to know who the paymaster was. But as for what a priest can and cannot do, you must ask one of them, not me. Sometimes it is not a matter of what is possible, but of what is right. Your justicar keeps a dead man hidden

170

beneath the earth where the sun cannot reach him to take his soul. That is not right.'

'There's always the witch-doctor down on the docks.' Berren watched closely again and this time he got his reward. Tasahre scowled.

'The creature that lives in the House of Cats and Gulls is a corrupter, an abomination. From men like that every word comes with a heavy price.'

'Is he a wizard?' *But he's been to see the grey wizard too! They got their own thing going,* that's what the Headsman's snuffer had said. Berren shuddered. The witch-doctor's house scared him.

'I do not know what he is. Evil. That is enough.' He'd rattled her somehow. Her timing was slightly off and there was a tension in her movement. 'Stop, stop! Stay as you are.' She dropped her waster and moved sharply to one side, kicking his front foot. 'Further apart! Your stance is too narrow.' She gave him a hard shove from the side, staggering him. 'See? Now, in guard.'

She went and stood behind him again. He felt her chest against his back as she reached around him and moved his arms. She was breathing a little fast. Her hands on his wrists felt hot. Berren's skin tingled.

A fat splat of rain landed on his arm. Both of them looked up. The clouds were breaking.

'Some say he's a sorcerer.'

'There are no sorcerers in Deephaven.'

'Why not?' *Keep her unsettled, unfocussed. Then catch her with her guard down!* Master Sy's last words of advice.

Berren felt another moment of tension run through her, down her shoulders to her hands. 'Because they're all in Varr,' she said. 'Because the Usurper's son desires a glimpse of the glories this world knew before the silver kings waged war on the gods. He scours the realms for any who are skilled in the fickle arcane.' Her hands fell away. Spatters of rain pock-marked the fighting circle. 'Guard! Again.' She came at him once more, faster than before.

'Is he a bad man, the Emperor?' Berren dodged and parried. He felt fast today. Alive. Maybe it was the rain, the talk of sorcerers, the feel of Tasahre's touch still on his skin, or maybe he was finally learning what she was trying to teach him. For a moment he was almost as quick as she was.

'I cannot say. As emperors go he has been wise and just and fair. But he is an emperor nevertheless and is set on his course. He follows the Usurper in turning his back on the sun. In the end he would not spurn a tool, however black, if its edge was sharp and could be turned to his purpose. So the abominations go to Varr and the Emperor's gold fills their pockets.' The rain was starting in earnest now. He could feel its coldness prodding at his skin. The skies were opening.

'A sorcerer saved my life once.' That was probably an exaggeration, but why did she call them abominations? 'Master Sy said the witch-doctor saved his, too. So is he a wizard?' Tasahre came at him hard, blow after blow. If she was holding anything back, it wasn't much. Still, he parried most of them and she was getting careless.

'Focus on the blade!' She feinted and caught him a bruising crack on the knee.

'I mean a *grey* wizard.' Heavier and heavier came the rain. Water ran down his forehead, out of his hair towards his eyes. He flicked it away.

Tasahre's face drew taut. Her waster snapped at his head with three sharp blows which he managed to block and then came a hard lunge to his ribs which he didn't. He tried not to wince. That one was going to hurt. 'The creature on the docks is worse than an abomination, it is an anathema. It is only a matter of time before it draws the wrath of the sun.'

He couldn't be *that* terrible, could he? The witch-doctor was a friend to Master Sy, and the thief-taker was hardly evil. Angry sometimes, and gods help you if you were on the wrong side of his steel, but he was still a servant of the city and Berren had seen kindness in him more often than spite.

They were both soaked now. Their light clothes clung to their skin. Most of the time, Tasahre looked more like a boy with her short cropped hair and the sunburst tattoo breaking the lines of her face; most of the time, but not now.

The prince's token around his neck seemed to burn, urging him away. Rain ran in rivers down his face, down his arms, and suddenly it was there, the opening he'd been looking for. Maybe Tasahre caught an inkling of what was on his mind, or maybe even sword-monks made mistakes from time to time. Whatever it was, Berren didn't care, because for an instant he was inside her guard. He dropped his waster, lunged and rammed her with his shoulder. He grabbed her arm, jabbed at her ribs with his elbow and reached a foot between her legs to sweep her over, all at once. She staggered, and then his foot caught her and she went down with Berren on top of her. He grabbed her other arm. She was still as quick as a snake, every bit as strong as him and he wasn't even much heavier, but this was what Master Sy had shown him, and he'd meant it to work on men twice his size. She almost wriggled free, but then he had her down flat on her back, sitting astride her, pinning her arms with his knees and his hands. Rain dripped from his hair into her face. She looked furious.

'What are you doing?'

His hands wanted to touch her, but that meant letting go and he didn't dare. 'Concede.'

She almost laughed at him. 'What?'

'Concede. Surrender!'

'Why?'

'I've got you.'

'You are as paralysed as I.'

'I'm on top.'

'If you move, I will be free. If this were a fight, how would you kill me?'

'I could bite your face off I suppose.'

'If you come close enough, I will bite yours first.'

He tried not to think about that. His heart was racing.

Beneath him, Tasahre bucked, heaving him upwards. The next thing he knew, she had her legs around his chest and a bear-like force had grabbed him, tearing him backwards, and then he was flat on *his* back and Tasahre was on top of *him*, arms and legs all tangled together, with two fingertips at his throat. 'If that was a fight then this is a knife and you are dead. Now get up.'

She seemed to pause for a moment more than needed before she sprang away. For the rest of their practice time she fought with cold unforgiving precision. The rain came down and made no difference at all. But afterwards, in the steamy evening twilight before sunset prayers, she took him back with her to the yard.

'Show me again how you did that,' she said.

21
THE WRONG PLACE AT THE WRONG TIME

Being a true novice, it turned out, was nothing like taking paid-for lessons in the day and then going home at sunset. Being a true novice meant you worked for your keep. He hadn't expected much by way of kindness or sympathy, but between his lessons with Sterm and his time with Tasahre, there didn't seem much time left in the day for more *work*.

He was wrong. Straight after practice with the sword-monks came twilight prayers – he had to go to those now. After prayers, the novices worked in the kitchens chopping vegetables, fetching, carrying, cleaning and sweating, serving the priests and the sword-monks with their supper; afterwards, they all sat together on long hard benches and got to eat whatever was left. There were a lot more novices than Berren had realised; a lot of them he'd never seen before, who'd never shared his class with Sterm the Worm or any of the others.

By the time he sat down, Berren was ravenous, but he barely managed to take a sip of gruel before a novice he didn't know banged into him, spilling it.

'Oops.'

'Oi!' Berren rounded on him. The boy must have been almost twice his size. He picked up Berren's bowl off the table and tipped it over Berren's head.

'Oops,' he said again. Then he looked at Berren. *And?*

Berren knew that look. The *What are you going to do about it, runt?* look. None of the priests had seen it happen. The other novices were all staring, eyes a-glitter. They hated him, they always had.

'Stupid!' they sniggered. 'Can't even drink from a bowl.'

Berren's face burned. This was what used to happen with Master Hatchet whenever a new boy was taken. He could see exactly where this was going. It was a challenge and it couldn't go unanswered; the years with Hatchet had taught him that.

As they filed out of the eating hall, he held back. Sure enough, when he went out, as soon as they were out of sight of any priests, there was the boy who'd emptied his gruel over him. Oops, or whatever his name was. He had a couple of friends with him too, just in case, but Berren didn't bother worrying about them. He threw himself straight at the big one, fists and feet flying. In the first second, he'd kicked the boy's legs out from under him and stamped on his knee to keep him down. Then he was on the ground too, all over the other novice, punching and kicking him while his friends were suddenly nowhere to be seen. 'Oops,' he said.

When the priests arrived with Tasahre to pull him off, everyone assumed it was all his fault. He was the one still standing, after all. Tasahre made his apologies to the priests, promised she would punish him harshly, and then she took him back out into the practice yard in the dark.

'Foolishness.' She shook her head. 'Words, not fists, Berren. That is the correct way.'

'Then why do you exist?' he asked.

'The threat of a sword so deadly means there is no need for it to be drawn.'

'Then that's what I was doing,' said Berren flatly. 'Showing off my sword. And now I won't ever have to do that again.'

She looked at him for a long time. Her eyes bored into him, searching for something, but her face gave him no clue as to what it was or whether she found it. 'I'm not finished with you,' she said in the end. 'Show me again how you threw me.'

So he did, and they wrestled and threw each other in the dark until she understood exactly how he'd beaten her and could do what he'd done with an ease and grace and speed that he'd never have. By the time they finished, he was battered and bruised and full to the brim with the touch of her, the smell of her. Afterwards he lay awake at night in the dormitory he shared with the other boys, listening to their snores, thinking of her and thinking of other things too. He'd been in a place like this before and the memories were of horrors and hurt and fear. What if Master Sy was wrong? What if he was killed? What then? Stay and fight his corner and spend half his days learning stuff he didn't care about, letters and gods? Or did he run?

The token around his neck felt cool against his skin. Run away from the sword-monks? From Tasahre?

As soon as he was sure everyone was asleep, he slipped out of the dormitory. Getting out of the temple was easy. Getting into Master Sy's house was easy too, but the thief-taker wasn't there. It was tempting to climb into his old bedding, with its familiar feel and its familiar smell and fall asleep, safe and away from the snores and the taunts, but that's what a boy would do, not a man, and so he crept back out the way he'd come, all the way back to his temple bed. He'd try again tomorrow, and again the day after that, and again and again until he found Master Sy once more, over and over until the thief-taker gave in and understood he *wasn't* a boy any more, that *he* was a thief-taker too and that whatever Master Sy was trying to do, he could help.

Tasahre was waiting for him in the morning. Oops, whoever he was, wasn't forgotten. There was a long lecture from the priest in charge of discipline in the dormitory. Berren got a whipping in front of all the other novices while another priest delivered a short sermon on obedience and humility. The whipping wasn't nearly as bad as he'd feared, a ritual humiliation more than anything else, a bit of pain but no real injury – he'd had worse beatings from Master Hatchet every week back before the thief-taker. After that, instead of lessons with Sterm and practice with the sword-monks, he spent the rest of the day with a grumpy old priest who growled at him and showed him around the parts of the temple where the other novices lived, fed him a dry crust and then gave him chores until his knees were raw from scrubbing floors. The old man hardly said a word. When Berren asked how long he would be punished, all he got was a clip round the ear.

'Stupid boy,' said the priest, and that was that. No one said anything more, but the meaning was clear. *Train with sword-monks or scrub floors. Your choice.*

That evening the other novices kept away. He saw them watching him. They eyed him up with fear and, here and there, a flicker of nervous interest. No one tipped food over him. When he finished eating, Tasahre was waiting for him again.

'You missed training,' she said.

He shrugged. She knew why.

'The presence of the sword is enough now, is it?'

This time he bowed. Not that he *had* a sword, but if Master Sy had taught him anything at all, it was when to keep his mouth shut. For that night and the two nights that followed she took him to the practice yard after dark, after supper and prayers. Away from the other monks, she battered him, taking what Master Sy had taught him and making it even better. Something had changed between them. He was catching her, slowly, and now when she spoke to him, he heard a quiet respect that hadn't been there before.

After four nights practising in the yard, Tasahre used what Berren had shown her to win two of her fights with the other monks. They looked bemused, uncertain of how they'd been beaten, while the elder dragon wore a frown deep enough to sink a ship.

'The teacher can learn from the pupil,' Tasahre said as she bowed, and Berren didn't know which pupil she meant – him or her.

He slipped away again that night, back to Master Sy's house. There was a lock on the thief-taker's door this time, shiny and new, which made him pause. Master Sy had never bothered much with locks before. *Locks mean keys and keys are always stolen* and Master Sy had shown that he knew all about stealing keys. *Better to keep with you everything you value.* That was another of the thief-taker's mantras, always trotted out with a twinge of bitterness; but here it was – a lock. Berren stood and stared at it. Then he climbed onto the handcart they'd taken to Wrecking Point, still resting against the kitchen wall, and pulled himself onto its low roof. From there it took all of a few seconds to wriggle open the catch on the shutters to his old room. He crawled inside and stood and listened. The house was silent, which meant the thief-taker wasn't asleep in his bed. Master Sy snored like a wounded donkey.

He crept down the stairs. The thief-taker's table was still covered in papers, dozens and dozens of them, spilling onto the floor, the papers they'd stolen from the Headsman's strongbox in the House of Records. Berren picked them up and leafed through them again, holding them up to the little windows at the front of the thief-taker's parlour, and to the moonlit sky beyond, peering at them. They were full of numbers and names and places, the same as before.

He frowned. They were inventories, he saw that now. The numbers talked about swords and arrows and spears. They weren't about ships, either, they were talking about places. He knew some of the names, parts of Deephaven where the Emperor's soldiers were barracked: The Old Fort, the Emperor's Docks and places along the coast, Mirrormere and Bedlam's Crossing. Torpreah. The City of Spires. There were other places whose names were dimly familiar and others he didn't know at all.

The more he looked, the more they started to make sense. The lists made a map, a map of the imperial armies.

He sniffed the air and smelled a slight whiff of tallow. Someone had burned a candle here not long ago. Then he checked the kitchen, looking for the crumbs and the fruit peelings and stones and where Master Sy would spit them. They were there and they were fresh. The thief-taker had been here, and not long ago.

He put the papers back and returned to the window, peering outside and wondering what to do. The yard was empty. This time, he decided, he was going to wait. He'd stay here until Master Sy came home again. He made his way back up the stairs, slow and careful so as not to creak the steps. Maybe he'd doze the night away in his old room, waiting for his master.

The door to the thief-taker's room was open. Berren stopped. It had been closed when he'd come down, he was sure of it. He couldn't bring himself to go in, but couldn't help but look either. Everything was there. The table, the bundle of letters tied with a ribbon, the box … Oh gods, the box and the cursed ghost-knife inside it, only tonight, the box was open and he could see the knife, it's cleaver-blade naked, gleaming in the moonlight that crept between Master Sy's shutters. Point glittering, curling patterns shimmering.

Downstairs, the front door opened. Berren froze. Footsteps moved though the parlour. He heard Master Sy's voice, muttering to himself. He started to move, but then he heard a second voice, a soft whispering.

'Tonight. Done and finished, Syannis. You really think so?'

'He's in the Two Cranes. We've waited long enough. We can get to him tonight. You lure him out. I'll be waiting for him.'

'And then?'

'Then Radek, that's what. Look!' Paper rustled.

'Someone has been here, Syannis. I smell them.'

'You're imagining things. Look! It's not proof, but when Radek comes it'll be enough to bury him.'

The voices receded, back outside. The door closed. After a few moments, Berren started to breathe again. He tiptoed to the window and peered down into the yard in time to see the thief-taker vanish into the gloom of the alley at the far end outside. He had someone with him too, cloaked in swirling darkness. Could have been anyone, but the voice wasn't one that Berren knew.

He took a deep breath and counted to fifty, enough time for Master Sy and whoever was with him to get to the end of the alley. Then he ran to the door, crept outside and listened. Silence. He paused a while longer and then slipped down the alley, following Master Sy's steps. At the end, where the thief-taker would have turned right towards Four Winds Square, Berren turned left for Weaver's Row. He started to run. It wasn't the quickest way to get to the Two Cranes, but an instinct told him that if Master Sy knew he was about, nothing would happen. This way he could still get there first if he ran, and then he could watch and no one would be any the wiser. He jogged up towards the night market and then cut into The Maze, darting from shadow to shadow, taking his chances with the press gangs. He passed the Barrow of Beer, Kasmin's old place before the Headsman had killed him. It was quiet and dark, its door closed and the windows all shuttered. Here and there he saw other shadows flitting through the dark. They left him to his business and he left them to theirs. That was the quiet rule of The Maze. After dark, you made sure to pay careful attention not to see anyone else who might be about and, if you could, you made quite sure that they *saw* you not seeing them. You left them alone and they didn't bother you. Still, he wished he had the sword with him tonight, the one that he'd buried up at Wrecking Point.

The Maze spat him back out onto the Avenue of Emperors and the docks, always busy and never mind the hour. He slipped in among the teamsters and the sailors there, across to the other side, towards the Kingsway, around the warehouse where the archer had been on the day Kol had told them about Kasmin. He passed the old watchtower and then slid back into the dark streets between the Kingsway and the Avenue of Emperors until he reached the back yard of the Two Cranes. There were snuffers down on the street, watching the back gates, so he climbed up onto the rooftops next door and jumped straight over their heads onto the roof of the stable block. From there it was easy enough to get up onto the roof of the Two Cranes itself. He slithered on his belly, slow and silent – underneath his feet, the attic of the Two Cranes was where the servants slept and if they heard a noise they'd surely raise the alarm. He waited, peering over the edge of the roof, watching the front doors, breathing slowly and steadily. Did the sword-monks still come, watching out for Master Sy? He didn't know. He scanned the shadows around the entrance but he didn't see any of them.

He'd been there for ten minutes when the thief-taker finally arrived. He came on his own and he walked straight past the entrance and the snuffers there, round towards the back gate. Berren crept back up the roof in time to see the thief-taker stop by the two snuffers guarding the yard. A purse changed hands. The snuffers opened the gate and moved aside and then the thief-taker was moving swiftly across the open space behind the inn. He went straight for the stables. His sword was drawn, naked in his hand.

Carefully, Berren crossed the roof and slid down the other side. As he dropped onto the stable roof, he heard a muffled crash and a strangled cry. Alive with the moment, he lay down, very slowly pried back one of the roof tiles and peered inside.

22
GETTING A HEAD

'**G**et in!'
There was a crash, the sound of someone being hurled across the room and then of wood splintering and Master Sy swearing. Then footfalls. A horse snorted. Berren heard a quiet splash of water, more quiet footsteps, then a loud one. There was some spluttering. He couldn't see anything. There were no lights inside the stables. He wrinkled his nose – even though there was almost no wind, the city stink of rotting fish was uncommonly bad all of a sudden.

'Kelm's Teeth! Who'd have thought that a life of rape and murder could leave a man so fat?'

That was Master Sy's voice. There was another, one he didn't know, the whispering voice from before, but then there was a coughing and a third, gulping, gasping for air.

'You!' The Headsman.

The realisation broke whatever spell was freezing Berren still. He needed to be closer. Gently, he slipped across the roof to a little shuttered window that opened into the stable attic. The shutters were loose. He pried them slowly apart, and then whipped one open and dropped inside, into the hayloft.

'What was that?' The voices down below fell quiet. All that separated Berren from the men below was a thin layer of creaky wooden boards and he had no idea which ones might squeak and which ones wouldn't. He lowered himself down, lay flat and pressed his ear to the floor, sweating and shaking. One whisper of noise and the thief-taker would know he was there, and then ... Whatever the *and then* was, he didn't want to know.

'Noises in the wind, Syannis. Ghosts and night-creepers, nothing more,' said the whispery voice.

More footsteps. 'You have a choice,' said Master Sy, as amiably as if he was commenting on the weather. 'Your life ends tonight, either way. I can do it quickly or I can linger. I'd like to linger. I've a decade of lingering to catch up on. So please, don't tell me who in Deephaven is a part of this. Let me take my time over you.'

'Time is dripping by, Syannis,' said the other voice. 'Wasting.' It was brittle, like old dry paper rustling in a breeze. 'Take his head and be done with it.'

'Treacherous necromancer!' The Headsman again. 'Cut me loose, bastard. We'll settle this the old way.'

'See?' Master Sy snorted. 'Saffran wants to do it his way. That *would* be quickest and we'd know the answer, but I want to see your face. I want to see your pain. I want to see it wrenched out of you as though I was tearing out your heart. So why are you here? Weren't Tethis and Kalda enough?'

Saffran? Saffran *Kuy*? The witch-doctor?

'Deephaven is not Tethis, Syannis.' The whispery voice sounded bored. Perhaps a touch impatient, but only insofar as it had better things it could be doing.

'Yes! So they would have accomplices within the city!'

'Armies would march from the fortresses around Varr, vast and fast, and how would we stop them, eh? The Emperor would smash us flat rather than lose us. Crush and rend us to ash and sand. How would you stop such a fate?'

Someone lit a lamp. Pale orange light flickered. Berren

moved his head and put an eye to a crack in the floor. He could see the top of Master Sy's head, slowly shaking, but he couldn't see anyone else. He could smell something, though. The smell of dead fish, even worse than it had been outside; stronger and richer, almost deep enough to make him retch.

'I want to hear it from him while he lives!' Master Sy moved out of sight, and then the familiar sound of fists pounding flesh began. Berren winced. He'd heard that too many times before, back when he'd been with Master Hatchet. 'This bloated turd has no more power than the Overlord here holds in his little finger! He's a foot soldier. Foot soldiers advance and die, sacrificed to save more potent pieces. I want to know who the Dragon is.' The edge to Master Sy's voice set flies fluttering in Berren's stomach – it was like steel being sharpened on a whetstone. He wriggled back and forth so he could either see the top of Master Sy's head again, or an occasional glimpse of the Headsman, sprawled against the wall. All he saw of the witch-doctor was a fleeting shadow.

The Headsman spat. 'Get on with it, bastard. You won't get out of here alive! Every snuffer here is mine. And even if you kill me, Radek is coming. When he does, it'll be the end of you!'

The thief-taker spat right back at him. 'Yes, I know Radek is coming. I delight in knowing that. In fact, the only reason I waited so long for this was to make sure, certain beyond any possible doubt, that Radek *will* be coming. Believe me, I'll be sharpening my sword every day in anticipation. All I need to know is when.' There was a pause, but whatever happened, Berren couldn't see. 'Yes, you overfed leech, I've been watching you for weeks. You have no idea how hard it was to wait. I know you murdered Kasmin.'

A harsh laugh. 'Kasmin was a thief and a liar.'

'He was a fine man once.' Master Sy's voice was flat.

'He was a killer and a drunkard. Putting him down was a mercy. Do you want to know how we found him?'

Everything went silent. Berren listened to his heart, pounding so hard it seemed that everyone must hear it. Then a crash shook the stables. The door flew open, kicked almost off its hinges by some heavy boot. Berren wriggled frantically, trying to see. Master Sy was moving. At least three more people had come in. More than that, Berren couldn't tell.

'The warlock!' a new voice called. 'Get the—' There was a crash. The lamplight died. Steel rang on steel. Berren heard a gasp, a shout, abruptly cut short, and then a screaming that went on and on, a screaming the likes of which he'd never heard. It was a keening, wailing cry of anguish and terror and dread and it ran through Berren and pinned him to the floor. Other noises pierced it: a crash, another crash, a shout, the smash of something thrown against a wall. But over the top, the constant howl held Berren fast. It took him a moment to realise that the noise was even human. It was the scream of something worse than death. He clamped his hands over his ears but even that didn't help.

He ought to run. He could slip back out to the roof and be away. No one would possibly hear him now. Yet he couldn't move. He could barely even breathe.

As suddenly as it had started, the chaos from below came to an end. There was no more crashing, no more shouting. The flickering light of a candle appeared.

'Men will come now,' breathed the whispering voice. 'Soon and fast.'

'All right, Kuy,' said Master Sy. 'We'll do it your way.'

Berren heard sobbing.

'You see, in the end, you fat feeble prick, I don't care why you were here. I don't care why you came. I don't care what you've got in your ship dressed up as crates of black tea. I don't care who or what or why or what war you're trying to

187

start and I don't care what you think you could offer me to leave you be. You took my life, you murdering shit.'

The Headsman's voice, when he spoke, was tight with pain. 'A pox on you, bastard! You say you're a godly man and you serve a thing like *that* ...'

'I serve my kingdom,' answered the thief-taker evenly. He punched the Headsman in the face, knocking him out of Berren's view. The Headsman lapsed into sobbing whines. Berren couldn't see either of their faces.

'I'll give you anything I have.'

'No, no. Gods! It's too late for *that*. All you have that I want is your silence. I want you to disappear. I want you to *end*.'

'Quickly, Syannis!' hissed the witch-doctor from the House of Cats and Gulls.

'I know about Radek! He's coming! He's ...'

The Headsman said no more. His last sound was a punctured sigh. Then there came a heavy thud. Try as he might, Berren couldn't find a crack in the floor wide enough to let him see what had happened.

'I know, I know,' said Master Sy softly. 'He's been looking for me for a long time, and now word is on its way to him that I'm here. We'll hear all about it later, won't we now.' Wet fleshy sounds floated up through the floor, mixed with the sort of crunching Berren was used to hearing from dogs when they were chewing on a bone. Very slowly, he eased himself to where there was a slightly bigger crack in the floor.

Master Sy was hacking through the Headsman's neck with his sword.

Berren's heart nearly flew out of his chest. He rolled away and stared at the ceiling and clamped a hand over his mouth, partly to stop himself from gasping and partly to stop himself from being sick. He lay very still, wishing he was invisible. Kasmin had been decent, Master Sy was right enough about that. He'd saved Berren's life once, back when Jerrin One-Thumb had been about. He'd become something of a gruff-but-kindly uncle and Berren wouldn't shed a single tear for the man who'd killed him. But still, hacking a man's head off? Why?

When it was done, Berren thought he heard the thief-taker and the witch-doctor, slipping away. He couldn't be sure. His ears were still filled with the terrible sound of Master Sy's sword slicing at the man's flesh. For a long time he lay where he was, flat on his back, not daring to move. What if Master Sy hadn't gone anywhere? What if he was simply lurking downstairs in the darkness? What if the witch-doctor was still there, waiting for him?

There were bodies in the room downstairs for sure. He didn't know how many, but more than one.

No, he needed to move, to get away, and as if to prove it, a gang of snuffers from the Two Cranes burst in, six or seven of them with lanterns from the inn.

'Holy Kelm!'

'Khrozus' Blood!'

He couldn't know what they were seeing, but he could imagine it. Three dead men and a fourth with his head missing, blood everywhere.

'Sun and Moon!'

'Well don't just stand there, you onion-eyed oaf! Go and get someone!'

'Who?'

'Gods! I don't know! Everyone! Don't touch anything!'

The snuffers moved back outside. As quietly as he could, Berren tip-toed back to the window. He slipped out and closed the shutters behind him and lay quiet and still on the stable roof. The little yard behind the inn had half a dozen snuffers in it now. He didn't dare move.

A few seconds later, they found the bodies of the two men who'd been guarding the back gate, the ones Master

Sy had paid off to let him in. That was enough. They ran back inside, filling the night with cries of murder and alarm. Berren waited until they were gone, then jumped down into the yard, bolted for the open gate, and fled into the night as fast as he could.

23
THE NEED TO KNOW

Berren slipped across the city, silent and unseen, back into the temple and crept to his bed. He lay there with his arms wrapped around his head, trying to cast out the sounds so that he could sleep; except, even when he did sleep, they came back in his dreams. That was worse. His imagination provided what his eyes couldn't. He saw himself watching Master Sy split the Headsman's head from his shoulders. In his dreams, the Headsman was never quite dead. His tongue lolled, his eyes rolled and strange noises escaped his lips. As his head fell from his neck, some last word guttered from his throat, so bent and broken that Berren couldn't understand what it was, no matter how many times he heard it. He woke up, sweating, his rough woollen blanket twisted around him. *This* was his thief-taker master? It seemed like madness. Master Sy was always so calm, always so assured. *Never kill unless you have to. If you draw a blade you have already failed.*

No, not always so calm. Underneath the surface was a rage like no other. Berren had seen it before. He'd seen more than a dozen men die on the end of his master's blade, and the thief-taker wasn't shy to use it once his ire was raised. But Master Sy had never chopped a man's head off his shoulders before. It had been so ... messy, that was the thing. Not a clean single stroke like an executioner, but hacking over and over, like a butcher with a cleaver having at a thick joint of meat. And the blood …

He was late to practice that morning, but once there, he immersed himself in it. He let his muscles do what they did every day, stopped thinking, turned his mind blank and in his head, he walked away from everything. By the end of the day, he'd had more curses and taps from Sterm's cane than he could count, and Tasahre was giving him the strangest of looks. He thought he might have fought unusually well when they'd sparred.

Why? Why had Master Sy taken the man's head? A ghoulish trophy? Kasmin was more than just a friend for Master Sy, but still – that wasn't the thief-taker he knew; no, there had to be a reason for it.

The dreams left him alone that night. The next morning, Tasahre was shaking him awake.

'A girl monk in with the boy novices?' he mumbled at her. 'Whatever will the elder dragon say?'

Tasahre glared at him. 'Come,' she hissed. 'Quickly.'

Outside it was still dark. On the eastern horizon, out across the estuary, the sky was tinged with pink. Today was Abyss-day, the day the old gods pierced a hole through the heart of the world. What did she want with him on Abyss-day? There wasn't supposed to be any training.

Outside, there were soldiers in the temple. Not just the usual ones in yellow with their sunburst shields but soldiers in the colours of the city Overlord, lots of them, passing yawns between them as though it was some sort of game. The other dragon-monks were there too, still as statues, watching, tense and prickling with hostility. At the open gates, he caught a glimpse of a man dressed in grey robes leaning quietly against the walls, his face hidden beneath a cowl. Grey was the colour of death. He thought he saw the man meet his eye and wag a finger, but then some soldiers passed between them and when they were gone, so was the man in grey; instead Berren saw someone else, almost the last person he'd expected to see, striding across the temple yard with a cadre of soldiers trailing behind him. Justicar Kol. Whatever this was, it wasn't about a naughty novice who played truant in the night.

'What's happening?' he asked.

Tasahre put a hand on his shoulder. It was a soft touch and yet it made him jump as though someone had set off a firecracker. 'I don't know. A man has been murdered. There is talk of conspiracy and treason and assassination, but it is all whispers. The elder dragon says we have a snake in our nest.' She sounded unsettled. 'They are looking for your master, too,' she added softly. She nodded towards the justicar. 'That one is here to speak with you.'

'What? Why? Why are they looking for Master Sy?'

'I don't know. Has he done something wrong?'

Berren shook his head. But shaking his head wasn't enough – the pictures and the sounds ran in circles inside him and he wanted to be rid of them. It would have been easy to tell her how he'd slipped out, how he'd lain in wait, and then how Master Sy had come with the Headsman and the terrible things that had followed. About the fight in the House of Records and the bodies they'd taken out to the Wrecking Point. It all wanted to come out. Right back to the archer up on the warehouse roof.

The hand on his shoulder tightened. 'If he has done something wrong, Berren, the crime is his, not yours. You are his apprentice, that is all. You have nothing to fear.'

Really? Nothing? Because it didn't feel like nothing.

At the gates, the figure in grey was there again.

'Let this city man ask his questions. I will be with you. Is he a friend? He says you know him.'

'Who's that?' He pointed towards the gates, to the man in grey. His finger was shaking. He wasn't even sure why, just that everything was wrong, every*one* was wrong, nowhere was safe and he needed to run away from all of them. The urge was building up inside him, irresistible.

'Who?' Tasahre frowned.

'There!' But the man in grey was gone again.

'Berren! Stop! You're shaking!' She reached out to him again. Her hand on his shoulder was firm and warm, and in her face, all he could see was concern for him. He felt the panic ebb away. 'What is it that makes you afraid, Berren?'

He wasn't sure. Losing everything all at once, maybe. He shrugged and shook his head. He couldn't give an answer that made any sense, and even if he could, he was quite sure he wouldn't want to share it.

'Whatever it is, you must find it and face it. Fear is the killer of thought.' She frowned and let go of him. 'There. It is fading. Come. You must talk to this city man who claims to be a friend and then he can go.' She kept looking at all the soldiers scattered around the temple, the Overlord's men. The other dragon-monks were prowling the temple yard like hungry tigers. He'd never seen them like this, never seen them so on edge. It was infectious.

'What's happening?' he asked again.

'I don't know, Berren. I don't know.'

Kol had seen them and was coming towards them. Maybe *he* would know. Berren tried not to think about what he'd seen at the Two Cranes. A part of him wanted to let it all come out – Kol was a friend, right? But he couldn't.

'Berren.' Kol stopped in front of him. He looked as nervous as the monks. He glanced at Tasahre. 'Is there somewhere we can talk? Quietly? Preferably alone.'

'I ...' Berren looked back at Tasahre.

'No,' she said. 'Berren is my student and I am responsible for him. I will hear your questions too.'

'You?' Kol snorted. 'What has any of this to do with you, monk?'

'This is my temple and we are outside your law,' she said, quiet but firm. 'Come.'

There were soldiers everywhere, and men Berren didn't know but who wore fine clothes and swords as though they were lords. Tasahre marched past them all, past a cluster of priests swathed in whispers who all stopped and stared as they passed. She took them to where the monks lived and slept, to their meditation room.

'Here,' she said. 'Speak your piece, city man, then go.'

Kol glared at her. 'I wish to speak to Berren alone.'

'I will not leave him with you. I don't trust you.'

'You do know who he is, girl?'

'Of course.'

The justicar was seething. At other times, Berren knew, he would never have taken this. He would have shouted at her, driven her away somehow, or else walked away himself, too proud to be defied; but those were other days. Today he was ... Kol was almost scared!

'Boy, send her away,' he hissed. 'Do it!'

Berren cringed but Tasahre stepped between them. She met the justicar's stare. 'He may do as you ask, city man, but I will not go. Ask your questions of the monks of the fire-dragon. Berren is within our circle for now. We are as one.'

'You can take that mystical crap and shove it up your arse,' growled Kol. He kicked over a stool. 'Fine. Boy, this isn't about you, this is about your master. Where in the name of the broken god is he?'

'I don't know.'

'Bollocks!'

Berren winced. If he had known, what would he have said? 'The last time I saw him, he was home.' There, at least that was true. *Sort* of true.

'You think I didn't look there? You know what I found at the Two Cranes yesterday? Blood, boy. A whole load of

195

it and someone missing a head. Ironic given who it was, and so I think you can guess who I'm talking about. You know the last place I went to where I saw that much blood? That would be the House of Records a bit over a week back. You wouldn't happen to know anything about that, would you? Think carefully, boy, because I know you were there.'

'You don't have to answer anything,' murmured Tasahre. Berren whipped round and glared at her.

'No? So when you ask all the same things as soon as he's gone, I don't have to answer you either, right?' He turned back to the justicar. 'Master Kol, I don't know where Master Sy is.' How much could Kol know? The thief-taker had been careful at the House of Records, careful about who saw what, at least. 'Yes. We went there in the night. About a week ago. Master Sy ... I don't know what he's been doing since I started my training here. He wouldn't say.' He'd tell the truth, as much of it as he could. He could almost hear the thief-taker whispering in his ear right now: *Never lie if you can possibly avoid it. No one can ever catch you out with the truth. Give enough of it to lead them astray and then let them run themselves aground.*

Kol tapped his foot.

'He wanted me to keep a lookout. He had keys. I didn't know we were doing anything wrong.' The justicar snorted. 'He spoke to the guards on the gates. They seemed like they knew him. We crossed the yard inside to another alley. I couldn't see what was down there, it was too dark. He told me to keep watch in case any men came. He told me that if they did, I was to give him a signal and then make myself scarce. He went inside and it wasn't long at all before people *did* come. It was like he'd been expecting them. There were snuffers, four of them, and a man with a cane. I don't know who any of them were. I gave the signal like he said and then I hid. They walked right past me but it was so dark they didn't see me. They went inside and then when they were gone, I ran, like he said.'

'And no one saw you leave?'

'I don't know, Master Kol. I went up and over the walls.'

'And why would you do that?'

Berren wrung his hands. 'I was scared, Master Kol. Scared of the snuffers. I've seen them before, the ones that work for the harbour-masters and they're evil. I didn't want ...'

'Yes, yes,' Kol growled impatiently. 'Fine. So you didn't see anything, don't know anything. How very useful. Very convenient for your master too.' He glared at Tasahre again. 'See what you have here, monk? This is a thief dressed as a lamb. One of Khrozus' boys. Put him back on the street and he'll be cutting purses again before you can blink.'

'Then best he stay here,' she replied. Kol twitched,

'When was the next time you saw Syannis, boy? The truth, now!'

'I saw him the next day. It was Abyss-day. There was something wrong, I could feel it. He wasn't hurt, but I knew something bad had happened. He said I had to stay at the temple all the time now. Said he had to go away for a bit. That was it.'

Kol glared at Tasahre again. 'Boy, think carefully now. Did he have any papers? Anything he might have taken from the House of Records? This is important.'

'Yes. There were papers.' Master Sy had taken fistfuls of them and for all Berren knew they were still on Master Sy's table in his front room for any fool to find. *Don't lie if you don't have to.* 'I saw some. They were lists of things. I didn't see much though. Not enough to know what they were. I ...' He hung his head. 'I don't read so well.' There. And *that* was the truth.

'And then?'

'Then I came here, Master Kol. Been here ever since. Haven't seen Master Sy. Haven't heard anyone say a word about him. Do you know where he is?' Truth had its limits.

'If I did, do you think I'd be asking you?' snapped the justicar. Another glare at Tasahre. 'Would you *please* go outside, girl. I'm not going to knife him.'

Tasahre didn't move. 'No.'

The justicar's knuckles were clenched white. 'Berren, you listen to me and you listen good. Syannis has been a friend to me and me to him for the best part of ten years, but he's on his way to a burial in stone right now. I have a shrewd idea who those men were at the House of Records and if the blood is anything to go by, I'd say your master killed the lot of them. I know exactly whose headless body I have on my hands and I'll eat my own sword if it wasn't your master who killed *him* too. Either would mean the mines for him at the very least, and quite possibly you too unless you help me. You see, what I think is that Syannis stole something or found something. Papers that are very important and might well have something to do with this lot.' He jerked a thumb at Tasahre. 'I want to know where he is, I want to know where those papers are, I want to know what's on them and I want to know where he got them. If you think you know anything about any of those things, you tell *me*. You don't tell some priest, you don't tell Master Mardan or Master Fennis or some ignorant novice who happens to be your friend for the day. And particularly, you don't tell *her*.' He took a deep breath and slowly let it out. 'This is much more than one thief-taker and his revenge for something that happened half a lifetime ago, and Syannis needs to get that into his thick skull before someone cracks it open with an axe. Did he give you anything, perhaps? Something for safekeeping? If he did, you find me and you tell me. No one else. They can't stop you from leaving.'

'He didn't give me anything, Master Kol, I swear it.'

'Right.' Kol stood up. He sniffed. 'Waste of time, aren't you, boy? Knew that from the first day I saw you.'

Berren bristled. Kol shrugged.

'Prove me wrong. So you don't know where your master is? Where might he go, boy?'

Berren's turn to shrug.

'Yeh. Waste of time. I don't believe you don't know anything. You come and you tell me. Else you're on your own, you and Syannis both. I wash my hands of you.' Kol stalked to the door.

'Master Kol!'

'Yes, boy?'

'Did you ever find out who bought Master Velgian?'

For a moment, Kol glared murder at Tasahre. 'No.'

He slammed the door behind him. Berren was left shaking. Then Tasahre had her hand on his shoulder again. Her touch was soothing, too soothing, as though she was doing some sort of priest magic on him to calm him down and he didn't want anyone doing *anything*. He shook her off.

'You should tell him, Berren, if you know the answers to his questions,' she said.

'But I don't!' Berren stamped his foot. He could almost scream with the frustration of it. 'I wouldn't tell him even if I *did* know, but I *don't know* where Master Sy is! I don't! I wish I did!' He looked at her, and there was that urge to let it all out again. He couldn't, though, he couldn't tell her about what he'd seen at the Two Cranes. No one could know about that. He took a deep breath. Somehow, hiding things from Tasahre was a lot worse than lying to the justicar. If anything, Kol had made it easy. 'I did see some of what happened in the House of Records though. It was like I said, I was keeping watch and everything, but I didn't run away. I saw them fighting. Couldn't watch Master Sy get killed and there were four of them, even if he'd stabbed one already. I was so scared.' No harm in telling her that much, as long as it was all true. Sword-monks had a sixth sense for lies. She probably already knew he'd lied to Kol about not seeing Master Sy afterwards. But she hadn't said anything. Why?

The day was a mess after that. There were no lessons, not from the monks, not from Sterm, not for anyone. Berren milled aimlessly with the other novices, watching the city soldiers do much the same, being herded away and out of sight by the priests, then slowly milling back to stare at the soldiers again. None of them had the first idea what was happening or why.

He fingered the token around his neck. He had a purse with a handful of silver crowns and a pocket full of pennies, enough to buy him passage up the river. One gold emperor for emergencies. He had a sword now too, hidden in its bundle up on Wrecking Point. For a while, he wondered if he should run. Maybe go to one of the taverns where the lightermen who plied the river went to have their fun, buy a few drinks and find someone who would take him up the river, quietly, no questions asked, and leave what happened after in the hands of the stars. Maybe he'd get to Varr and just freeze and die when winter set in and the snow fell thick and heavy enough to crush whole houses flat. Or maybe he'd find his fortune. There'd be no Master Sy, no Justicar Kol, no Headsman and his ilk, no Tasahre. Just him.

But if he ran, he'd be running away. By the middle of the morning, he knew that as surely as he knew the sun would rise, and he knew that what he ought to do was find Master Sy and find him first, before Kol. He needed to understand what was happening and warn his master that the whole world was looking for him, if he didn't already know. That was his place – at his master's side. He tried to think where the thief-taker would go. Not to the justicar, nor any of the other thief-takers, that much was obvious. Teacher Garrient at the moon temple? But Kol would surely have been there already and Master Sy wasn't *that* stupid. Kasmin was dead, so what friends did the thief-taker have left? None?

No. There was the House of Cats and Gulls.

He shivered. There had to be somewhere else, but if there was, he couldn't think of it, and the more he thought, the more he saw Velgian hanging from the edge of a rooftop. *You've got to tell Syannis one thing for me. You tell him that Saffran Kuy is not the friend he thinks.* Only he hadn't said why. Maybe it mattered. Maybe it had something to do with this. Or maybe it didn't.

He slipped out of the temple. It was easy; if anyone even noticed him, no one stopped him. *Find your fear and face it. Fear is the killer of thought.* Easy words to say, not so easy when you had to go and do it. He tried to think where else he could look as he hurried down to the river docks and vanished into the market crowds there; and he was still trying to think where else he might go when he was standing at the door to the House of Cats and Gulls at the end of the docks where the crowds thinned to nothing. The air was ripe. Dozens of green and amber eyes peered out from nearby alleys and all the dark corners. A scattering of fish parts littered the ground.

Fear is the killer of thought. He swallowed hard and banged on the door. Something hissed at him.

The door opened. Berren didn't recognise the man standing behind it, but there was only one person it could be. The witch-doctor. Saffran Kuy – the Headsman's grey wizard who could make the dead speak and who'd been with the thief-taker on that night. For the first time, Berren saw the witch-doctor's face, old and watery-eyed, pale white skin like the men from the far north. Like a ghost. He was clean-shaven with strange tattoos on his cheeks and on his neck, disappearing down beneath his robe.

The death-man, the witch-doctor. Berren took a pace backwards then stopped himself. He was a man now, not a boy, and he had no cause to be afraid of anyone.

'I'm looking for Master Sy,' he stammered. 'I mean Syannis. Syannis the thief-taker. Is he here?'

Kuy looked him up and down. He beckoned Berren to follow then turned and withdrew. Berren went after him. The door closed as he passed. Outside, the sky was clear and the sun was bright; inside, the darkness was so thick you almost had to push your way through it. The windows were boarded and shuttered, a few pale and feeble rays of sunlight poking through the cracks and that was all. Candles lit a short hallway and then an expanse of space, a huge black room filled with shadows and shapes and more candles, candles everywhere, so many of them and yet all so dim. Despite their little flames, most of the witch-doctor's home was lost to the gloom.

Saffran Kuy turned to look at him.

'I've been expecting you,' he said.

PART THREE

THE WARLOCK

24
THE HOUSE OF CATS AND GULLS

Kuy settled into a stiff high-backed chair. 'Syannis. He comes here in the middle of the night, asking his questions. Full of them, and so are you. Black powder, disguised as black tea: who would have thought it? And traitors in your temple. Have you noticed, Berren, how the pure are always so full of sin. *Sit!*'

The command carried a force that made Berren drop where he stood and sit cross-legged on the floor.

'You saw us. The Two Cranes. Then back to your nest of liars in blindfolds.' He shook his head. 'You're a fool, boy, if you think an open door stays open. I know what questions brought you here and I have answers for them, for some of them, but they are answers you will not like. They are answers not to be shared, not before the year begins its slow slide to death. They will close doors and bar them firmly shut. They will make you mine and you will wonder if you were a fool to come to me. Are you ready for such answers? *Do not move!*'

Berren had started to rise. He fell flat as though he'd been kicked in the chest by a horse.

'So you're looking for Syannis are you? Yes, we came here. I haven't seen him since. Would you like to see what we brought with us?'

Berren shook his head. Last he'd seen of Master Sy, he

was hacking the Headsman's head off his shoulders. 'I ... I just wanted to know if he's here.'

'And I've told you that he is not, but that is not the answer you're looking for. It's not the one that dares you to come here. Is it?'

'Do you know where he is?'

'Thief-taker Velgian, that is what brings you here, with his cold dead seducer song and his warnings that lure you onward.' Kuy raised an eyebrow. 'Yes, I take answers from the dead. From their spirits or from their flesh. From wailing ghosts and cold gibbering heads. Would you like to see the one we brought back with us?'

Berren shuddered. He couldn't move. Wanted to but couldn't.

'Tush! And I'd taken you to be one of those young men with a fascination for the ghoulish, for the macabre, for the touch of cold damp skin. Here you are, full of questions and you don't want my answers? You will have them though, wanted or not.'

Berren shook his head. *All I want is Master Sy.* But his mouth stayed firmly shut.

'I know all about you, Berren. Syannis talks of you. He's proud of his little lookalike bastard brother with the mistake in his head. Come, Headsman, speak! Show the young man that we can do what we say we can, yes?' Something rolled across the floor of its own accord, something the size of a head. 'Berren, the ghost of Aimes. I've waited many nights for you to come with your questions and now that you are here, you must look!'

Berren shrank away. The Headsman's severed head was on the floor at the witch-doctor's feet. He wanted to run but his legs weren't listening. Kuy's mouth gulped air like a fish. 'Berren, Berren. You might have stayed in your bed with your head on your arms and gorged yourself with dreams, but what then?' For a moment Kuy hesitated. Then, in the gloom, a smile twisted across his face. 'He's full of answers, this one. I can show you how to make him tell.'

Berren shook his head again. 'I just want ... Master Velgian ... He knew something. Maybe. Whose gold did he take? Do you know?'

'Do you have his head?'

'No!'

'A part of him? A part of what was his? Anything?'

Berren gulped. 'No. I'm sorry. I didn't know ...'

'Didn't ask!' The shadows around Kuy began to move, closing in on Berren, pressing him down like sticky sheets and nets as heavy as lead. They nailed him to the ground, killing his desires and dulling his thoughts. 'Where is your offering, Berren? You have no fish to nourish my eyes and my ears!'

'I ...' He tried to get up but his legs refused to move. 'I can go and get some! I thought ... I thought you were Master Sy's friend.'

'Friend? A craftsman and his tool and now I have a better one.' Kuy's bloodless lips grinned. Berren bit his tongue.

'Pluh ...' *Please.* He didn't know who he thought he was talking to. The gods? He had to fight these shadows. When he blinked, they were gone, just figments of his imagination, but when he blinked again they were heavy as stone once more.

'Here you are and you ask for something and yet you have brought me nothing! Ignorance! Rude boy! So now you are here you will listen. I have power. You feel it. You fight it but you mustn't. Let it be a friend to you. Let it in. Be its master. It will show you how to fight in ways you've never dreamed. I know nothing of swords, not even a tiniest little part; but you're to be a killer, that is certain. Great things wait for you. The Bloody Judge. Gods and ice and lightning and the bringing of the black moon, all of that. You bring me nothing and so I have no answers for your questions, yet I offer you a gift, a marvel. I will show you how to ask those questions of the dead ears who will know. I could show you more if I had a mind to, much more. Speak with the dead? You could raise them from their ashes.'

Berren shook his head again. A sorcerer? Him? Sorcerers were wicked people, that's what the priests at the temple said. What had Tasahre called them? Abominations! Anathemas! He was still powerless. He couldn't even lift his hands off the floor. His fingernails dug into his palms.

'Sorcery?' Kuy shook as though he was silently laughing. He left the head where it was, lying on the floor, shrouded in its own shadows only a few feet from where Berren sat, and shuffled away into the darkness. He came back clutching strips of paper, a quill and some ink. 'Now, boy, what was the first thing your master tried to teach you?'

Letters. Those were the lessons Master Sy had tried to give him when he'd first started as the thief-taker's apprentice. They'd been a disaster.

'Take them!' Kuy stood over him, thrusting the quill forward. Berren's arm rose of its own accord. His fingers uncurled to take it, then a strip of paper, as long and as wide as his forearm, then another. The second had strange symbols written across it. 'Open the lips of the dead. A simple sigil and every secret in every splinter of the world is yours for the taking if you can find the right mouth to speak it. You want to know where to find Syannis? This one knows where he will be in days to come. He will not give it willingly, but you can take the answer from him. So do it!'

Shakily, Berren's hand started to move, copying the signs and strokes. He felt distant from himself, as if he was watching while his hands and fingers moved with a will of their own, painting the lines and shapes in their own special order. *Why? Why am I doing this?* Yet he was. He was powerless and had been from the moment he'd crossed the threshold into the witch-doctor's domain. And in truth, a part of him watched his own hands with awe, amazement, and yes, with a hunger and a desire. Make the dead talk? Could he do that? What could that mean to a thief-taker? How much was such a gift worth? Priceless, surely!

When he was finished, Kuy nodded. 'Place your mark upon his skin, boy. See his lips fold back and grin, even though he might be dead, still his secrets will be said. An old rhyme for children. Now you will see its true meaning.'

Berren crawled on all fours towards Kuy's feet, to where the Headsman's face lay on its side. The worst of it was hidden by the gloom, but he caught the glisten of a dead eye. The Headsman had been close to bald, so at least there was no hair to brush away. Berren screwed up his face, sneaking a last glance. His hand fumbled towards the severed head. As he touched it, the paper seemed to leap with a will of its own. Berren scuttled hastily away.

'Good, good! Now ask it! The dead cannot lie, Berren, not like the living. For the living, lies grow like flowers in spring. Ask him what he knows about the dragon-monks. Or why he's here. Or your lost prince, Syannis from across the sea, where is he? Anything you want, Berren.'

'Whu ... Why? Why, who?' Berren's tongue was so dry it kept sticking to the inside of his mouth. He could taste his own blood. He was starting to notice the smell again and it was threatening to make him sick.

'Ask!' Kuy steepled his fingers. His pale face smiled. He made a gesture and then sat down a few yards from where Berren still squatted on the floor, and Berren couldn't have said whether the warlock's chair had actually been there or not a moment before. He thought not.

'Ask! Call his name! Headsman! Make him answer!'

'But he's dead.'

'But he's listening.'

A shiver prickled across Berren's skin, crawling from his shoulders, down along the length of his arms and all the way to his fingertips. Kuy was watching closely.

'You can ask a question, Berren. It's simple enough. Mister Headsman, sir, why did you come to Deephaven? You see. Words. That's all.'

'Mister Headsman, sir ... Why did you come to Deephaven?'

The head moved. Berren almost jumped out of his skin. He skittered back and fell over and then stopped, paralysed again as the dead man spoke.

'To bring letters of greeting from Radek of Kalda to the Autarch of Torpreah and the priests of the sun.' The words were slow and flat and dead. They didn't sound like the Headsman at all.

Kuy growled. 'Foolish man! Tell the boy what they wanted, these priests you saw?'

'They wanted mercenaries from overseas to seize the city.'

'Yes.' Kuy bared his teeth. 'Tush tush. Kind old men with never a harsh word. Serpents! Liars!' He rounded on Berren. 'Talk, boy! He is yours! Ask him! Whatever you want!'

'You ... you're the Headsman,' Berren stammered.

'You're Syannis' boy,' said the head slowly. 'Well well. This one, he'll cut a piece from you, just like he cut a piece from me. I see that. The dead see what the living don't. Why have you called me back?'

He almost ran, right then. 'Why did you come to Deephaven?'

'You know that answer.'

'Where's Master Sy?'

A low groan blew out from the cold dead lips. Kuy snapped his fingers. The head rolled across the floor to his feet. Kuy picked it up. Held up by the warlock's hand, the Headsman's face was clearer now, pale and dead with ragged flesh hanging where Master Sy had hacked it apart. It was horrible. Berren couldn't look, but he couldn't *not* look either. 'I'm dead. He killed me. How could I know what has become of him since, boy?'

Kuy shrugged. 'Radek is coming. He knows where Radek will be and that is where Syannis will be too. That is all he has for you. Until Radek comes, Syannis hides.'

The head leered. 'How can this poor corpse know, eh? Syannis will take his revenge if he can, of that I am sure.' It laughed and its eyes rolled. 'Syannis. Clever clever like an eel. Deephaven is his home. He knows it like a lover, all its crannies and sweating crevices. No one will find him.'

Kuy held the Headsman in both hands now, facing Berren. Berren felt cold and sick. He shook his head. His world was smashed up enough. 'Ask, Berren! Ask! Where will Radek be?'

'Abyss-Day. The first night of the Festival of Flames. Radek will have his ship at the Emperor's Docks for the start of it.'

'And why?' Kuy's eyes gleamed. The Headsman moaned.

'He comes with magic Taiytakei rockets for the city. A gift to light the skies as the Night of the Dead draws to an end and the festival begins. His thanks for the chests heaped with gold that the priests of sun will load into his hold. Heh!' Another hoot that might have been a laugh. 'If you want to know the real price of all that gold, ask a priest. Ask Sunbright Ansinnas. Yes, you ask. They all deserve what's coming to them. And now you know, Berren, apprentice of Syannis. That's what I told him, so that is where he will be. Before and after I'm as blind as the living.' The head lolled its tongue. 'Radek would pay a pretty price to take Syannis

211

home with him. You might think about that, boy. Now let me go. I have nothing more for you.'

Kuy cackled. 'You'll not find Syannis, my boy.' He lowered the head. 'The priests will kill him if they can. Your sword-monks? Do they know what's been happening under their noses? Was that why they came? Or perhaps they know nothing at all. Perhaps their eyes are blinded by their own light. The city Overlord might be grateful, but Syannis knows too much and he's not an easy man to quiet. While autarchs and emperors claw each others' throats, lesser men simply die. A stab in the dark would be the easy way. The mines for the men he's killed if the justicars catch him, a swift sword for what he knows if a dragon-monk reaches him first. So he hides and neither you nor I will see him until Radek comes. There will be swords and blood and one must fall and no other way is allowed by fate.' He gave a cold laugh. 'The Autarch never came. Five thousand swords await across the sea. Do they sit there, furious, raging at their betrayal? Radek is coming. Syannis knows the time and place. No, Syannis is not for you, boy, not for now. Master Velgian, though? Let that be your morsel. Your temple fools will not ask him questions because they fear for his answers and so no one knows why he did what he did but now *you* have the means. Ask if you wish, if *you* do not fear to hear the answer.' He laughed again, scornful and derisive. 'Priests of the sun? Followers of the light? Who wants them? Hypocrites! Door-closers! Blind to everything but their own righteousness, wearing bands across their eyes.' His head snapped to the doorway through which he and Berren had entered. '*Aren't you?*' He jumped up and hurled the Headsman a fraction of a second before the door smashed open and the brightness of the day flooded the hall. In silhouette, there she was. Tasahre. Her swords were naked in her hands, the sunlight like a halo around her.

25

THE WARLOCK IN HIS OWN DOMAIN

The severed head was already in the air, aimed straight at Tasahre's face. She ducked, fast as lighting, and it sailed over her out onto the waterfront. Berren started to rise.

'Berren! Run!' she snapped and charged. Berren scrambled away towards the door. Tasahre ran straight at the warlock. Kuy didn't move, stayed sitting exactly where he was as Tasahre leapt through the air and drew back her swords to strike. 'Abomination!' She landed, both feet at once, right in front of him.

And stopped, frozen and quivering, held in place by some force Berren couldn't see. Kuy's voice dripped with hate. 'Today I came to your temple and stood among you. Now you come into my domain and you dare to threaten me? Your kind are even worse here than you were in Caladir.'

Berren stood at the door and stared. Every muscle in Tasahre's body was straining, shaking as she tried to break free of whatever the warlock had done to her. But she couldn't. She was held fast. He edged towards the door, slowly and steadily until he was close enough to bolt.

'You ... cannot ... stand ... against us!' Tasahre's words came out between gritted teeth.

Kuy's voice rose again. 'The more you struggle, the tighter it binds! Let it have you and you will be free, but that was never the way for your sort. You are so *pathetically easy!*' He picked up a knife with a cleaver-like blade. His eyes flicked to Berren. 'Call this lying spider friend, do you? Stay! See what becomes of such dull bags of sightless flesh!'

Berren hesitated. He was almost at the door. 'Don't! Let her go!'

'Let her go?' Kuy almost shrieked. 'Let her *go*? This creature came here to kill me and you ask me to let it *go*? Hear me boy, for I will do no such thing. You brought this here and if you leave now, I will do far worse than kill her. And then I will come for *you*.'

'We ... will ...' The effort of speaking was too much for the monk. Berren stood in the daylight coming through the bashed-in door. This time it was his head that wouldn't let him move, not his legs. He stared in disbelief at the knife in Kuy's hand. It was the one with the golden hilt, the one from Master Sy's room.

'Get my head back, boy. Then sit and watch and learn!' Kuy turned back to Tasahre. 'You! You will do nothing, monk! In a while I'll send you home to tell all your bright and blind little friends that the witch-doctor down by the docks is just a harmless old fool. Best to leave him be and not waste precious time on such a small thing, not when there are emperors to overthrow, eh?' A gleeful grin washed over the warlock's face. 'Look, boy, look! She doesn't know!'

'Never ... !'

'Yes! You will serve me! My little toy!' hissed Kuy. He raised the knife.

Berren leapt. Not away, as his head said he should, but back in. He slammed into the warlock as the knife came down. Tasahre screamed and fell, twitching on the floor. Kuy staggered, the knife still in his hand.

'Boy!' His face turned pale, his hands too, while charcoal smoke whiffed from his fingers. Berren rolled back to his feet, torn between running away and helping Tasahre. She was still moving, still alive ...

Kuy raised his hand. Black shadows curled around it. Berren drew his waster and threw it, hitting the warlock in the chest. Kuy staggered back; the shadows around his hand dissolved into the air and Berren ran at him again. He didn't have a choice any more; he couldn't leave, not with Tasahre on the floor, and so he crashed into the witch-doctor a second time, both hands clamping around the wrist that held Master Sy's knife. Kuy's skin had turned white as milk, almost translucent so that Berren could see the bones beneath the skin of his fingers. He grinned at Berren as they struggled.

'You betray me for this? For that?' He spat in Berren's face. 'You betray your master? Oh, how we have punishment for naughty little boys like you! Yes, yes, for this is no knife that you would understand, Berren. This blade cuts souls and now I will show you how. Foolish boy! You will make a slave of yourself and then you'll do the same to her!' The blade turned slowly and inexorably towards Berren's face. With every moment, the witch-doctor seemed to grow stronger. His eyes gleamed with madness. Berren felt the edge of the knife touch his cheek. Kuy's face was inches from his own, teeth bared, gleaming at him.

'Dragons for one of you! Queens for both! An empress! Touch it!' The razor edge pressed into Berren's skin. Shadows roared in circles around them. 'The future, boy! See the horror it holds! See the black moon!'

Facing him, no more than a few dozen yards away, he saw himself. He raised his javelin, ready to throw. His own face stared back at him, wild eyed, spattered in blood.

'Well? Are you going to throw it or not ... ?'

Berren slammed a knee between the witch-doctor's legs. Kuy grunted. The vision faded.

'I have seen my own, too. It showed me. I saw my

apprentice kill me. But not you. Ah, my poor brother Vallas. Both of you such hunters!' Kuy bore down on him with the knife. With a last fling of strength, Berren pushed the witch-doctor away. He cast wildly about for anything he could use as a weapon. The warlock still held the knife. He was grinning like a madman, pointing at Tasahre. 'Look at her!' Shadows swirled around Kuy like a maelstrom now, while the witch-doctor himself was as white as a ghost. In flashes, Berren could see right through him to the candle-flames and the gloomy shapes beyond. 'For Syannis I will let you live. But her?' He slashed the golden knife through the air. 'You brought her here, Berren. What would you give to save her, little traitor?'

Give? Berren's mouth ran dry. There was nothing here that he could use to fight, there were no weapons, at least not as Berren would understand one.

Behind Kuy, Tasahre moved a fraction. Her head turned. Her eyes opened. She looked at Berren.

'Well? A leg? An eye? A voice? A day? Three lovers you'll never have? An emperor? *Take it!*' He pressed the golden knife forward. Berren collapsed, helpless. The way the ghost-face of the warlock was looking at him made his insides squirm.

Tasahre was starting to rise. Berren's hands reached out of their own accord and took the knife, just as they had taken paper and quill before. They clutched the hilt together. Slowly, no matter how hard he tried to tell them not to, they turned the blade towards him. He knelt forward.

'Yes! Now *see!*' The rage of shadows around Kuy was fading. He was using all of his power on Berren now. Tasahre was almost on her feet.

He couldn't help himself. The knife jerked, the blade pushing into his skin, his own hands pressing it deeper and deeper towards his heart. He screamed but there was no pain. Instead he felt a pressure in his head and suddenly he could see himself, as though he was looking in a mirror; but he wasn't seeing his skin, he was looking at what lay underneath, at his soul, an endless tangle of threads like a spider's web wrapped within itself.

'Tell the knife! Make it your promise: *You will be unswervingly loyal to my desires*. And then cut, Berren, cut! Three little slices. You! Obey! Me!'

With each command the knife sliced a little piece away from Berren's soul. His own hand was making him into the warlock's slave! Even as he cut, he could see it working, see how each thread mattered, how each strand made up what he was, how each cut made him more of a slave. The knife showed him all of it, exactly as it was and would be. Kuy crouched over him. He threw back his head and laughed. 'Stupid boy! I could have given you everything and you throw it in my face and for what? For a monk? For a *girl*? Stupid, foolish—'

Tasahre rose behind him and drove both her swords into the witch-doctor's back. He screamed and staggered away, wringing his hands, looking down at himself, at the two sword-points sticking out of his chest.

'What have you done?' Darkness poured from the corner of his mouth. Berren hoped it was blood. He scrabbled backwards to get away, still on his hands and knees.

Kuy's voice grew stronger and full of fury. An invisible force clamped itself around Berren's throat, strangling any thought of protest. 'I am no hedge witch! You cannot do this! Not here! This is *my domain*!' As Kuy's words rang out, the candles that lit the room seemed to burn ever brighter, yet the air itself was turning black. Unseen hands gripped Berren, holding him rigid. Forms grew out of the blackness in the air; they swirled around the warlock, shifting and morphing so Berren caught only glimpses of what they were, but those glimpses were of monstrous terrors, with eyes that glared and teeth that snapped, of claws and spines and withered hands that would reach through flesh to scar his soul. The nightmares strained, as though somehow tethered to the warlock. Horrors.

Kuy lurched forward and slashed at Berren with the knife. He *was* like a ghost now, a translucent milky white, half there and half not, but the knife was still real enough. Desperately, Berren threw up a hand to ward off the blow. Pain seared down his left arm. 'They hunger,' shrieked Saffran Kuy. Black mist poured out of his mouth. His voice had become something else, a deep growling thing that seemed to come from the walls themselves and filled every corner of Berren's head. 'They have your scent! They will find you! However far you run, they will seek you out and gorge themselves on you! Do you understand, boy? You can't just walk away from here, not from me!'

Behind him the room filled with light, sunlight pouring in through the broken door. Tasahre had two fingers raised, held out towards the warlock. She was quivering with tension, while the sunlight flowed around her. Her outstretched hand shone so bright Berren had to squeeze his eyes shut.

'Shadows be gone!' cried Tasahre. The nightmares vanished and Kuy reeled away, staggering, still with Tasahre's swords stuck through him. His voice broke to his usual whisper.

'Destiny!' He staggered away into the darkness. Tasahre strode after him, burning with light. Berren followed after her.

'Be gone!'

Kuy stumbled away, crashing past crates and boxes and piles of books, knocking down candles. A bundle of old parchments tumbled together and caught aflame. 'You will die twice, boy! At your own hands each time!'

The warlock was falling apart, his hands dissolving like smoke. He lurched down a hallway and into another room at the end, as cavernous as the first.

'*Be gone!*' Tasahre was closing on him. One by one, candles flickered and died, plunging the room into darkness except for the light that shone from her. The warlock was half vanished, his arms and legs formless stumps, shadows swirling around him. But here he stopped and turned.

Tasahre's light flared. '*Be gone!*'

'No!'

The warlock's face twisted. The shadows around him began to swirl, slowly at first, then faster and faster.

'Tasahre!' Now was the time to run, Berren had no doubts about that. Whatever the warlock was doing, he wasn't dying.

She flared again but not as brightly as she had at first. Berren could see the sweat on her now. She was drenched, almost steaming. The shadows around the warlock recoiled but they didn't vanish.

'Tasahre!' His hand felt as though it was on fire where the warlock's knife had cut him. Daylight! There was no daylight here, that's what it was, there was no sun, none at all! This was the warlock's place, his domain, his heart! He grabbed Tasahre's shoulder and pulled at her. The light shining from her skin flickered and failed. They were in darkness now, and a faint glimmer from where they'd entered was the only light.

She screamed at him: 'What are you doing?'

'It wasn't enough!' He pulled her to the door and then they were both running, sprinting away as fast as they could, out of the House of Cats and Gulls with Tasahre's swords still in the warlock and the warlock still alive and flinging curses in their wake. Out into the glorious daylight, into the afternoon rains come early, up the Godsway towards the temple. Halfway there, he remembered that his hand was hurting.

It was the little finger of his left hand. Half of it was missing.

26

SOME THINGS CAN'T BE HAD

Berren was almost sick when he saw the damage to his hand, but Tasahre pulled him on. He paused long enough to tear his sleeve and wrap some cloth around his hand, then ran the rest of the way dripping blood behind him. They didn't stop until they were standing in the gateway to the Temple of the Sun.

They were holding hands. He didn't remember when that had happened.

Tasahre jumped away. They were wet, both of them, soaked through. The air smelled of the rains, but the sky was clearing again, the sun breaking through the cloud.

Berren looked at his hand and whimpered. It burned. The last joint of his little finger was gone. He felt faint.

'Thank you,' she said.

Berren blinked. What he'd expected was a torrent of anger for pulling her away, or for having gone there in the first place, or for a hundred and one other things he'd done wrong.

Tasahre put a hand on his shoulder. He couldn't meet her eyes. 'You were right,' she said. 'He was too strong for me.' She winced and screwed up her face, put a hand to her head. Berren looked at her then. Looked at her eyes, searching for any trace of what the warlock had done to her. There were no marks, no scars, nothing. She was scared, that was all, scared like he was.

His head throbbed, a searing ache that pushed through the pain of his finger and slowly devoured it.

'Why did you go to that place, Berren?'

'I thought I might find Master Sy. I'm sorry. You saved my life.'

'And you mine,' she said. 'Come. You have unmasked a monster. It cannot be allowed to escape.'

'No.' Berren shook his head. 'You go.' The more he looked at her, the more it hurt that he'd have to leave again. He would though. He couldn't stay here. The House of Records, the Headsman, now the warlock, they were all too much. No, he couldn't stay. 'You tell them. I can't ... Look, I just can't. There'll be lots of questions and I'm so tired. I can't.' His head was crippling him.

Tasahre stared at him and he didn't know what to make of what he saw in her face. Longing? Or was that just a reflection of his own? She touched his cheek. 'Stay here. I won't be long.'

Master Sy had said something like that. He nodded, knowing full well he'd be gone before she got back.

'Stay,' she said again.

He bit his lip. Made to touch her and then thought better of it.

'Your hand!'

She took his hand in her own and looked at it, and then all of a sudden he was telling her everything, right from the start. The prince, the assassin in the scent garden, Kasmin, Kol, the Headsman, the papers they'd found and what he'd seen in the Two Cranes and what the Headsman had said after he was dead, all of it. It was too much to keep inside him any more and he had to let it out. He watched her as he spoke, looking for any sign of what she already knew. When he was done she looked at him, brow furrowed and face fierce.

'Show me the wound.'

Berren held out his finger. It was hurting badly now. Blood was oozing out from under his makeshift bandage. He didn't dare look. Thinking about it made him shiver and feel sick.

She looked at him then shook her head. 'This needs to be dressed, and properly. Come!'

'It'll be all right. Don't you need to go tell someone about the witch-doctor?'

'More likely than not the abomination has already fled, if he has the power, and this will not take long. Today is the day of the Abyss, the day of the dark, a bad time to face such a creature. Perhaps that's why my strength was not enough to break him, even as wounded as he was. Come!'

The practice yard was empty. The clouds had unveiled the sun and the sky was bright again. All the monks and the priests and the novices were closeted away in their temples. Tasahre took Berren into a small low hut with a sliding door, the place where the monks kept the tools and devices they used for training along with their weapons; and, it turned out, other things. Berren stared, wide-eyed. He'd seen lots of swords in one place in the Armourer's Quarter, certainly he'd seen bigger swords there, but here ... there were so many! Straight swords, curved swords, swords with a hook on the end, all short-bladed and in pairs to be used the way the dragon-monks liked to fight. He'd never seen so many different styles and designs.

Tasahre smiled. 'When an elder dragon merges with the sun, his swords are left to the order. That is how we have remembered those who guide us for more than five hundred years, since before the schism. Since before the first of the sun-king's ships with their Taiytakei guides cast anchor in Aria.' She opened a small chest by the entrance, filled with neatly arranged pots of powders and salves.

Berren tried to grasp how long that was and failed. He started to count the pairs of swords instead but there were too many. There must have been close to a hundred.

'Every sword has its story.' Tasahre sat Berren down on a bench. Several of the swords were missing their twin, he noticed, and a few had clearly seen a good deal of fighting. 'Berren! Look at me!'

She jabbed him in the neck with one finger, somewhere near where his jaw met his ear. He gasped, paralysed and swamped by a pain that ran up the entire side of his face as though all his skin had been torn off. After a second or two it ebbed and he could breath again.

'What ... ? What was that for?'

Tasahre dangled something in front of him. He was starting to notice that his hand hurt. Really hurt. Warm blood was running down his palm and dripping onto his legs. Oh Gods – now she'd ripped his makeshift bandage off him.

'Distraction,' she said. She dipped into the chest and set to work, sprinkling powders into the bleeding wound, pressing a gobbet of black mud over the top and then wrapping a piece of cloth tightly over everything. 'You have seen how we train. There are accidents, at times. So we learn to dress them. This is how a sword-monk treats a wound, Berren. See the difference.'

He tried but there were tears in his eyes. It burned like acid and he thought he might be sick. Tasahre stood back. She held his wounded hand in her own and touched the first two fingers of her other hand gently to it. Berren winced and almost whined, squeezed his eyes shut, fearing what would come.

The pain began to recede. In the dim light of the hut, he saw, her fingers were glowing. Not much, but enough that there was no mistaking it. It was the way she'd glowed when she'd chased down the warlock.

'You're ...' The pain was almost gone.

'The blessing of the sun,' she breathed. 'A priest would do

it better, but this will suffice. The wound will heal quickly and the pain will be tolerable. You will not lose more than you already have.' Then she picked up the bandage she'd taken off his hand and sniffed it. 'You know I cannot be silent about what you've told me. Where is your master, Berren? Truly now, do you know?'

Sword-monks could smell a lie, that's what everyone said. They could sniff them out, easy as smelling out a dead fish. Tasahre was looking at him, eyes hard, straight into him.

'That was the only place I could think of. He wasn't there.' The Headsman had told him where Master Sy might be, but the Festival of Flames was months away. 'I don't know where else to look.' And that was true, and if he had known, right there and then, he would have told her too. 'How did you know where I was?'

'I followed you through the city.'

'You tracked me? What, followed my footprints on the cobbles or something?'

'I followed *you*, Berren. It seemed you might go looking for your master after Justicar Kol came to ask his questions. You were not truthful when you spoke with him. I watched and then I followed. It was easy enough.' Tasahre's eyes narrowed. 'What are your master's dealings with that monster?'

Berren shrugged. 'He never says. I think ... I think ... The Headsman – he said he was bringing soldiers to the city for you from across the sea. He said the priests in this temple were going to start a war. Is that true?'

Now it was her turn to look away. 'I cannot answer that, Berren. The city men who came here today think the same. That is why they were here, and that is why they are looking for your master who they say holds the proof. They cannot say who has done this, so they point their accusations at us all. I came to Deephaven to bring the word of the Sun.

I came to serve the Autarch and to protect him. That is all.'

'But he hasn't come.'

'I know.'

Berren swallowed. 'Velgian. He was dressed like a sword-monk. Was he one of you once?'

Tasahre shook her head, almost laughing. 'We heard the story. Not then, but later. You threw a bowl of porridge at him and then hit him on the nose with a waster and he ran away, yes?'

Berren nodded. 'He had swords like yours.'

'Perhaps he meant to be seen? Do you think, Berren, you could have hit a true sword-monk on the nose? Even now?'

He thought hard about that. No, there was the answer. He'd spent nearly two months with Tasahre and her brothers and sisters, and no, he couldn't have hit any of them on the nose, or probably anywhere else. Not then, before the training, and probably not even now. He shook his head.

'He was never one of us, Berren. In your heart, you know this. We do not murder men in their sleep. That has never been our way.' She took a deep breath. 'I remember His Highness coming to the temple and ordering me to train you. I thought the sun was punishing me for something. I didn't know what it was but I hated him for doing that to me, for separating me from my brothers and sisters, for giving me such a burden. I didn't want anything to do with you. I thought you were a stupid idiot boy.' She laughed. 'And sometimes you are. You are uncouth, rude, you have so little respect for our ways that you could never be one of us and you would never want to be. I thought all you wanted was to learn how to kill so you could strut about like the snuffers this city seems to breed like rats. And in part, it's true that you do, and don't try to tell me it's not.

But we are taught to take whatever the sun passes down upon us and carry it without complaint. So I did as I was asked, and in the end you were not such a heavy stone around my neck.'

Berren got up. His hand throbbed but it wasn't so bad now. His skin tingled. He wanted to throw himself around her and hold her close to him. He took a step closer but she stopped him, a hand against his chest, gentle and firm.

'It would not be right.'

He took her hand in his own. Pressed it to him. He could have cried. 'I want to ...' Wanted to what? Run away with a sword-monk? Yes, but that wasn't ever going to happen.

A sad smile flickered over her face. 'The crossing of our paths will be a fleeting one. The time will come when you will leave and I will stay. When you are gone, I will remember you fondly, as you will remember me. I am glad to have met you, Berren.' She reached out with her other hand. Two fingers glowing with a faint light in the gloom, warm and yellow like the sun, touched his brow. 'The sun's blessing be with you.' For a moment, her fingers lingered. He half raised his injured hand to touch her arm and then stopped. 'We should go now. The priests will need to decide what to do. I must tell them everything you have told me. I will have no say in what is to be done, but when they are deciding your fate, I will do what I can. When the abomination turned his power on me you had a chance to run. If you had, I would have been lost, but you didn't. I will not forget that.' Gently she withdrew and smiled one last time. 'I am sorry about your hand.'

'Tasahre, who is Sunbright Ansinnas?'

She laughed and turned to look at him with a smile. 'You've been in this temple for more than a year and you don't know who Sunbright Ansinnas is? Ansinnas is the Sunherald's aide.'

A chill ran down Berren's spine. 'What does he … what does he do?'

'*She*, Berren. The Sunbright looks after the Sunherald. Come!'

'What does that mean?'

'It means that if the Sunherald desires to visit the City of Spires, Sunbright Ansinnas will be the one who makes it so. If someone wishes to see the Sunherald, they will see the Sunbright to ask for his time. Come! We must tell the priests the truth of what lurks by the river.'

'He did something to me.' Berren shivered. The pain in his head and in his finger were receding now, but there was still the knife. The vision of his own soul, laid out before him, cutting a tiny piece out of it with his own hands. 'He made me …' *Made me into something. But I don't know what!* 'I saw some of the papers that Justicar Kol was looking for,' he murmured. 'In Master Sy's house.'

Tasahre shook her head. 'Then give them to him. The Emperor is no friend to our path but we do not start wars. That is not what we are for. Come. The priests will know what to do.' she smiled once more, and he watched her walk away through the afternoon sun towards the temple doors. He made as if to follow but lagged behind a little. She didn't look back, didn't wait for him but kept walking, as though she believed he was at her side.

Sooner or later, Master Sy would come looking for his old friend Kuy again.

He stared at the temple gate. He couldn't shake the sense that there was somewhere he was meant to be, somewhere that wasn't here.

He turned back to Tasahre, still walking away with the sun on her back, still not looking over her shoulder towards him. She was letting him go, he knew, letting him run if he wanted. She was letting him be free.

No. This *was* where he was meant to be. He'd made

228

his choice, back in the House of Cats and Gulls, even if he hadn't known it.

He trotted across the practice yard and followed Tasahre into the temple.

27

ERRANDS ON ABYSS-DAY

The monks didn't wait for the next day. Berren watched them go, seven of them with the elder dragon himself, as many priests and a score of temple soldiers. Tasahre went with them. They were gone the next day too, Sun-Day, all of them. When Tasahre came back she had her swords with her. She held them up to Berren. 'They were lying on the floor,' she told him. 'The abomination has disappeared.' And that was all she had to say. For the rest of that day she worked him hard, mercilessly hard; the more questions he asked, the more she pushed him. Twice he tried to ask her about the golden knife, whether it had been found, tried to find the words to ask about what the warlock had done to him. Both times she came at him with a sword for an answer. *Gone*, he slowly pieced together, meant vanished gone. Not dead gone. Not *finished*.

And that was all there was. Neither of them talked about what they'd seen there. No one came with questions about Master Sy. There were no visits from Justicar Kol and for the rest of that day it was as though nothing had ever happened; at least until the next sunrise when Berren found himself being shaken out of bed.

'We have duties,' Tasahre told him. Once he was dressed, she told him they were going back to the House of Cats and Gulls.

'No.' Berren shook his head.

The look she gave him was a strange one, half sadness, half affection. 'Yes, Berren. Yes you can and you will. We are both going. We will not be alone, it will be daylight, and the abomination is gone. He is merely driven away for now, but my brothers and sisters are hunting for him and they will find him and end him. You have nothing to fear while we are close to you.'

Berren shook his head again. 'If he's not there, why do we have to go back?'

She looked away. 'We must face our fears, Berren. That is what makes us strong. He touched us both and we must take back what is ours.'

However true that was, it wasn't why they were going. Berren waited.

'I cannot tell you,' she said after a bit. 'I have sworn I would not. Your master had dealings with the warlock. There may be papers. You said you had seen some.' An uneasy look crossed her face. 'There may be other things, too.'

Like the golden-handled knife. Berren shuddered.

'Please.' She looked him in the eye, full of earnest hope. 'I cannot offer you much in return, but I will teach you what I can while we are there.'

They'd have more time together. Yes, he'd like that, but not spent in some stinking gloomy old warehouse.

'We might find where your master is hiding.'

They wouldn't, but he followed her anyway, out to the practice yard and the dawning sun where a few priests and a dozen temple soldiers were already gathered. The priests gave him hostile stares. One of them was Sterm. That made Berren smile.

'They will cleanse the house,' Tasahre told him, which made him wonder why they needed a sword-monk at all, until he realised that they didn't, what they wanted was

231

him, and because they wanted him, Tasahre had to be there as well. They were most of the way down the Godsway before he'd worked that one out.

'I'm sorry,' he said.

'Why?' she asked.

'For making you be here.'

She laughed. 'Are you *making* me be here, Berren? Are there shackles around my feet? Do you lead me in chains? I am here because the elder dragon commands it and because I choose to obey. There is no reason for you to be sorry.'

'But it's still my fault. You wouldn't be here if it wasn't for me.'

'The sun put you in my path, Berren.' She put a calm hand on his shoulder. 'Should I rail against the sun? What use is there in that?'

Which made him want to press her even harder. How could anyone be so calm, so accepting of whatever happened? 'What if I *had* run away when I had the chance? What if I'd left you there with him, eh? What would have happened to you then?'

'I don't know. The abomination would have destroyed me. Turned me against my path, perhaps.'

'Would that have been the sun's fault too?'

'Fault?' She laughed again. 'If that was to be my fate then yes, I suppose so. But you didn't run, Berren.'

'But I might have.' She'd never know how close it had been. Or maybe she did and maybe that was why she was smiling at him.

'But you didn't,' she said again, and then they were at the bottom of the Godsway and by the door to the House of Cats and Gulls and the air was full of the stink of dead fish. He watched the priests wrinkle their noses, watched Sterm screw up his face, and tried not to giggle. When you came past the River Gate often enough, eventually you got used to the stink. Sometimes, when he'd been on his way back

232

from Sweetwater with Master Sy's buckets pressing into his shoulders, he'd even put them down for a quick rest. He had an idea that the cats and the gulls knew when someone was coming out. He'd watch the cats gathering, vying for dominance. The gulls would flock to the warehouse roof, its windows, anywhere they could find purchase; and then someone would come out and leave their basket and hurry away and the frenzy would begin. A short, violent free-for-all between the feral cats while the air filled with gulls, wheeling in to steal whatever they could. The cats hissed and clawed at the gulls and each other alike, and the gulls snapped at anything and everything.

That had been back when he'd carried water up to Master Sy's house every Abyss-Day morning. He'd come down the Godsway just like this, right about this time of day. Now those days were gone forever.

He took a deep breath. The eyes were there, the cats, skulking in their shadows, watching, the gulls on the window ledges and on the roof. There wasn't much of a door left after what Tasahre had done to it. There were baskets, though, baskets that hadn't been there the day before. Like the priests, the warlock had his faithful. How he got them ... Berren shivered. He didn't want to think about that. When he closed his eyes he could still see the web of his own soul, spread out before the golden knife. His life wouldn't be his own, one way or another, until Saffran Kuy was dead. That alone was a good enough reason to be here, helping these priests.

'Come.' Tasahre led the way. There were other smells inside, smells of old and musty clothes, of decay and damp. As Berren and the priests walked cautiously from room to room, a reek of rotting flesh wafted past and then was gone. Berren thought he smelled burnt hair once. Some of the rooms were dark, the windows still shuttered and boarded; once the priests saw that, they mumbled amongst themselves and then had Tasahre and Berren rip off the last remaining boards, flinging open the shutters and letting in the light. In the deeper rooms where there were no windows and no place for the sunlight to enter, they lit candles laden with incense. The warehouse became a feast of smells, burning tallow and sulphur and a hundred scents that Berren couldn't name adding themselves to the ever-present stink of rot and decay. The richness of the air seemed all the more imposing set against the dullness of any other sensation. Even as the sun rose higher and shone through the warehouse windows, the grime and the gull excrement on the dim glass reduced the light inside to a dull brown glow. Everywhere Berren went the walls were greasy to the touch. They found no sign of any food, any drink, not even any waste. Not even a pisspot.

'Was there another place?' Tasahre asked Berren. 'Did he live somewhere else?'

Berren could only shrug. He watched the priests gather papers and put them into piles. They burned most of it and they never asked Berren if he recognised a single sheet; then they took artefacts and skulls and bones and smashed them methodically to powder. They sprinkled salt in circles on the floor and bathed the walls in sunlight. Several times, Berren saw one of the priests glowing the way Tasahre had flared two days before, though not as bright. After a bit, he wandered away. Tasahre came with him – she was always beside him, his watcher, his keeper, his minder. He wasn't sure whether she was there to keep him safe or to keep him honest or whether it was both, but he didn't mind. He wouldn't have wanted to wander a place like this on his own. He wouldn't have dared.

'Is there anything we should look for?' she asked him.

'There's that golden knife he had. Did more than cut my finger. Worth a bit, too.' Maybe if they found the knife, the priests would know a way to undo what the warlock had done. 'There's that head he threw at you. Could tell you a bit, if any of your priests really can talk to the dead.'

She gave him a hard look and shook her head, and then it crossed Berren's mind that the Headsman's secrets were all about some sun-priest and so the temple was hardly likely to go digging after them.

He stood where he and Tasahre had last seen the warlock, where shadows had swirled around him just before they'd turned and run. There wasn't any sign of him now, but Berren could feel Kay's presence, watching him. It didn't seem to bother Tasahre so he supposed it must have been only in his head, but that didn't make it any better. After a bit, he had to go back to the door, out to the docks outside, just to be in the light and away from the smells. The dead fish stink didn't bother him – you got used to that, growing up in Shipwrights' – but the rest, the rest made him want to be sick. The incense that the priests were using. It was so ... rich. It was making his head spin.

He could make the Headsman talk. Whatever those symbols were that he'd drawn, he was certain he could make them again. He could make the Headsman talk and make Tasahre listen and understand the truth.

Or he could run – some part of him still wanted that. He didn't even know why except that running was what he'd always done. Running was how a boy from Shipwrights' stayed safe. Old habits died hard.

He must have dozed, leaning against the warlock's wall in the summer sun, because the next thing he knew, it was Saffran Kuy standing in front of him, just his head and his shoulders, his arms and the rest of him crumbling into a fine white powder. Berren jumped with a start and a scream, and then Tasahre was there, hands on his shoulders, staring into his eyes.

'What did you see?'

'I saw ...' He gulped. 'I saw Kuy.'

235

She nodded. 'I smell it. A bitterness on the air.'

'Please can we go back? Please!' *If he comes, I have to do what he wants. He'll make me!*

Tasahre nodded pensively. 'I must defer to the priests,' she said after a moment, 'but I can ask.'

She went back inside and Berren was alone again. He took in a deep breath and forced a smile. It was the middle of the morning. The sun was shining and there was a slight wind brushing his hair. For a moment, he imagined he was free, that Kuy was gone and Radek too and everything was finished. No Master Sy, no nothing. He could just get up and head out the River Gate, off to the Poor Docks where the little fishing boats that plied the river mouth were moored. He had enough silver to buy a trip to the City of Spires. After that it would be walking. Maybe he'd get to Varr before winter and maybe he wouldn't, but no journey ever got anywhere without a start, right?

His eyes slipped over the nearer jetties of the river docks, looking at the barges, the lightermen who might carry him all the way. Then across the glittering water with its smattering of estuary boats going back and forth, to what lay beyond, a low line of stilted houses built on the tidal mudflats. Siltside, home to the mudlarks, the people who scraped a living through whatever they could dig out of the mud or what they could steal from the ships anchored on the city side of the river.

He frowned and fingered the token around his neck. Siltside was a refuge for people who had nowhere and nothing. *Really* nowhere and nothing. And that wasn't him.

'Hello, Berren.'

He jumped. There he was, thinking of running away when no one was looking, and now here was Sterm the Worm, almost as if he knew, as if he had a sixth sense. Sterm didn't have his cane out here but his tongue could be quite sharp enough.

'Teacher.' A while back he wouldn't have said it was possible for Sterm to think any less of him, but that was before he'd been found consorting with a warlock.

Sterm gave Berren an awkward pat on the back. 'If there's anything you need, anything that Tasahre cannot give, I promise not to make you answer questions about Saint Kelm.'

Tasahre came back outside. She smiled at Berren. 'It is agreed. There is too much here to be addressed in one day. We will find crates and summon wagons and take this wickedness back to our temple where it can be properly examined and destroyed. We will do as we intended, but we will do it in our sanctuary.' She stretched and tipped her head up to the sun, soaking up its warmth and its light. 'Finding wagons will surely be a simple matter so close to the river docks.'

'What happens after that?' What happens to *me*? That's what he was thinking.

'Another sunrise, Berren. And with every sunrise comes another hope. Come!' And before he could say anything else, she'd grabbed his arm and was bounding away with him up the Godsway.

28

AND WITH EVERY SUNRISE

In the second week of the month of Lightning, a ship came from Helhex, the closest port in the far south to the holy city of Torpreah. Sunburst flags flew from its masts and word swept through Deephaven like a fire: the Autarch had come at last! But no. The ship stayed in the harbour for two weeks and then it slunk away again. Some said the Autarch had been aboard but had been too afraid to step ashore. Others that it was just a ship, that the Autarch had never left his sacred island at all. Berren wasn't sure he cared much one way or the other, but a disappointed gloom fell over the novices and the priests, while the sword-monks were even more tense than ever. The city rumbled and grumbled. No Autarch, no holy teeth of Kelm, nothing at all except a company of fire-dragon monks who were slowly wearing out their welcome. In the temple, Berren learned swordplay and letters as before. Master Sy had vanished and the warlock had disappeared too, and without anyone quite saying it, he knew he was expected to stay within the temple walls until Kuy had been destroyed. And that was fine. He was safe there from whatever the warlock had done to him, and he knew in his heart that Kuy hadn't lied about Syannis. He might find the thief-taker on the night before the Festival of Flames, but he wouldn't find him before.

The relics from the House of Cats and Gulls were laid

out on sheets in the same rooms where the monks kept their weapons, their Hall of Swords where Tasahre had bandaged Berren's hand. No one stopped Berren from going in to look, although he was somehow never alone there for long. There were all sorts of things he didn't understand. Most of it he didn't even want to. The golden knife wasn't there, and that was all he needed to know. None of the priests understood what Kuy had done to him. He wasn't sure that any of them even believed him, any of them except Tasahre.

They had the Headsman, shrivelled and lying in a corner. His dead staring eyes and his gaping mouth were always there, always the first thing Berren saw every time he went inside. Hideous.

Kol came once more. Berren told him everything this time. The priests had been through the papers salvaged from Kuy's house by then, but there was no sign of whatever Master Sy had stolen from the House of Records.

'Watch them for me boy,' Kol hissed, before he left. 'That Headsman fellow, I *know* he had dealings with this lot. The Emperor and the Autarch have been circling each other like gladiators all year. There's another war coming. I can smell it. You keep your eyes open.'

Berren watched him go. Keep his eyes open for *what*, exactly? But Kol didn't come back.

In time the month of Lightning gave way to the month of Flames. The mornings were full of fierce summer heat; the afternoon rains grew heavier, the evenings became long, the air thick and humid. Master Sy had been gone for four weeks, then five, then six, with no word, no sign, no sound, nothing. The priests still searched for Saffran Kuy and Berren still felt the hole inside him where the golden knife had cut a piece of him away. Was it healing? He wasn't sure. The priests told him that whatever the warlock had done, it could be undone with prayer, which Berren didn't

239

believe for a second. Tasahre suggested long days of hard and honest work and a truthful tongue, which sounded more likely. Thing was, though, how would he ever know? It was always there, a scar inside him.

The Festival of Flames drew closer, weeks away and then mere days, and Deephaven prepared itself to celebrate as only Deephaven could. Every night, Berren fingered the Prince's token around his neck. He felt restless. No one had said anything, but the monks would leave before long. They'd only been there for the Autarch, the Autarch had never come and so they had no reason to stay. And, as Kol had predicted, the city was tiring of their honesty.

'After the summer,' Tasahre said, when he finally plucked up the courage to ask when she was going. 'With the Harvest Tides.'

'Can I come with you?'

She smiled and shook her head. 'I would not mind it myself, but the elder dragon would never allow such a thing. Dragon-monks are chosen as children. You are quick, I will admit, and you will make a fine swordsman if you practise with discipline. But there is more to us than swords, as you have seen. The priests here will look after you. Your master was once a friend to many here and they will easily believe that the abomination drove him to his crimes. They will keep you safe. Now. Guard yourself!' She drew a waster.

'I don't want keeping safe! I want ...' *I want you*, he was about to say, but then what? A smile and a shake of the head, that's what. 'I want to learn swords.'

'There are other teachers,' she said, and then showed him why none of them would ever be good enough.

'I want ...' There was more to it than simply how to fight with a sword. He was beginning to see that now. All those things Master Sy had tried to tell him. Learning about how to use a sword, that was one thing. The grip, the stance, the footwork, the cut and thrust and parry and riposte, how to read your opponent's blade and how to read their eyes and how to watch both at once without ever giving anything away – he'd been learning all that from Master Sy for years, he could see that now. But there was more. There was something Tasahre was teaching him that no other sword-master ever could. Not the *how* of how to fight, but the *why*. But he couldn't think of a way to put it into words, not in some way that wouldn't make Tasahre laugh and smile – which was all for the good – and then tell him that a priest could teach him that far better than a monk – which was not so good, and also happened not to be true.

He still hadn't worked out the right words when a gong sounded. Over Berren's shoulder, the temple gates swung open and a company of armed men marched in. They came two by two, dressed in the Emperor's colours, the flaming red imperial eagle on their chests framed in black and moonlight silver, with breastplates and pouldrons polished until they shone like the sun. Strutting behind them came a man in golden robes, then more soldiers and a spread of rich-looking men like the ones Berren had seen in the Golden Cup with Master Sy, each flanked by their own guardsmen. Behind followed a small cart covered in a shroud with a man walking beside it, and then more of the Emperor's soldiers. They all marched in with their heads held high, into the centre of the temple yard. The rich folk made a show of inspecting the statues.

Berren's eyes went back to the man who was walking beside the cart. It was Justicar Kol.

Tasahre paused from smacking him in the ribs. One of the soldiers started to shout at the sky. 'His Imperial Highness Prince Furyondar, Overlord of Deephaven, Marshall of the Seas, Commander of the Seventh Legion, Regent in the Emperor's Name and Speaker of the Emperor's Word!'

Berren froze on the spot. Overlord? *The* Overlord?

He turned and stared at Tasahre. Her eyes were as wide as his. As they stared, a priest came running out of the temple. He stopped in front of the soldiers and bowed. The soldiers parted and the Overlord in his golden robes stepped between them. Whatever was said, the words were too quiet to reach Berren.

'Why is the Overlord here?' He couldn't stop looking. He'd never seen the city Overlord before, not even half-glimpsed from a distance.

Tasahre shrugged. 'I do not know. Now attend! They are no concern of yours.'

Berren burst out laughing. How could she say that? 'But ... But that's the Overlord! He's the next thing to the Emperor!'

'I am aware, Master Berren, but you are blades drawn against a disciple of the fire-dragon. Until our time is done and I let you go, nothing short of the sun falling out of the sky should be of more concern to you than the point of my sword. Now guard!' She jabbed him in the ribs.

They sparred for a few minutes more. Berren tried to turn the fight so he could see what was happening in the yard. When she realised what he was doing, Tasahre tried to turn the fight so that he couldn't. After a while she stopped, withdrew, saluted and bowed.

'I give up. I release you.' she shook her head and Berren couldn't tell whether she was more amused or annoyed. 'Go! Listen at doors or whatever it is you mean to do.' She glowered. 'I will forgive you, but only if you remember that we are not done for today. So you will come back and tell me all that you have heard, yes?'

He turned and ran, chasing after the Overlord and his soldiers as they vanished into the temple dome, racing into the atrium in time to see the inner doors slam shut. Temple soldiers in their yellow sunbursts barred his way, along with two soldiers in imperial eagles.

'The temple is closed, novice.' A soldier glared at him. The temple soldiers generally took their lead from the priests in not having much love for Berren. 'The Sunherald is in private session.'

Berren gawped. The Sunherald? The highest priest in Deephaven? A priest who answered only to the Autarch himself? The Overlord was here to see the *Sunherald*? But then, who else would the Overlord come to see?

'Oi! Novice! You deaf?'

He obviously wasn't going to see or hear anything from *this* door, but there were plenty of others. He skipped back outside, all ready to run to the back of the temple and one of the other ways into the great dome. But outside he almost ran straight into Justicar Kol and his wagon, parked in the shade around the corner from the grand gates.

'Berren.' Kol wore a grim smile. 'Well, well. Fancy seeing you.'

'Justicar.' Berren looked from side to side. 'What's happening? That's the Overlord!'

'Yes.' Kol raised an eyebrow. He seemed unusually pleased with himself. 'I noticed.'

'What's he doing here? What are *you* doing here?'

Kol grinned. It was a nasty grin, the sort a cat might give to a cornered mouse. 'Where's your master, boy?'

Berren shrugged.

'And if you did know, would you tell me?'

Berren shrugged again. 'Not if he told me not to, Master Kol.'

'That's *justicar* to you today, boy. You know I could have you sent to the mines just for that, just for not telling me things that I want to know.'

This time Berren sniffed. 'Might as well send the whole city then, Master Kol, because it's packed full to bursting with people who don't know where Master Sy is hiding.'

Kol bared his teeth some more. 'You think you're safe in

here where I can't touch you, but you won't be here forever, and I'll always be waiting. One by one I'll bring you in. I don't know whose side you think you're on, Berren, but for as long as you're not telling me what it is that you know, it's not mine. And that's a bad place to be.' His eyes gleamed. 'Tides ebb and tides flow. The Autarch rests in Torpreah, the Emperor still has an heir, armies have stayed in their castles and it seems there is to be no war after all, not this year; so our Overlord finally grows a spine and climbs off his fence. And so now I'm here, with the one and only man in this city who can command the priests of the sun, and at last we get to the truth.'

'I told you everything I know, Master Kol. All of it.'

Kol snorted. He pulled back the shroud on the cart. Underneath was a body, someone who'd been dead and drying out for months.

'I haven't forgotten you and your master, Berren, but today I have my eyes on a different prize.'

It took Berren a moment to recognise to corpse, and even then, it was the clothes he recognised more than the dried peeling leathery face.

Master Velgian.

29
CURIOSITY AND ITS CONSEQUENCES

He ran straight back to Tasahre, who was sitting at the edge of their fighting circle, legs crossed, eyes closed, with a smile on her face.

'They've got Master Velgian's body! They're going to call his spirit and make him talk! Or something like that.'

'Good.' She unfolded her legs, stood up and tossed a waster at Berren. He caught it without thinking. 'Now can we resume our practice?'

'It's Master Velgian! They're going to bring him back from the dead!' Practice? This was no time for practice! Berren hopped from one foot to the other. 'Don't you want to be there? Don't you want to hear what he says?'

'No.' She came to him and lifted his arm so he was holding his waster out straight. Then she balanced her hourglass on the end of his blade and took her own position across the circle. She stared at him down the length of her sword. 'Calling back the dead is ... it is an unclean thing to do. A necessary evil perhaps, and it will be kind when this is done to give the assassin's body to the sun at last. But no, I do not wish to witness such a deed.'

'I do! I want to know who made him do it!' Berren grinned. He couldn't ask the priests of course – *they* wouldn't tell him anything and he'd just get a telling-off for being nosey. Even following a few around trying to eavesdrop on his way back to Tasahre hadn't helped.

'To what end? What difference will it make?' She was trying to sound severe but there was a twinkle in her eye that Berren had come to recognise. One that said *we are more than just a teacher and her student*. One that said they were friends.

'You want to know too!'

For a moment, Tasahre's sword wobbled, actually wobbled, and Tasahre's sword *never* wobbled. It took Berren a moment to realise why. She was trying very hard not to laugh.

'What?'

She shook her head and then she couldn't stop herself from smiling. 'Of course I do. But it is forbidden.'

'Forbidden? Why?'

'A sword-monk does not dabble in such things.'

They stared at one another. Berren glanced at the glass on his sword: five minutes left.

'But shouldn't you be there? I mean one of you? Sword-monks can smell a lie – that's what they say!'

'Yes, Berren, we can, as you very well know, but from the living, not from the dead.' For a moment he thought he caught a slight stiffening in Tasahre's face. She was always hard to read, but there was an air of unease to the way she stood.

Two minutes on the hourglass. Berren watched the sands trickle down. 'I'm going to go and listen,' he said.

'They will not let you in.'

Which made him laugh. 'I know more ways to get about this temple than the rest of you lot put together. I was raised a thief, Tasahre. There's nowhere I can't go.'

She raised an eyebrow. 'And here we are, teaching you swords too? I shall begin to wonder if that is wise if you continue to say such things.'

He shrugged and beamed. 'I could say nothing. Wouldn't make it any less true.' One minute. 'Tasahre?'

'Berren?'

'Come with me.' Thirty seconds. His shoulder was starting to go, the tip of his waster just beginning to wobble. Behind Tasahre, the great gates to the temple dome were opening and there was Justicar Kol and his cart. Berren watched it roll slowly inside and the doors close again. The last grain of sand trickled through the hourglass. Berren didn't move. After another minute, Tasahre gently lowered her own sword.

'I cannot.' She stepped smartly away. 'Now! Guard!'

Berren lowered his waster. 'You'll have to catch me first!' He dropped it and bolted across the yard, dodging around Tasahre and heading for the dome.

'Berren!' It took her a moment before she was after him, swift as the wind. He ignored her, pelting past the closing doors of the dome and round to the back where the bulk of the temple joined it, the dormitories and the teaching cloisters and the kitchens and the priests' tower. He sprinted for the kitchen, up onto the roof of a low drying shed and then shimmied to the top of the teaching cloister. He smiled. Tasahre was right behind him. Somewhere under his racing feet, Sterm was teaching a class full of novices. Telling them all about some saint who simply didn't matter any more, most likely.

'Berren!' Tasahre called him again. 'Stop! You cannot!'

Oh yes I can! His smile spread through him, making him run even faster. He vaulted a chimney block and then hurled himself at the high roof of the dormitory, gripping the edge with his hands and swinging his legs up onto the tiles a whisker of a second before Tasahre could reach him. He paused for a moment and looked down at her. 'Admit it – you can't catch me!'

She jumped, a standing jump, high enough to reach the edge of the roof with her hands while the rest of her followed in one fluid movement. Berren dashed across the top of the sloping roof towards the dome. There was a walkway that ran around it, an easy climb from the dormitory. He vaulted up and ran to the little door that led into the inside, to a catwalk that ran high around the dome above the altar. No one ever guarded the temple rooftop.

At the door he skidded to a stop.

'Berren! Don't!' But she wasn't close enough to stop him. He opened the door and slipped inside, creeping now. Below him, the centre of the temple dome was filled with people, forty or fifty of them. The cart was empty now. There were soldiers, the Emperor's men in their pale silver, carrying Velgian to the altar of the sun. Berren moved quickly and silently away from the door and then crouched to watch. There were shadows up here. If he was still, no one would see him, even if they thought to look up. He just had to be quiet, that was all.

'Berren!' Tasahre came through the door. She hissed at him but she didn't shout; instead, she came quietly to crouch beside him and grabbed his arm, tugging him. 'Come! You cannot be here! It is forbidden!'

'Why?'

'They will expel you! *I* cannot be here!'

'Then go away!' Berren jerked his arm away from her.

'Berren!' She was getting angry. He'd never seen that, not once in all the time he'd been with her. She grabbed his arm again.

'Get off!' Below, the soldiers had Velgian on the altar now. They stepped back, leaving space around the dead thief-taker. The Overlord in his golden robe was standing beside an old man in sunshine yellow, the Sunherald of Deephaven himself. The Emperor's soldiers and the temple guardsmen eyed each other with twitching suspicion. But it wasn't the Sunherald who stepped towards the body, it was a woman, dressed in the same brilliant yellow robes as the Sunherald.

'Who's that?' asked Berren.

'The Sunbright,' whispered Tasahre. Her grip on him eased.

'What, Ansinnas?'

'Yes.' She let go of him. It seemed odd to Berren that with so many of the Emperor's soldiers in the temple, the priests hadn't called in their sword-monks. But they hadn't. Apart from Tasahre, he couldn't see a single one.

'Is that usual?'

'I wouldn't know. I have never seen such a thing as this.'

'When the warlock made the Headsman talk, he said she was the one he'd met with.'

Tasahre hissed. 'And you would believe the spirit of a dead murderer, conjured by a warlock?'

Berren didn't say anything. He could feel her unease, though. She wasn't sure. There was doubt in her, just a crack of it, but enough to make her stay. 'This is all a farce!' she growled.

The Sunbright bent over Velgian. Light flowed from her hands, bathing him.

'What's she doing?'

'Berren! I do not know!' He'd never seen Tasahre so tense before.

The Sunbright stepped away from the body. The light faded from her fingers.

'I have spoken to the spirit of the murderer,' she said, loud and clear enough for everyone in the dome to hear. 'He could not stand the decadence and the arrogance he saw. It was his decision to try and to kill Prince Sharda Falandawn. His alone.'

A rumble of discontent swept the men below. The overlord was shaking his head and looking at Kol. The justicar was shaking his head too, harder, almost trembling with anger. The Sunherald was smiling.

'It's not true!' shouted Kol. 'He wouldn't! I know him – knew him. Someone paid him!'

'He acted alone,' said the Sunbright again.

Berren hissed. 'It's not fair! She's lying! She must be! He *told* me there was a purse full of emperors ...' He looked at Tasahre, but the sword-monk had gone white. She was staring down at the Sunbright and at Velgian's body. In the corner of her eye, a tear crept loose and began to roll down her cheek. She touched a finger to her nose.

The Overlord and the Sunherald were glaring at each other, exchanging quiet heated words. The soldiers around them stirred uneasily. Hands slipped to sword-hilts.

Tasahre stood up, very slowly. She moved to the edge of the catwalk and leaned over, where anyone who looked couldn't fail to see her. Kol was pushing his way towards the Sunbright, his face bright with fury. Temple soldiers moved to be in his way and grabbed at him. Kol went for his sword. Around them, the Emperor's men began to move. Another sword came out of its sheath.

Tasahre drew a blade from across her back and pointed it down at the temple altar. 'Liar!' she screamed, and the whole of the dome seemed to ring with her voice. Below, everyone froze. They all looked up. 'Sunbright Ansinnas! Your words carry the stink of falsehood!' And then she jumped, right over the edge of the catwalk. It must have been at least thirty feet to the floor, and the whole temple shook as she hit it. Berren rushed to the edge, because surely no one could fall so far without breaking a bone at the very least – Velgian's fall from the roof had been less and that had killed him! But Tasahre was already up, striding towards the middle of the temple, both swords out now, one held straight out in front of her, aimed right at the Sunbright's face.

'Traitor! Assassin!' shouted the Sunbright. 'Stop her!'

No one moved. They all seemed paralysed. The soldiers

who stood in Tasahre's way, the temple guard and the Emperor's men alike, backed out of her path. She stopped in front of the Sunbright. The tip of her sword hovered between Ansinnas' eyes. 'Liar,' she said again.

'I speak as the spirit told me,' said the Sunbright. Her voice was shaking, but maybe that was just because she had a sword in her face.

Tasahre sniffed the air. 'Liar,' she said again. 'You did not speak to the spirit of this man at all. Every word you spoke, every single one, was false. You knew, before you even began, that this man did not act alone. How did you know that, Sunbright? The truth, Sunbright!'

Ansinnas started looking for a way out. Berren couldn't see her eyes, but he could see the twitching of her head.

'Did you pay for foreign soldiers to come to Deephaven? Did you?'

'No!' The Sunbright was quivering.

'*Liar!*'

The Overlord's face had transformed. He'd gone from anger to the look of a cat who, quite unexpectedly, had cornered a mouse. He nodded towards the nearest of his soldiers. They moved towards the Sunbright.

'No!' The Sunbright shrank away from them. 'Guards!'

Tasahre turned on the temple guard. 'The first one of you that raises a blade, I will cut you down. Any of you.'

The Emperor's men took hold of Ansinnas. They marched her away and no one moved to stop them. The Overlord and his followers and Kol all trailed after them. The Sunherald turned and walked out the other way, without a word to Tasahre. The priests and the temple guard went with him. Tasahre stood alone bedside Velgian's body.

When everyone else was gone, Berren walked around the catwalk. On the other side of the dome, a tiny set of steep steps led down. He crossed towards the altar, but as he came close, Tasahre whipped round and pointed a sword at his face. It was the same thing he saw for ten minutes every day across the fighting circle, yet here and now, the sight almost stopped his heart. He froze, paralysed with a moment of utter terror.

'And now you see,' she said, as the tip of the sword held his eyes, 'the power that this holds.'

As his heart remembered to beat again, he looked at her. Tear-tracks marked her cheeks.

30

SOMETIMES THERE IS NO ONE ELSE

They went through the rest of their daily routine. She worked him as hard as she always did, and the more his mind wandered, the more she pushed him. Sometimes he liked that, losing himself in the sheer physical energy she demanded from him. She still beat him at almost everything but he made her sweat to do it now, and there was no taking anything for granted any more. He had no idea, after what had happened in the temple, how she could put that aside and go back to the simple motions of the fight, thoughts unclouded by the fears and anxieties of the world. Yet he saw no guilt, no fear in her, only a deep sadness.

But today his timing was off, his footwork sloppy, and not just because of what Tasahre had done. Today was Moon-Day. Abyss-Day was tomorrow, the night before the Festival of Flames, the day he'd been waiting for ever since he'd fled the warlock. Tomorrow he'd find Master Sy again, and now the sight of Velgian had left him thinking of the thief-taker, of where he might be and what he was doing and why, and why did it matter so much, and what was it that Velgian had wanted him to know? He *still* didn't know.

When they were done, Tasahre held him back for a moment. She didn't say anything, but her eyes did it for her, fixing his feet to the dirt while she sheathed her swords behind her back. She came towards him and held him, her hands on his shoulders, and stared at him, and then touched her cheek lightly to his, almost as though she knew their time was coming to an end. Maybe she was right. After today, maybe she'd be sent away. Or after tomorrow, maybe it would be Berren who left, off on some ship far away with his master, running from the justicar who was once his friend and the city he used to serve.

'I do not know if I will be here in the morning,' she whispered in his ear. 'You have it in you to be a good man. Hold fast to that.' She let go of him and left.

He watched the priests, later that afternoon, moving Velgian out of the temple before dusk prayers. They took him over to the same place they were keeping the warlock's things. Berren went to prayers like a good novice, unsure whether the priests knew that Tasahre hadn't been alone when she'd challenged the Sunbright. If they did, no one said anything, but still, he'd keep his head down for the rest of the day in case. He did his work in the kitchen, saw Tasahre come in and eat with the other sword-monks as she always did, and then when they were done, settled down to his own supper. It bothered him, not knowing what would happen to her, same as it bothered him with Master Sy, but with Tasahre he knew there was nothing he could do. Nothing he *should* do.

Velgian. Right here in the temple.

He tried never to think about what had happened between him and Kuy before Tasahre had run the warlock through, but it was always there in his dreams or when he closed his eyes. Mostly what he remembered were the strands of his soul, laid before him, and cutting them and understanding every part of what he was doing – that was the nightmare that woke him with a cold sweat when he was asleep and made him shudder when he was awake, wondering how else he might have changed, whether without those missing pieces he was still the same Berren he'd been before.

But he remembered the rest too. He remembered the symbols he'd been forced to write, the ones that made the dead speak.

He picked at his food. The answers he wanted were there to be had. He almost got up, right there and then, to go and look for Tasahre, to ask her to come with him. Then he changed his mind and ran through the way that conversation would go.

I want to see Velgian.

Really? Why?

I can make him talk.

How?

Oh, there's just this thing that the evil warlock showed me.

A spell?

Yeh, I suppose, if you put it that way, yeh, it's like a magic spell.

That you learned from the abomination?

Yeh. From the evil warlock who tried to kill you and made me cut out a piece of my own soul. Yeh, that one. But we're not evil, we're good, so that's all right, isn't it? A necessary evil, like you said.

Yeh. And Tasahre would be just fine with that, and then his long-lost father who just happened to be king of the silver faeries would come to the temple disguised as a rainbow and shower him in gold!

Maybe it would be better to just do it and tell her afterwards. If he could find a way to not mention the part about making dead people talk. Or maybe he shouldn't tell her at all. Hadn't he got her into enough trouble already? Maybe he should just leave Velgian alone.

He needed someone who wasn't Tasahre, someone who wasn't Master Sy, someone who could let him think it through for himself without telling him the answer. Tasahre would say no, it was wrong, it was sorcery and

255

never mind what they might find out, never mind that it might save Master Sy, never mind that even the Emperor himself was said to study the arcane. Master Sy, on the other hand, would tell him to get on with it. Use the best tool for the job, that's what he'd say. How you got to where you got didn't matter: what mattered was where you found yourself when you were done.

He picked at his food. He did his chores and he went to bed. And in the night, when everyone else was asleep, he got up and crept outside again to where Velgian was waiting. He crossed the practice yard, darting from one shadow to the next. No one was about this late but he felt eyes everywhere. At any moment, someone was going to shout out: *Boy! What are you doing?* and then he'd be caught and they'd find out and Tasahre would know and everything would be bad.

But there were no shouts; and then he was inside the Hall of Swords and it was dark and the warlock's things were all around him and he didn't dare even light a candle. He waited, letting his eyes get used to what little moonlight filtered in through the open windows. He already had a quill and a strip of paper, stolen while he was cleaning the classrooms. He found an old book to write on, a shaft of light to see by, dipped his quill in his stolen pot of ink …

And paused.

It didn't feel like he was doing something wrong. He didn't feel like he was damning his soul or committing some terrible crime, yet if Tasahre came in now, if she saw him like this, he was quite certain she'd do almost anything to stop him. She'd fight him if she had to, for his own good, not that it would ever come to that.

No. He *wasn't* doing anything wrong. Maybe he was trying to stop something terrible. Maybe it was nothing. Maybe all Velgian wanted was for Master Sy to know that he could keep Velgian's book of poetry, but it had something to do with Saffran Kuy and he'd never know unless he did this, and Master Sy and Tasahre had both told him in their different ways that he should trust his instincts. Well here he was, that was what he was doing and tonight his instincts were all he had.

He started to write, one symbol and then the next and the next and the next. Four altogether. The Headsman was staring at him, all bulging eyes, waiting for him where he always was. Berren went past to the table where they'd put Velgian. They'd burn him tomorrow.

Just as before, the paper almost flew out of his hand as he reached to touch it against the dry dead skin. The smell wasn't as bad as he'd thought it would be.

He held his breath. Nothing happened for a moment, and then the eyes opened and a low groan came from the poet thief-taker's lips. The air changed and grew colder. Berren shivered away, but there was no turning back, not now.

'Velgian?' he stammered.

Velgian's body didn't move. His head didn't turn, but his blind dead eyes rotated towards Berren. 'What is it? Why have you called me back? Why can't I rest?'

Berren kept his distance. 'I'm sorry, Master Velgian. They'll burn you tomorrow. They wanted to know who paid you.'

The head moaned softly. 'How long have I been gone?'

'A couple of months, Master Velgian.'

'It feels like years. Paid me?'

'To kill the prince in the Watchman's Arms.'

'It was a priest from the temple of the sun. I don't know which one.'

'It's all right, Master Velgian. They found her. That's why they'll let you burn tomorrow.' He paused. The dead had to obey the living, that was what Kuy had said, wasn't it? And they couldn't lie, not like priests. He glanced over his shoulder. They were both whispering but in the stillness of the night every word made him flinch. 'Master Velgian, do you remember when you were chasing me across the rooftops?'

'Yes. I'm sorry, Berren. I didn't want to have to kill you. If only you'd let it be, eh?' The head made a funny noise. Velgian was laughing, a bitter twisted laugh.

'I'm sorry too,' said Berren. 'Before you fell, you said there was something I had to tell Master Sy. About the witch-doctor at the House of Cats and Gulls. But you didn't tell me what it was. What was it, Master Velgian?'

'He's not the friend your master thinks he is.'

'You don't need to tell *me*.'

'He gave Kasmin to that Headsman fellow.'

'What?' Berren couldn't hide his disbelief. Of all the things ...

'I was there. In the Barrow of Beer. I saw them come in. I heard what they said. The witch-doctor sent them there. He knew exactly what he was doing. He sent the Headsman to the temple priests too. Told him what to ... Ahhh! Quick, boy, let me go! He's coming!'

The head made a strangled noise. The eyes rolled again, round and round, and then they stopped, and slowly Velgian's face began to change. His voice, too.

'Berren. Berren, Berren! Boys who think they are men, never doing as they are told, always thinking with the dangly flesh between their legs. Wants a monk, can't have a monk. Want to run away from Kuy, don't you. Always always thinking it. Hard work, hard work. Hiding away from me, but I will find you. Where, boy? Let me smell you! Where?' The eyes rolled again. Berren gasped. He snatched at the paper, the one with the sigils on Velgian's head, but it was stuck fast and wouldn't come away. Velgian's eyes rushed from side to side, up and down as if he was desperately looking for something.

'Holes in roof! Water is the moon. Slovenly promiscuous

258

night-lord! Cold and still and dark. Dark under the dark where nothing changes, that is what we are. *Where are you, boy?'*

He almost ran, but then what? Someone would find out what he'd done. He grabbed Velgian's head and closed his eyes, trying not to think about the dry dead skin flaking under his fingers. He held it in one hand and pulled at the paper with the other.

'*Where? Where are you? I feel you, boy!'*

The paper ripped in two. Velgian's eyes fell still, his mouth slack. With a shudder, Berren let go. His heart was thumping in his chest hard enough to be hammering a new way out. He was shaking. He ran outside and leaned heavily against the wall, gasping for breath. He had to bite his tongue not to be sick.

This, *this* was where someone would catch him. Red-handed, shaking and gasping, too scared of what he'd done to try and come up with some sort of story. And what *had* he done? What would the priests do if they found out? They might throw him out! Gods! No, that wasn't what he wanted, not now, not any more. Outside, with nowhere to go and Saffran Kuy looking for him? If the warlock caught him … he didn't want to think about what would happen then. Something worse than death!

No. He forced himself to move, climbing back over the temple roofs to slip unseen to his bed. He lay there, wide awake. *Now what?*

The Festival of Flames. Abyss-Day. Tomorrow. The night of the dead. Throughout it, across the city, people would burn effigies of their ancestors and of the sun and drink themselves stupid until dawn, when the first line of fire on the horizon across the river heralded the Solstice of Flames.

And in the dark, on the Emperor's Docks, Master Sy would come, sword naked and heart filled with murder.

31

MORE THAN A SWORD OF THE SUN

He lay in bed, tossing and turning, wondering what he should do. He wanted to tell Tasahre, somehow, without losing her trust, without her hating him, but what business was it of hers? Kuy selling Master Sy's oldest friend to the Headsman? That was between Master Sy and Kuy. Maybe the thief-taker knew a way to kill a warlock.

No, he had to find Master Sy. He had to get to the Emperor's Docks first and be waiting for him, to try and stop him, or else to help him. Try and stop the thief-taker from murdering Radek of Kalda, or else help his master kill the man who had destroyed his life. One or the other. And then tell his master how one man he called friend had helped to murder another.

The thought made him pause. What if someone came to Deephaven right now? What if they killed Justicar Kol and every thief-taker in the city and murdered Tasahre and the other monks? What if they burned his home and ... no, not that, he wouldn't care too much about Deephaven getting burned. But what about the rest? And then they hunted him down for years, trying to murder him? What would *he* do if he met that man again, ten years later?

Kill him. He didn't need to think about that. That's what he'd *want* to do.

Wanting didn't make it right, though.

He crept out of bed for the second time. For once, as the sun came up, he was down in the practice yard, already sitting there in the dark as the sword-monks filed out for their sunrise vigil. He watched with them in silence as the pinks and purples in the sky over the River Gate grew brighter and blossomed into reds and oranges as the sun lit the horizon.

And when he *did* find Master Sy, what then? The thief-taker wouldn't be staying in Deephaven, not with the justicar after him. He couldn't. He'd have to leave and Berren would have to choose, either go with him or stay and let the thief-taker leave him behind.

He stared at Tasahre. She was sitting still, legs crossed, hands on her knees, watching the sun. His heart clenched. She wasn't like the women up on Reeper Hill, all lips and smiles and curves and exotic scents. She was as different from them as it was possible to be, and he wanted to be with her more than he wanted all the rest of them put together; and now he was going to have to leave her.

She'd be going soon anyway, he reminded himself. Even if they didn't send her away after what she'd done, it wouldn't be long before she was gone. With the Harvest Tides with the rest of the monks. How long was that? Another month? Two? He didn't know. He furrowed his brow to try and work it out, but every time he did, all he could think of was her.

The dawn vigil ended. One by one, the sword-monks rose and left, all except Tasahre who stayed exactly where she was.

'It's Abyss-Day, Berren,' she said, without taking her eyes off the dawn. 'You have no lessons today. You're supposed to rest. If what I hear is true, you're rarely seen much before the middle of the day.'

'Couldn't sleep.'

'You're troubled, then.'

Berren shivered. He nodded. 'And you aren't? After what happened yesterday?'

'I am saddened, Berren. Saddened that one of my path has fallen in such a way. I pray to the sun for her, as I pray for everyone.'

He almost asked her right then to come to the Emperor's Docks with him this evening. They could stop it, the two of them. *Just* the two of them. They could make Master Sy relent, make him see that killing a man wouldn't change anything, make him let it go. With the Sunbright taken, the Headsman's plot and Radek's part in it, that would all come out, wouldn't it? Maybe they could get Radek taken in by the city justicars for what he'd done? He understood it now. The papers Master Sy had taken from the Headsman's strongbox, they showed it all. The mercenaries he'd hired, the black powder brought in secret to the city, the disposition of the Deephaven defences. The Headsman was dead, but Radek wasn't. The city justicars would be all over him, and all over the Path of the Sun too, as soon as they were done with him. The Path who stood opposed to the Emperor.

The mines for the men he's killed if the justicars catch him, a swift sword for what he knows if a dragon-monk reaches him first.

He looked at Tasahre and wanted to cry. She was so … so beautiful, in her own way. He couldn't ask her to be a part of this. She'd never come with him alone. She'd do what she thought was right and she'd tell the other monks and the priests and …

No.

'Are they going to send you away?' he asked.

'Yes. On the next ship to sail for Helhex. After the festival.'

'I want to show you something,' he said and got up. He blundered towards the Hall of Swords.

'What is it?' She was following him. The hall was filled with sealed pots and jars, with tiny glass bottles. There were sacks full of something that looked like manure but smelled a hundred times worse and crates of metal ingots that he couldn't even lift; strange devices, glass flasks full of oil with lumps of greasy white stone inside them, other things he didn't begin to understand. He stared at them all. The warlock's artefacts from the House of Cats and Gulls. He had no idea why he'd come here.

'Berren?' Tasahre was in the doorway, framed by the light. 'What is it? You are troubled.'

Desiccated dead rats. He remembered those. He and Tasahre had found them, laid out in a sinuous pattern, weaving in and out among circles of ash and sand, of salt and charcoal. A glint of silver caught his eye from an open knapsack.

'Berren! What are you doing?' She came in towards him. 'You shouldn't touch such things!'

Memories of what he'd seen swirling around the warlock's head filled him. He pushed them away. He went to the bag and reached inside. There was a purse filled with strange silver coins that he didn't recognise.

'Berren!'

Underneath the purse were three small vials, carefully packed in a wooden box lined with straw. One by one, he pulled them out and peered at the tiny words, carefully etched into the glass. *Poison*, said the first. *Blood of the Funeral Tree. Enough to kill six men. Secrete in food or drink.*

Berren almost dropped it.

Let them drink this and fall asleep. Whisper a name three times in their ear, that that name may become the object of their obsessions and desires.

A love potion? He almost burst out laughing. He looked at the last one.

Three times this will stay the hand of fate when otherwise your life would end.

A potion to cheat love. A potion to cheat death. And poison, a potion to cheat life. Underneath the potions were more notes, scrags of vellum, some rolled up, some crumpled into balls, all covered in the warlock's spidery hand.

'Berren! Stop!' Tasahre was next to him. She laid a hand on his, gentle but firm. 'Stop,' she said again. 'You shouldn't be in here.'

Carefully, Berren put the warlock's potions back as he'd found them. He put the purse back too.

She had her hand on his, pulling him, still gentle. 'Come away.'

'I wanted to show you something,' he said again.

'Then please do so and let us be gone.'

'As you wish.' He reached out his other hand and cupped her face. 'I know our paths were never meant to join, and it makes me want to raise my fists against the gods, but I won't do that, because I know it would make you sad.' They weren't even his words. Just something Velgian had recited one evening while Master Sy and Kol and the other thief-takers had jeered at him. 'You are the best thing in my life. I wish ...' The lump in his throat wouldn't let him say any more.

Tasahre didn't move. Her hand stayed on his. She didn't push him away. He leaned forward and kissed her, softly on the lips, as the ladies from Reeper Hill would do. He kissed her lips and he kissed the corners of her mouth. His hand on her cheek slipped slowly to her neck.

'Stop!' She pushed him away, took a step back and shivered. The expression on her face was a strange one, full of confusion. He'd never seen her anything but certain. Angry, before she'd confronted the Sunbright, and sad afterwards. Scared as they'd fled from the warlock. But unsure? Never.

She sniffed hard and half-smiled. 'Is that what you wanted to show me?' There were tears in her eyes.

'I wanted you to know,' he said, with a quiver in his voice. 'Just in case …'

There. He couldn't finish that sentence or he'd be crying like a little boy.

'In case … ?'

He shook his head. 'I'm sorry. Shouldn't have.'

'No.' Now there was a tear on her cheek. 'No, you shouldn't.'

He'd ruined everything. He turned away.

'Berren?'

'Tasahre?'

She was standing there, arms limp at her sides, eyes glistening, half smiling, half full of sorrow.

'I …' She shook her head. 'You are so …' She looked down at her feet, then looked up again. 'It is Abyss-Day, is it not?'

'Yes.'

'And tomorrow begins the Festival of Flames.'

'Yes.'

'And so tonight you will go to the Emperor's Docks to look for your master, because you know that he knows that his enemy will be there, and you hope to find him. If you do, will you stop him?'

She knew? But of course, because he'd told her everything the Headsman had said after they'd fled from Kuy. She hadn't forgotten, then. He swallowed hard. 'I will try.' So she knew he wasn't coming back then. She'd see that, surely.

'Then I hope I will not see you again.' She took a deep breath.

'What?'

'Give me your hand.'

He held out his hand and she took it and pressed it against

265

her cheek, just as he had done, and sighed and closed her eyes. 'What do you mean?'

'It means I hope you will succeed. I hope you will sway him and be away, both of you. It means I hope you will be safe. You know this cannot be.'

He nodded.

She lifted his hand gently away and kissed it. 'But thank you for giving me this moment. Thank you for showing me that there is more to this monk than what you saw of me yesterday, that I am more than a sword of the sun.' She laughed, shaking her head, and there were tears running down her face. 'And now I will go, before one of us does something even more foolish. And you should go too. I would ask you to stay in the temple tonight, of all nights, but I know you won't unless I tie you down, and I will not do that. Please, be safe Berren.'

With that, she turned and almost ran out of the door.

Yes, he thought. *I will. But I'm coming back. I promise. I will find a way.*

32

THE EMPEROR'S DOCKS

He stood, frozen to the spot for a time with a head so full that he couldn't think. Outside, as he walked across the empty practice yard, he felt a lightness on his shoulders and a spring in his step. He'd go to Justicar Kol, that's what he'd do. They'd go to the Emperor's Docks while it was still light with a company of the Emperor's men. Kol could take Radek away and Berren could sit there and wait for dark. That's when Master Sy would come, and then he'd tell the thief-taker everything and no one would get murdered and just maybe they wouldn't have flee the city and he'd get to come back to the temple for the last week before the Festival of Flames ended and Tasahre sailed away, and that was enough time that anything could happen, right?

The thought of his hand on Tasahre's cheek made him shiver as he walked past the temple guard, out through the gates. Even so early in the morning, the city was getting ready for the summer festival. The days were at their longest, the nights hot and humid and short. He crossed Deephaven Square, still quiet at this hour, and went down the Avenue of the Sun to Four Winds Square which was anything but. He smiled to himself. It seemed like almost forever since he'd been out in the city crowds. They felt like an old and loved shirt, easily slipped on and immediately comfortable. For no better reason than he could, he made a game of it, pretending there was a whole militia gang after him. He zigged and zagged his way around the square. Everything felt so *right* today.

He crossed in front of the courthouse and turned down the street that ran beside it, past the fountain and into The Eight. He stood on the threshold and savoured the familiar smells – good strong beer, pipeweed, damp wood, earth and the ivy. For a moment he felt a pang of sadness. The Eight was a familiar place. Now he was here, he missed it. It had always felt safe.

It was also empty. Thief-takers, he reminded himself, were night people and it wasn't even mid-morning. Although it *was* early enough that some of them might not have gone to bed yet ...

He breathed a sigh of exasperation. Maybe it wasn't such a bad thing. If Kol was looking for the thief-taker then there'd be gold on his head by now and there might be a crown on Berren's as well. Finding the justicar was one thing, but running into one of the thief-takers he barely knew, maybe that was another. He tried to think. He had no idea at all where Justicar Kol lived and the courts, where he might have asked, were closed on Abyss-Day. He wandered aimlessly down through the backside of the Courts District, skirting the edge of the Maze until he reached the sea-docks, right down the end by the Reeper Gate where the harbour-masters lived beside their House of Records. For a while he lost himself among the crowds there. He made his way to the harbour wall, to all the little jetties stuck out into the water and sat for a while, watching the boats going back and forth to the ships out in the bay. He bought himself a bun stuffed with pickled fish, the sort that he and Master Sy used to eat together when they came down to the docks, then slipped inside a warehouse when the guards weren't looking, climbed up to the top, out through the open windows and onto the roof. It was barely mid-morning and now he had to wait for dusk and the Night of the Dead and the start to the Festival of Flames before Master Sy would come. He settled back to eat his bun and doze a little in the warm summer sun, fingering the token around his neck. One day. One day, that was where he was going. If they had to flee Deephaven, at least they had a place to go, up the river to Varr. There could be rewards for what they'd done, if he had the right of it.

There had to be some way, didn't there? Some way to take Tasahre with him? He mulled the thought over, looking at it from every way he could imagine, until suddenly the middle of the morning had become the early afternoon and he was stiff from sleeping too long on the hard uneven roof.

He yawned and stretched and eased himself back into the warehouse and down to the docks again, slipping past the half-drunk sentries as easily as though they were statues. On the Day of the Dead before the Festival of Flames, no one in Deephaven was going anywhere in a hurry. Even the constant stream of wagons between the river and the sea, the pulse of the city, had stopped. The air was already rank with sweat and smoke and sour cheap wine, filled with raucous shouts and the occasional scream as someone accidentally set themselves on fire. Past the entrance to the Avenue of Emperors Berren pushed his way onwards, up the Kingsway and down the other side of The Peak. In time, the ground under his feet changed into the worn hard stone of the Old Fort Road. The jetties and the boats and the hustle and bustle they brought with them gave way to jagged stone. The crowds shrank to scattered clumps of revellers, mostly drunks who'd started the day far too early. Further along the shore, right at the far end of the estuary, stood Deephaven Fort. The city had had a navy once, Master Sy said. A small fleet that had guarded the mouth of the river, there to stop the Taiytakei slave-galleys and the sun-king's war-galleons from sailing the river towards Varr. Batteries of light ballistae and stone-throwers had once lined the shore. The ships and most of the stone-throwers were gone now – the sun-king might have been a threat a hundred years ago, but Aria had grown vast and almost immeasurably powerful. The Emperor had sorcerers now.

The fort was still there though, still filled with the Emperor's soldiers. Around it the Armourer's District had grown. Toolmakers Square. Sword Street. The infamous Forge Tavern. Every other alley was a this-smith or a that-smith. Hammersmiths' Passage was the one he wanted, the one that led to the Emperor's Docks, otherwise no different from any of the rest. It wasn't a part of the city that Berren knew well, and he had no idea whether anyone still made hammers here, or swords or shields or anything else for that matter, or whether they'd all gone away with the stone-throwers and the ballistae. No one used the Emperor's Docks any more; hardly anyone in the wider city even knew they were there, but they were: tiny, exposed, but the one place in Deephaven where a tall ship could anchor right up against the land if it didn't mind taking its chances with the winds and the tides and the rocks of the Blue Cliffs.

Old instincts forged in the rough streets of Shipwrights' guided him off the Old Fort Road and into the side streets. They were wide here, broad enough for the carts that used to carry charcoal and ore from the docks to the smithies. The river brought steel now, forged somewhere far to the north, and the streets were quiet and empty. Militia gangs kept order in most districts, but as with The Peak, the Overlord took a more direct hand in this part of the city.

He was still a good few streets from the docks when he spotted the first of the Emperor's soldiers, distinct in their pale silver shirts and flaming eagle crests. They were heading the same way as he was, carrying bundles of festival torches. Berren flitted back across Old Fort Street, never quite letting the soldiers out of sight but never getting any closer than needed. They crossed the wide open space of Royal Parade, the old city's version of the Avenue of Emperors, and reached the Fort, on the river side of Toolmakers' Square.

Three more soldiers came the other way, broadswords jangling at their sides. The two groups stopped outside the district courthouse, laughing and joking together. The smell of beer wafted around them as Berren walked past, and then he was there: Hammersmith's Passage. He turned into its shadows. The cobbles sloped steeply down towards the river. His skin prickled. He was close. Master Sy would come, sooner or later.

Water shimmered at the end of the passage. The great river, bright in the midsummer sun. A moment later he rounded the corner of Hammersmiths' and the Emperor's Docks were right in front of him. They were so small! He'd never seen them before, but he'd always assumed they were at least a *bit* like the other docks, huge and sprawling. But no, they were small and cramped, a thin cobbled strip squeezed in between the rocky shore of the river and the steep slope up to The Peak. There was one ship tied up alongside, towering over everything. Wooden steps ran down from the ship to the dockside. At the bottom of the steps, a handful of soldiers stood about, bored. Berren stared at them. He'd never seen soldiers like this – they were dressed in bright breastplates, and around their waists they wore long skirts made of overlapping strips of thick hard leather, coloured a deep green. Instead of swords they carried pole-arms, strange things with spikes and curved blades on both ends. Berren walked closer but the soldiers paid no attention to him. They weren't drinking, not like the Emperor's men he'd passed on the way here. They were tense.

Apart from the soldiers, the dock was quiet. A few

people walked back and forth along the waterfront, but the festival was further down the river. There was no one here juggling torches, no one selling hot fish strips or roasted roaches.

He moved to a quiet corner, out of the way but in clear sight of the ship, and sat down in the sun. Out on the river, little boats sailed to and fro across the estuary. If he strained his eyes, he could just make out the line of Siltside across the water, the gleaming mud and the patchwork of little huts on stilts.

He hadn't been there for long, eyes half closed, when a shadow loomed over him.

'Berren.'

He blinked. 'Tasahre?' She sat down beside him. He shook his head, trying to work out whether he was really awake or whether he'd fallen asleep and this was a dream. 'What are you doing here?'

She smiled at him. 'A glorious day, is it not? It never rains on the Festival of Flames. Not for a hundred years. Did you know that? Almost every day in the summer, the rains come in the afternoon, yet never on the Day of the Dead. Not once.'

He touched her lightly on the shoulder to make himself believe she was real. 'But what are you doing here?'

'Radek of Kalda is on that ship. So I knew you would be here.'

'But still, why?' He didn't understand. 'Are you all here? What about the others?' The other monks! If Master Sy saw sword-monks, he'd never come! He'd turn back and slip away and wait for another day!

'Only me, Berren. If your master comes to kill this man, this Radek, do you think he will listen to you?'

'I don't know.' Berren shivered. 'I thought ... I thought after the Sunbright ... maybe there would be some other way. I came to go with him, one way or the other.'

She took his hand. 'I know.' Out in the water, one of the little boats was sailing towards the docks. 'And I found I was not content to let you go when I could share your company one last time.' She took his hand and squeezed it gently. 'I did not ask any others to come. Together we will be enough, I think.' She laughed. 'Perhaps I am here to protect you from the press gangs! I am told more men become sailors after the Day of the Dead than over the rest of the year!'

Berren wasn't so sure of that and he wasn't so sure about them swaying Master Sy from killing Radek either, but to have some company through the afternoon, waiting for the night when Master Sy would come, that was a pleasure he couldn't deny. He smiled back at her. The warmth of the sun on his face was a delight. Maybe she was right. Maybe when the thief-taker came slinking through the shadows later, the sight of his apprentice and a sword-monk would be enough to make him pause. For a moment, he felt himself at peace.

A band of players came out of Hammersmiths'. They walked slowly along the docks, men and women with painted faces and bright clothes, juggling balls and dancing and playing pipes. Three of them were dressed as knights, with jerkins decked like armour and swords and long brightly painted lances made of wood. They walked past where Berren and Tasahre sat and smiled at them. Berren smiled back.

'May the festival bring you joy!' one of them cried and waved. Berren blinked. That voice – he'd heard it before!

Beside him, he felt Tasahre tense. 'That is odd,' she said.

The players wandered on towards the ship. As they did, their music grew louder. They started to dance and sing. On the river, the little boat with the sail drew closer. Berren scrunched up his face, trying to work out why the man

273

had sounded familiar. 'What's odd?' he asked after a bit. Tasahre was staring out at the water.

'Those men. Their swords. They were real.' She stood up. The players had reached the soldiers with the leather skirts. They were dancing around them, teasing them. The men played their pipes while the women offered up skins of wine and then snatched them away again. Abruptly Tasahre stood up. 'He's here! Your master! He's here!'

Berren looked up and down the docks, searching. 'What?'

The old harbour watchtower. The day he and Master Sy had climbed it to look at the ships and they'd seen the Headsman's flag. *That* was where he'd heard the voice before!

'There.' She pointed out to the water, to the little boat with the sail.

It had turned. It was heading straight in for the docks.

33

A STACKED DECK

Tasahre was up and running. A shout came from somewhere up on the ship. The soldiers by the steps turned, confused, and then several of the players, the men who'd been singing and dancing and making music just a moment ago, drew swords and attacked. The soldiers fell, caught by surprise, the swordsmen too close for the soldiers to use their long axe-spears. Three of the players, the ones with swords, ran up the steps; the rest bolted for the far end of the docks and vanished into the alleys there. Out on the river, Berren couldn't see the little boat with the sail any more. It had vanished behind the bulk of Radek's ship.

He leapt up and raced after Tasahre. More shouts rang out from the ship. He saw her ahead of him, bounding up the narrow rope-and-wood steps and disappearing onto the deck. She made him feel slow even though he knew he wasn't, molasses to her lightning. He didn't even have a sword. Just his stupid waster. They certainly weren't going to stop the thief-taker, that much was already clear.

He pushed himself faster, jumping over the dead soldiers sprawled at the bottom of the steps. If they'd had swords then he might have stopped to take one, but he hadn't the first idea what to do with their stupid pole-arms so he let them be and raced up the steps. The deck of the ship had become a swirling melee. There might have been a dozen men fighting on each side, more of Radek's soldiers pouring up from inside the ship only to be met by men climbing over the side from ropes thrown from the little ship with the sail. There were already bodies, a few of them, some lying still, others crawling, hauling themselves to some semblance of shelter and leaving thick dark streaks of blood on the deck behind them. There was an air of desperation. As Berren watched, one man fell, another reeled away with half his arm missing, screaming. Berren's eyes sought Tasahre.

Master Sy! Even in the chaos, Berren knew the thief-taker from the way he moved. He cut down one of Radek's men and moved straight at another, howling curses all around him. 'Tethis! For Tethis!'

The rest of the men fighting with him could have been anyone. City snuffers, maybe, although they fought with a grim determination and hardly any of them had swords; they had clubs and boat-hooks and knives. At the top of the steps, on the edge of the deck, Berren stood, frozen, wondering what to do.

'Stop!' The shout came from above him. He looked up. Tasahre was standing up in the rigging, ten feet above him. 'Stop! Now!'

For a moment, the fighting paused, but the one person who didn't falter was the thief-taker. The soldier in front of him hesitated. Master Sy opened his throat and went straight on to the next, hacking the man's arm off at the elbow. 'Tethis!' he screamed.

The soldiers in their leather skirts faltered. The thief-taker pushed forward. There were sailors, too; some of them had picked up clubs and hooks of their own, but now they were backing away, keeping behind the soldiers. Some were already shimming down the ropes that tied the ship to the dockside.

'No!' Tasahre jumped onto the deck, her swords in her hands. She walked through the fight like a ghost. No one, soldier or sailor, dared to go close. 'Thief-taker!' she cried. 'Thief-taker! Stop! Stop now! I cannot let you do this.'

Back on the docks, another gang of men came spilling out of Hammersmiths' Passage, screaming and waving their sticks. They ran towards the ship, howling. Master Sy rained blow after blow at the last soldier in his way. The man kept his halberd down, forcing the thief-taker to keep his distance for a moment, but then the thief-taker was inside the soldier's guard. Blood sprayed across the deck and the soldier went down, clutching his throat.

And then Tasahre and the thief-taker faced one another.

'Thief-taker!' With deliberate care, she sheathed both her swords. She stood completely still, lit up by the afternoon sun, yellow robes streaked with blood from the men dying around her. In that moment she seemed to glow.

Behind Berren, at the entrance to Hammersmiths', a new commotion broke out as yet more men came down from Toolmakers' Square, soldiers this time, the Emperor's men. Berren thought he saw more sword-monks too.

'Master!' Berren shouted. 'Master! Stop!'

For a moment, the thief-taker paused. He stared at Tasahre and then at Berren. The fighting on the deck faltered, and then Berren saw Tasahre stiffen. Her head snapped towards the doors beneath the spar-deck. A man was coming out. He was old, not a greybeard yet, but his face was weathered and his hair was thinning. His clothes were rich and the hilt of his thin sword was jewelled. To Berren, his face seemed pained. Around his throat, a black scarf of shadow fluttered in the breeze, and he walked as though the shadow was a knife held at his throat. Master Sy bared his teeth and almost leapt straight at him, but Tasahre was looking straight through this man that Berren knew must be Radek of Kalda – for behind Radek, something else had stepped out of the gloom. It wasn't even a man, but a creature, a creature made of the shadows themselves. Berren's throat tightened. A silence stilled the deck. The fighting stopped, although the commotion on the docks behind Berren went on.

'Radek!' hissed the thief-taker.

'Warlock!' Tasahre had her swords in her hands again. The shadow-thing pointed a wispy tendril at her.

'It is my day, monk,' hissed the wind. 'Abyss-Day. Fall on your swords and die!'

No one moved. For a moment, Tasahre stood frozen. Then she raised one sword towards the sun. 'Look above you, demon! Your power is not greater than mine, not today, not under this sun.' She took a step towards him and flared with light. 'End!'

That was as far as she got before the thief-taker let out a roar.

'No! You'll not stop us, not now, not even you!' The thief-taker lunged at her. Tasahre darted sideways, caught the next swing with her own blade, and then the two of them were a blur of swords. Around them, Radek's soldiers surged forwards. On the docks behind Berren, *that* fight was breaking up. The crowd of men who'd first come down Hammersmiths' weren't after a fight any more, just an escape, bolting for the tiny alleys that wound up the hill from the other end of the docks.

Kill her!

The command rang inside his head.

'Syannis!' Berren thought he heard the justicar's voice from somewhere in the midst of the chaos behind him. At the steps to the ship.

Kill!

He had no choice. The sword-monk was going to kill his master. He had to stop her! A little part of him screamed and screamed, but there was a piece missing from inside him, and so the rest of him didn't hear. The rest of him knew, with a cold certainty, what he had to do, no matter how much it pained him.

Kill!

There were men running up the steps, the heavy boots of the Emperor's soldiers. But Berren was already halfway across the deck.

34
SWORDS AND THEIR CONSEQUENCES

Tasahre jumped away from Master Sy, holding her swords out towards him. 'Drop your weapons,' she called in a voice that rang the air.

'Do it,' shouted Kol. He was standing at the top of the steps, surrounded by the Emperor's soldiers who were swarming aboard. The thief-taker's men were crowding together, forming a circle around Master Sy. Their eyes darted from side to side as they fought, looking for an escape. Radek still stood frozen by the spar-deck door. Berren ignored them all. His eyes were set on Tasahre.

Kill!

The Emperor's soldiers were pushing Radek's men out of the way. Swords came out. One of Radek's soldiers jabbed at one of the Emperor's and got skewered and then suddenly there was fighting all around Berren again. Once more the thief-taker's men surged forward. Master Sy and Tasahre were staring at each other.

Very slowly, Tasahre put her swords down onto the deck. Berren skittered away from one of Radek's sailors who swung at him with a hook. The sailor came at him again. This time Berren blocked it with his waster, jumped at the man and clocked him on the head, dazing him long enough to dart past.

'End this, thief-taker,' said Tasahre. Her voice was calm, yet it still carried across the fight.

Kill! Berren dived out of the way of a soldier with a halberd. One of the Emperor's men came bellowing past. The thief-taker howled with rage.

'And why should we? So you can send us to the mines? Do you know what this man did to us? Did to all of us? He killed our fathers. He killed our mothers. He killed our brothers, our sisters, our sons, our daughters. He killed our king and our country. He killed our faith. He killed everything!'

The thief-taker lunged at Tasahre. As he passed her, he snatched up one of her short curved swords in his spare hand. Tasahre leapt straight up into the air. Master Sy stabbed at her, but she curled and twisted away from his steel. Then she was back on the deck, facing him.

Kill!

Berren pushed past a soldier and one of the thief-taker's men, grappling each other with knives in their hands. He was yards away now, yet he paused. He'd seen Master Sy take three armed men down in as many blows; Tasahre didn't even have a weapon, yet she ran right back at him and she was so unbelievably fast. The curved sword stabbed out, so quick that even Tasahre couldn't have avoided it, yet somehow she did; her foot caught the other sword off the deck and kicked it into the air and into her hand. For a moment, the two of them stood, swords in guard, facing each other.

Kill! Now!

He clenched his teeth, gripped his waster. The screaming inside him was getting louder, starting to break through. 'Master! Tasahre!' They were going to kill each other. He knew that look in Master Sy's face. There was no coming back from wherever the thief-taker was.

A dark stain was spreading out across Tasahre's robe. She hadn't dodged Master Sy's blow after all. The other monks and the overlord's soldiers surrounded them all now.

The fight was petering out, Master Sy's men pressed close around him, tense but not yet defeated. As far as Berren could tell, the ones that had fallen had fought to the death.

'Prince Syannis.' Tasahre held her one sword straight out in front of her, pointing at Master Sy's face, just like she and Berren had done in the practice yard. Whatever wound she'd taken, she wasn't showing it. 'Hold.'

'Syannis! This fight is done.' That was Justicar Kol again. 'I can't save you, not from this, but you can save your men. You can save your boy. He's right here, you know.'

Master Sy held still for a moment. Berren kept walking, slowly, slowly closer, fighting to hold back each and every step.

'I know the story.' Kol spoke slowly and clearly. The Emperor's men were swamping the ship now. Most of Radek's soldiers were down, the rest had surrendered their arms. Radek himself still stood paralysed by the spar deck door, the scarf of shadow around his neck. Kuy, if that's what the other shadows had been, had vanished, but Berren knew he wasn't far. He felt the presence inside him, the guiding words, the desire he had no choice but to serve. 'You think I don't know half the men here? Of course I do. Came from the same place you did, one by one. Good men, most of them. Now look at them. You did this. They made lives for themselves here. It could have stayed that way. Now put your bloody sword down.'

Berren was in front of the thief-taker's men, who had formed in a wall around Master Sy, against the edge of the ship, penned by Kol's soldiers. They held their swords and their clubs ready. Their faces were hard. Whoever they were, they were set on dying. As Berren came close, one of them lunged.

Come! Come to me! Berren lurched. For a moment, he was confused, as the silent scream inside his head faded. *Come to me* – so much easier. He pushed his way between the

Emperor's soldiers, watching over his shoulder all the time. Everyone was looking at Tasahre and Master Sy, waiting to see what the thief-taker would do. His eyes were wild. They moved from one face to another. He barely seemed to recognise Berren. His gaze moved to the ropes that ran down to his own ship, and then back to Radek. Berren could see the thought forming in his head – Radek's corpse on the end of his sword or a way out – which one?

Come, Berren. Come here! Come to me!

Radek. But Tasahre must have seen it in the thief-takers eyes before he even knew it himself. She launched herself at him a moment before he would have jumped. Sparks flew between her sword and Master Sy's, but she forced him back, further and further towards the edge of the ship.

As Berren reached the frozen Radek, Master Sy seemed to falter. Tasahre stepped in to finish him. As she did, Master Sy slipped inside her guard to take her down, exactly the way he'd shown to Berren.

And exactly the way Berren had shown to Tasahre. Her weight shifted. She danced around the thief-taker. The pommel of her sword cracked him on the back of his head. For a moment, as he staggered, he was helpless. Tasahre was right behind him, sword poised to run him through.

Kill! Kill Radek! Now! Kill him now!

The warlock's demand tore though him like a hurricane. Berren screamed. 'Tasahre! No!' Even as he screamed, his hands had snapped his waster high over his head. Radek didn't even flinch. And then he brought the wooden stick crashing down on Radek's skull.

Tasahre's stare flicked to him. She hesitated. The horror on her face burned his eyes. He turned, finally, to see Radek slumped around his feet, his head staved in, his blood pouring out all over the wooden deck. He gasped and stepped back in horror. *What have I done?* He looked for the warlock's voice inside his head, but Kuy was gone, vanished without a trace as though he'd never existed.

'Berren!'

Berren span around to Tasahre, and as he did, the thief-taker lashed out. The tip of his blade sliced across the exposed skin of the sword-monk's neck. *Always strike where you can see flesh, Berren. That way you know there's no hidden armour.* Berren screamed again.

'Tasahre!' She staggered. Blood poured down her robe, half of it already stained dark. It dripped from the cloth onto the docks. The thief-taker took a step away. He looked at what he'd done, looked shocked, then turned on Berren. His eyes were wild.

'Come on, Berren! Run! Run! We have to run!'

The nearest of Kol's soldiers snatched at Berren, half grabbing his shirt. Berren tore himself away. Tasahre fell to the deck. The thief-taker was backing quickly away, back towards his little ship.

'Tasahre!' He was the first one to reach her. He'd never seen so much blood. The thief-taker's sword had cut half-way into her neck. He grabbed her hand. Squeezed.

'Berren!' The thief-taker was at the edge of the deck now, beside a rope down to the other ship, looking at him, holding out his hand. It was covered in blood. So were his arms, his shirt. All about, the fighting began again, the Emperor's men and the last of the thief-taker's. At the top of the steps to the docks, Berren glimpsed the yellow of another sword-monk pushing forward. He knew the look, the tension. He stared back at Master Sy.

'...' Whatever words Tasahre had left, they died in a gurgle of blood.

'For the love of the sun, Berren, come *on*!'

'You! You ... You killed her!' If he'd still had Stealer, Berren would have stabbed the thief-taker without a thought. Stabbed him in the heart, over and over until he stopped moving and then stabbed him some more.

Tasahre's hand shuddered and fell slack.

The thief-taker's men were folding, crumpling inward, abandoning the fight and jumping over the side. The other sword-monk was almost on them.

Inside Berren, something broke. He jumped up onto the empty spar-deck, leapt across the water onto the docks and ran. Amid the screams and the clash of steel, he thought he heard the warlock. Laughing.

35

THE ROAD TO VARR

'*Berren!*' That was Master Sy, as he fled, but Berren
didn't stop. The sword-monk ignored him and
went for the thief-taker, or else to Tasahre,
Berren didn't know, and for the moment he didn't care.
All that mattered was to get away. He landed hard on the
docks, rolled and sprawled, thumped his elbow and his
knees and got straight back up and ran on. The soldiers still
on the waterfront seemed too stunned by what they'd seen,
or else Berren looked too fierce. Whatever the reason, they
were too slow and too late. Berren barged though them,
past them, back to Hammersmiths' Passage at the end of
the Emperor's docks and into the empty streets beyond. He
didn't stop racing away until his legs were burning and his
lungs heaving and he was all the way up the hill and on the
edge of the festival crowds in Deephaven Square itself.

There were soldiers here too, always were, standing
guard around the centre of the city's wealth. And there he
was, hands and shirt covered in blood that wasn't his. He
darted for the nearest shadows, up against the sides of the
Golden Cup of all places. He took deep breaths. His heart
was pounding so hard it felt as if he was going to explode.
It was still light. He had to hide. Hide until dark, until no
one would see the blood all over him.

Tasahre. Master Sy.

What have I done?

He'd gone to the docks to tell Master Sy that the witch-doctor had sold Kasmin, and he hadn't even managed *that*. He started laughing and the laughs turned at once to sobs. He sank into the deepest shadows he could find and held his head in his hands.

Later, as the sun finally set, he looked back down the Royal Parade. There wasn't much to see, but he could hear the distant sounds of celebration echoing up from the river, just as they sounded out from the square and the streets up on The Peak. He couldn't go back down there, not like this. The thief-taker was ... The thief-taker was a murderer. He'd killed a sword-monk. He'd killed Tasahre. They'd hang him now, or they'd chop off his head and send him in bits to the mines, and Berren would cheer as they did it.

No. *He* was a murderer. He'd killed a man he didn't even know, and he didn't even know why, except that he'd had no choice, none at all. The warlock had made him do it, but no one else would know that. Kol would hang them both.

He couldn't see where he was going. There were too many tears in his eyes. He hadn't even noticed he was cry-ing until now.

He couldn't go back to the temple. They'd all hated him there anyway, all of them except Tasahre, and now he was a murderer and she was dead and it was his fault. If it hadn't been for him, she'd be alive. If he hadn't used the warlock's magic to talk to Velgian, if he hadn't gone to the docks, if he'd stayed at the temple like she wanted, any of those things and she'd be alive. If he hadn't ...

He'd see her everywhere now, he knew that. And he wouldn't see her with his hand on her cheek, but with blood spraying out of her neck.

Evil, that's what he'd seen.

Tasahre. Gods! Why? *Why?*

He slipped away, across Deephaven Square, around the

back of the Golden Cup. He tried to ignore the delicious smells and the raucous sounds that came out, the salacious laughter of fat old men with pockets full of gold, groping the girls who worked there. Tasahre was right. The city was rotten.

Or maybe it was the thief-taker who'd told him that once.

He pushed his way down the Avenue of the Sun to Four Winds Square, oblivious to the drunken crowds that surrounded him, and made his way out into the back streets, into The Maze. This was his old home, the place where he always used to go when he needed somewhere safe. He had money. He could buy food, hard biscuits and salted meat and other things that would last. He could carry enough to keep him alive for the first few days. He could hide out in the Maze then slip out through the Reeper Gate in the dark and make his way towards Bedlam's Crossing. The nights were warm enough and there were woods to hide in during the day. He could be there in three days if he walked hard, maybe four if he had to dodge anyone on the road. Then he could buy himself some deck-space on a barge going up the river. He could have done the same from the river docks in Deephaven but he wasn't going to chance that, not from outside the witch-doctor's door. He wondered what the city would do to punish a murderer. Something slow and painful. Khrozus! Would all the way to Varr even be enough? A barge would take a month to get there, which made it seem a very long way away. Yet Berren knew there were other places that were even further.

He fingered Prince Sharda's token. No. That's where he was going.

The night wore on. The docks heaved with revellers. Reeper Hill was choked with men staggering between a parade of carriages. He made his way out to Wrecking Point, stumbling in the dark down the path to the broken stone cliffs at the edge of the harbour. It took an hour of searching, but the sword was still buried where he'd left it. He wrestled with it to pull it out of its scabbard. Brown streaks marked the blade; he wasn't sure whether they were blood or rust. The leather in the belt and harness was cracked and hard but it was still a sword and the edge was sharp. Berren put it on. Swords. He'd wanted to have one for as long as he could remember. Now he did, mostly what he wanted to do was take it off and throw it high into the air, away into the sea. But he couldn't. They were bound together now, him and the sword, like it or not.

He sat still, staring at the waves. Deephaven had been his home. For all its sins, it had given birth to him. The city and the sea. He'd probably miss the water. The sound of it, even the smell of it. The jaunty river men and the surly mudlarks, the rainbow breeds of sailors from across the oceans, the warm sultry nights and the winters where people didn't freeze to death. The colours, the way the markets always held something he'd never seen before, every single day. Yes, he'd miss all of that.

But not the thief-taker with his hands covered in blood. Not Tasahre, lying soaked in crimson, head lolling sideways. Not the shadow-thing that called itself Saffran Kuy.

He kicked himself. He was going to Varr. He was going to serve a prince, a *real* prince, not someone who got kicked out of his palace a decade and then some ago. If the worst came to the worst and this Prince turned out no better than the last, there was always work on the city walls. The whole world could work on the walls of Varr and they'd still never get finished. Apparently that was a joke. He'd heard it said and heard people laugh, too. Didn't see it himself.

The sky started to lighten. Nights were short in the summer. Over in the city the crowds were thinning as people either staggered to doze in a temple to the sun somewhere or else passed out in the streets, fodder for the press gangs.

He got up. When he tried to walk, the sword and its scabbard kept getting between his legs and tripping him up. In the end he wrapped the sword back into its bundle and ran across the city with it slung across his back.

He went down the back of Reeper Hill and Shipwrights' and towards The Maze. Lilissa lived there now, somewhere. His first love, gone to be with her fishmonger. He didn't know exactly where; Master Sy wouldn't tell him and Lilissa didn't want him to know. All in all that had probably been for the best. Everything to do with her seemed so childish now.

Tasahre. A part of him had died with her. Or maybe she wasn't dead after all – maybe that sword monk had reached her in time and touched her with a mark of the sun, like the elder dragon had done to Master Sy, and turned her at the brink and brought her back. Maybe? Could something like that have happened?

No. No, he couldn't even start to make himself believe it. She was dead and no one was going to miss him. Hardly anyone would even notice except Master Sy, and Berren would never be able to look at the thief-taker again without seeing Tasahre. Leaving was nothing to be sad about.

He walked through the Sea Gate into the docks. They looked like a battlefield. Clusters of drunks huddled together. Others shambled aimlessly towards the temple near the gates. A few were laid out flat, some of them already being dragged towards boats, bobbing on the sea. Berren skirted around the edge of all that. The Maze, that was his place. He knew exactly where he was going: to the half-collapsed cellar of the old Sheaf of Arrows, the place he used to go when he ran with Hatchet's gangs. It was as good a place as any to hide for a day.

He turned a corner and walked straight into a gang of men pushing a handcart. He stumbled and almost fell.

'Hey, lad. Careful there!' One of the men reached out, offering him a hand. Berren took it without thinking.

'Ever thought of going to sea?' asked another one behind him.

The grip on his wrist was strong, pulling him up. Very strong.

He had a moment, just long enough to realise who these men were, before something hit him round the back of the head.

ACKNOWLEDGEMENTS

For some reason this was a hard one to get right. Thanks to my editor at Gollancz, Simon Spanton and to my wife Michaela, both of whom earned their keep putting up with me through this.

I should also mention The Boxer Rebellion, who provided a substantial part of the soundtrack to my life while this was being written.